Praise

CW00590007

'The "what-if-this-happ
the F
Guardian

'Brilliantly imagined, fiercely authentic and wholly gripping'
Literary Review

'Wonderfully plotted, fast-paced and refreshingly original'
Nelson DeMille

'A distinctly atmospheric thriller'
Mail on Sunday

'Beguiling mystery'
New York Times

'Adam always handles his massive canvases with real panache. The
requisite pulse-racing action is wedded superbly to the serious theme'
Good Book Guide

'Brilliantly researched and informative... a turbo-charged, white-
knuckled thriller by a brilliant storyteller'
Daily Record

'Mystery fans and music lovers alike will be captivated by Adam's
excellent contemporary thriller'
Publishers Weekly, starred review

'The story is told with uncommon grace, clarity, and wit'
The Denver Post

'An enthralling mix of Italian ambience, history
and – most of all – music'
Booklist

Paul Adam is the author of twelve previous novels for adults, and the Max Cassidy series of thrillers for younger readers. He has also written television and film scripts. He lives in Sheffield and is married with two sons. For more information visit www.pauladam.com

THE HARDANGER RIDDLE

Paul Adam

Endeavour Publishing

First published in Great Britain in November 2019
by *Endeavour Publishing*

Copyright © Paul Adam 2019

A CIP catalogue record for this book is available
from the British Library.

ISBN 978-0-9571913-7-2

Printed and bound by CPI Group (UK) Ltd, Croydon, CR0 4YY

Endeavour Publishing
19 Bents Drive
Sheffield
S11 9RN

ONE

I do not think that growing older has brought me any great wisdom – though I am undoubtedly wiser than I was when I was, say, eighteen or twenty – but in my sixty-five years, I *have* learnt one thing: the key to fulfilment in life is to give something back. To our families and friends, to our neighbours and communities, to strangers who have need of us.

I don't mean to sound smug or trite, to spout clichés like the message inside some nauseating greeting card. I mean it from the heart. In a time when hatred and mistrust and intolerance are becoming increasingly widespread, I believe that we should put aside our divisions, try harder to understand others and share what we have with them. We have far more in common than we sometimes think and recognising that fact allows the good side of human nature to break out and blossom.

Each day, when I turn on the news or look at the paper, it's hard not to get depressed about the state of the world, to see what's wrong yet feel utterly powerless to do anything about it. I'm not naïve or arrogant enough to think that I have any answers on a global scale, but I *can* look after my own tiny part of the planet. I *can* tend and nurture my own garden – in both the literal and the metaphorical sense.

I grow fruit and vegetables and flowers on the land behind my house. I plant seeds. I feed and water the soil and reap the benefits of my labour – though sometimes the slugs and birds do better than I do. Then, outside my home, I try to do the same – with my children, who, though grown up, still occasionally need my help, with my friends who need support and with the students I teach at the *Scuola Internazionale di Liuteria Cremona*, the international violin-making school in the city.

I've taught part-time at the school for nearly thirty years now and, increasingly, am finding it a more and more rewarding part of my life. I still get enjoyment and satisfaction out of making my own instruments, but I do not delude myself that the world is beating a path to my door. No one really needs another Giovanni Battista Castiglione violin, much though I might like them to. But my students, with them I feel I can make a difference. I can share with them my experience and knowledge. I can stop them making mistakes, save them time and effort and maybe inspire them to create something truly wonderful.

And in return – for teaching is a two-way street – the students give something back to me. They take me away from the isolation of my workshop, they give me the pleasure of their company, the stimulation of their inquiring minds. They keep me young and they keep me interested in my craft with their enthusiasm and

2

talent. Above all, in my autumn years, they make me feel useful.

I've lost track of how many students I've taught. It's certainly well into the hundreds. They've come from all over the world, from Europe, from Asia, from the Americas. The school has a well-deserved reputation for excellence, and there is still a considerable cachet attached to studying in Cremona, the home of the great masters. Like any group of people, they have been a mixed bunch of personalities. Some, I admit, have been more difficult than others – a little bit odd or eccentric and, occasionally, downright weird – but I can't remember any that I actively disliked. Violin making is not a profession that generally attracts the brutes and the bullies, the ambitious careerists and the greedy, driven thugs. If you want to conquer the world and acquire riches, there are probably more promising routes to follow.

Many of the students have kept in touch with me, even if only through an annual Christmas card or intermittent emails. Some have settled in Cremona and set up their own workshops, others have returned to their home countries to continue their careers. A few gain such reputations as luthiers that they are invited back to the school to give a talk to the current students. Rikard Olsen was one such distinguished alumnus.

Among all the many students I've taught, Rikard was one of the most memorable. He had a real gift for making instruments, but what made him stand out in particular was his striking appearance. He came from Norway and was not only young and very good looking, but he had fine blond, almost flaxen, hair that in Italy is guaranteed to make heads turn.

The girls went mad for him, and the feelings were usually reciprocated. Rikard became known – or should that be notorious? – for his passionate liaisons and equally fierce breakings-up, the latter nearly always instigated by him. There were lots of tears, lots of heartbroken women hanging around outside the school to confront him, Rikard – to his shame – sneaking out the back entrance to avoid them. It became quite a soap opera at the time. The principal had to have an awkward word with him about his conduct, but Rikard never really changed. Women kept falling in love with him, and he kept using them and abandoning them.

Twenty years have passed since then, but looking at Rikard now, I could see only a few signs of ageing. He still had the same trim figure, the same conspicuous blond hair. There were maybe a few more lines on his face, but he was still a very handsome man – in his early forties rather than his early twenties, but some people might find that attractive.

"I see what you mean, Gianni," Margherita leaned over to whisper in my ear. "He *is* quite dishy."

"Don't let him break your heart," I replied.

Margherita laughed. "Me? Good Lord, he wouldn't even look at me. I'm old enough to be his mother."

"Mothers can still be susceptible to a man like Rikard."

"Hmm," Margherita murmured thoughtfully. "That's not a bad idea. It might be fun."

"That's what all his old girlfriends thought."

Margherita smiled and squeezed my hand. I smiled back. She was looking very beautiful this evening, her short, dark hair neatly combed, her small sapphire earrings gleaming in the soft light that filtered in through the windows down the side of the hall.

We were in the chapel of the Palazzo Pallavicini Ariguzzi, the restored fifteenth century palace in which the international violin-making school is housed. The other parts of the building have been converted into workshops, classrooms and offices, but the chapel – a modest, unadorned room with a high, wooden-beamed ceiling – has been kept as a place for communal gatherings, for formal ceremonies like the annual presentation of prizes and for talks like the one Rikard Olsen was about to give. He'd already done it once that afternoon, exclusively for the students, but this evening's event was open to the general public, part of the school's outreach programme to make its work more accessible to the wider community.

Rikard was at the front of the hall, standing by a portable white screen that only partially hid the glass cases in which prize-winning student instruments are displayed.

"Good evening ladies and gentlemen," he said smoothly. "Thank you for coming. It's a pleasure to be back in Cremona, and at the violin-making school in particular."

He hadn't forgotten his Italian, I noted. When he first arrived two decades ago, he could speak barely a word of the language, but he'd quickly picked it up. All that pillow talk, I suppose.

He was into his preamble now, telling us what happy memories he had of his time at the school, how difficult it had been for him to go home after graduation, to leave his many friends and return to the cold and the dark of Norway. I glanced around the chapel, wondering whether any of his jilted lovers were here, but I couldn't see any obvious candidates in my direct eye line. What I could see, however, was Vincenzo Serafin, the slippery Milanese violin dealer with whom I occasionally do business. He was over to my right, two rows in front, only his profile visible – his large, slightly hooked nose and sleek black beard. Sitting next to him was a man in his fifties with what looked to me like classic Nordic features – a round face, high cheekbones – and a full head of silvery blond hair that rivalled Rikard's.

Rikard was moving on from his polite introduction into the body of his talk, a presentation about the Hardanger fiddle, a violin that is unique to Norway, especially to the south-west of the country. He held up two instruments. In his left hand was a standard violin, in his right a *hardingfele*. They were both of a similar size and shape, but the differences between them were immediately apparent. While the standard violin had a plain brown varnished front, the Hardanger fiddle's was embellished with an intricate black pattern of swirls and curls and loops that spread out over the wood like a climbing plant. Its ribs were similarly decorated and the fingerboard and tailpiece – plain black ebony on the standard violin – were inlaid with a geometric design in iridescent mother-of-pearl.

The scrolls, too, were different, the *hardingfele* having a carved woman's head at the end of the neck. It also had a longer pegbox to accommodate the extra strings – four on a standard violin, but nine on this particular Hardanger fiddle for the *hardingfele* has four strings above the fingerboard but another four, or often five, understrings that aren't played with the bow but vibrate in sympathy, giving the instrument its distinctive sound.

The details on the fiddle were hard to make out from a distance, but Rikard had that problem covered: Powerpoint slides on a laptop that he projected onto the screen beside him. He started with the scroll.

"This is one of the main differences between a standard violin and the Hardanger fiddle," he said. "The scroll can be anything. On a lot of fiddles it's a carved animal. I've seen bears and dogs and lions, but one of the most common is a dragon's head. Makers over the years have liked putting dragons on their instruments. Or women's heads. This, as you can see, is one of those."

He jumped to a slide showing the scroll in close-up. It was an exquisite piece of craftsmanship. The young woman's face – and she was clearly young – had been carved in fine detail, the light varnish and underlying white wood giving a golden hue to her hair. Was it a sort of fantasy woman, or had it been modelled on a real person, I wondered. Whoever it was, she was captivatingly beautiful.

"I didn't make this fiddle, by the way," Rikard explained. "The standard violin is one of mine, but not the *hardingfele*. I *have* made Hardanger fiddles, but I brought this one to illustrate my talk because, well..." He shrugged modestly. "It's better than anything I've ever managed. Just look at the marquetry."

He moved onto other slides that showed the inlay in the fingerboard and the front and back plates.

"I've tried this," he said, "and, believe me, it isn't easy. This is extremely skilled work, and incredibly time consuming. It must have taken months just to do the fingerboard, let alone all the rest. Look how small are the pieces of mother-of-pearl, how complex the design. This whole fiddle is a monumental work of love."

He tapped a key on the laptop and took us through more slides, some of the fiddle, some showing drawings of the constituent parts with measurements and other technical information on them that went over the heads of most people in the room. It was a tricky line to walk, trying to be informative to luthiers whilst holding the interest of the lay people in the audience, but I think Rikard did a pretty good job. He didn't linger too long on construction issues, but soon addressed the question that most people were asking themselves: what did the *hardingfele* sound like?

Not all violin makers are also players. The two skills, after all, are quite different. Some of the best luthiers I've ever encountered couldn't play a note on the instruments they made, but were just exceptional craftsmen. Others were competent violinists or even very good. Rikard was in the last category. I remember in classes, when students wanted to try out their work, Rikard was the first person they turned to. He'd run up and down the strings with a flamboyant flourish, or play some Bach or Beethoven from memory. He wasn't professional standard, but he was certainly a better-than-average amateur.

"Let me play you something on the standard violin first," he said. "So you can compare the sounds of the two instruments. This is a piece by Ole Bull, the Norwegian Paganini, who was heavily influenced by Hardanger fiddle and other folk music. It's called *Saeterjentens Søndag*, The Herd Girl's Sunday. In Norway it's very famous, almost like a second national anthem, but you may never have heard it before.

"It's a descriptive piece, intended to evoke a young girl up in the high mountain pastures with her sheep and cows. She's lonely. Far below her in the valley, she hears the church bells ringing and pictures the boy she loves going to the service without her."

Rikard put the violin under his chin and began to play. The music wasn't unfamiliar to me. I have a collection of Ole Bull's compositions at home and used to play them with my late-wife Caterina. Bull was one of the most celebrated virtuosos of his day, but The Herd Girl's Sunday isn't a bravura piece. It's simple, but heartfelt – like its subject matter.

Rikard played it well, letting the gentle melody ring out around the room. It seemed a little strange, imagining a shepherdess in the wild Norwegian mountains from our plastic chairs in a grand Renaissance chapel, but it was easy to do, easy to let the sound of the violin transport us up the fjords to the summer meadows beneath snow-capped peaks, to see the lonely girl gazing longingly down from a crag and share her feelings of isolation and yearning.

A round of applause greeted the end of the piece and Rikard nodded his appreciation.

"Now let's hear the same piece on the *hardingfele*."

From the very first note the sound was different. The melody line was unchanged, but underneath it you could hear the five drone strings vibrating, sometimes in harmony with the tune, but sometimes clashing with it, giving a discordant edge to the music. If you closed your eyes, it sounded as if two people were playing. But it was very effective. The understrings gave

9

the impression of church bells ringing in the distance.

"That doesn't really do the fiddle justice," Rikard said when the applause had died down. "You need to hear something that was written specifically for the *hardingfele*. Remember, Hardanger fiddle music is dance music. It was played by local musicians or by travelling players who moved from village to village, providing music for the Saturday night dances. It was frowned on by the Church, who regarded it as the Devil's music, used to accompany drinking and merry making and men and women having a good time. Until the twentieth century, the *hardingfele* was banned from all Norwegian churches.

"But it influenced some of our greatest musicians. Ole Bull I've already mentioned, but listen to this. Does it ring any bells?"

He plucked the understrings of the fiddle, calling out the pitches as he played them. "A, F-sharp, E, D, E, F-sharp. You recognise the tune?"

Probably everyone in the room did. It was the melody of "Morning Mood", from Grieg's *Peer Gynt* Suite.

"Grieg took that from the *hardingfele*, though he transposed it into a different key. He borrowed other bits of folk music for some of his other compositions, too. Traditional music was important to him, part of his identity as a proud Norwegian. The Hardanger fiddle players – *spelemenn*, we call them – were all over the villages of south-western Norway when Grieg was alive. One of the most famous was a man named Torgeir Augundson, who's generally known as Myllarguten, the Miller's Boy. This is one of his pieces, called *Siklebekken*, the Trickling Beck, though he probably didn't compose it. *Hardingfele* music wasn't generally written down in the nineteenth century – it still isn't today. It was passed on by ear from generation to generation, often from father to son, and each player would add their own touches to it, embellishing and improvising while they performed. See what you think."

It was another simple piece, intended as a musical representation of a babbling brook, the theme repeated over and over in slightly different forms. The bridge of a Hardanger fiddle is flatter than on a standard violin so it's easy, indeed essential, to play on more than one string at a time, usually two, but frequently three or even all four. And underneath, the sympathetic strings are singing too, so the overall effect is of multiple chromatic sounds, which is quite jarring on ears – like ours – which are accustomed to a single melodic line. As he played, Rikard tapped the floor with his foot in time to the music, as if there were couples dancing out in the hall.

For me, and I suspect for nearly everyone else in the audience, this was a first. I'd never heard a Hardanger fiddle played before, even on a recording, and I wasn't sure what to make of it. I glanced at Margherita, seated on my left, but her eyes were fixed raptly on Rikard – whether captivated by the music or his looks I couldn't be certain. Then I turned the other way. Guastafeste caught my eye and pulled a face. He waited until the piece had finished and his words were covered by the noise of clapping before he said, "Is it just me, or is this terrible?"

I suppressed a guffaw. I've known Antonio since he was a baby, forty-five years ago now, so I'm accustomed to his blunt, matter-of-fact nature – partly his innate character, but mostly the result of his quarter of a century as a police officer.

"You don't like it?" I said.

"Well, I've heard nicer violin music. Even *you* playing, Gianni, is better than this."

"It's just unfamiliar," I said. "You have to give it a chance."

"Do I? I'm not sure my ears can take it."

The applause was fading away. Rikard lifted the *hardingfele* to his chin again.

"Oh, no," Guastafeste murmured. "He's not going to play something else, is he?"

He was. Three more pieces, in fact, each one illustrating the unique characteristics of the instrument. When it was all over, we got up from our seats and shuffled along the row to the side of the hall.

"What did you think?" I asked Margherita.

"It was interesting," she said non-committally.

"Interesting?"

"You know, different."

"I can think of other adjectives," Guastafeste said sourly.

"Now, now, Antonio. Don't be so narrow minded. It probably takes a while for the music to grow on you. Give it time."

"Life isn't long enough," he growled.

Margherita laughed.

"You agree with him?" I asked.

"Not exactly. But it *was* rather... harsh at times. The violin can be so sweet, but that was almost shrill. And a bit repetitive."

"All dance music is repetitive," I said. "It's not meant

to be listened to in a concert hall. You're meant to be in a barn somewhere, holding a partner with a few litres of beer inside you."

"Speaking of which," Guastafeste said. "Shall we go for a drink?"

"Don't you want to meet Rikard first?"

"I thought you'd never ask," Margherita said.

We weren't the only people wanting to meet the visitor from Norway. There was quite a cluster around him at the front of the hall – mostly women, but I'm sure that was a coincidence. I could understand his appeal. He had that alluring aura around him that some men exude. He was good looking and had the exotic – in Italy, at least – attraction of his blond Nordic colouring, but there was more to him than that. He wasn't just a pretty face. There was substance there, too, and a solid masculinity that men as well as women would find engaging. He had a look that combined the sensitive, creative artist with the rugged outdoorsman – reinforced by his checked shirt, black jeans and scuffed work boots. You could see him crafting violins, but you could also see him striding across the Hardanger Plateau with a rucksack on his back.

He was showing the group the *hardingfele*, passing it around so they could take a closer look. He saw me approaching and smiled warmly.

"Gianni!" He broke through the crowd and shook my hand. "It's good to see you."

"You, too. I enjoyed your talk." I introduced Margherita and Guastafeste and they shook hands.

"It was fascinating," Margherita said. "I've never heard music like that before. You played it so beautifully."

"Thank you. But you flatter me," Rikard said. "You

13

should hear some of the real *hardingfele spelemenn*, and women. Then you'd know what it should sound like. I'm afraid I'm pretty much a beginner."

"You didn't sound it."

"How are you, Rikard?" I asked. "You've barely changed in all these years."

"You're looking pretty good yourself. You're still working, I assume?"

"As much as I want to. I could do more – the work's there – but I like to do other things, too. You're earning quite a name for yourself, I hear."

He shrugged. "I'm doing all right – for now. But you know the business, things could dry up at any moment."

He glanced over my shoulder and I saw his face cloud for an instant. I turned round. Vincenzo Serafin and the middle-aged man with the silvery blond hair had come up behind me. The blond man said something to Rikard in Norwegian and he replied briefly in the same language. I couldn't understand the words, but I sensed immediately from the body language that they didn't like each other.

"Gianni." Serafin nodded at me curtly.

I waited for him to introduce his companion, but basic courtesies have never been one of Serafin's strong points, so I made the move myself.

"Gianni Castiglione," I said, offering my hand. "Are you a friend of Vincenzo's?"

"He doesn't speak Italian," Serafin said. "And I doubt you've got much Norwegian. You'll have to speak English."

I repeated my introduction in English and the blond man gave a nod.

"Ingvar Aandahl," he said. "Not so much a friend of Vincenzo's as a professional colleague. I'm a violin dealer, too."

"Ah, I see."

He had the same affluent appearance as Serafin: expensive, well-cut suit, silk tie, the self-satisfied, preening manner of a successful businessman who's made his money from other people's labours. His face and hands had a deep suntan that I didn't think had come from the Norwegian climate.

"You know Rikard, too?" I went on.

"We're acquainted. Bergen's a very small place."

"You came all this way to hear his talk?"

"I came to see Vincenzo on business. This was just a diversion, an evening excursion from Milan."

"Do you deal in Hardanger fiddles?"

He gave me a horrified look, as if I'd suggested he trafficked women.

"There's no market for those things," he said with a sneer. "They're passed down through families, or from one musician to another. Almost no one in Norway plays them, you know. Or listens to them, for that matter. You see them at the odd country festival or on Constitution Day – our national holiday – but the rest of the time they're unseen and unheard."

"Which is perhaps as well, considering the noise they make," Serafin interjected with his customary tact.

"Not everyone shares that view," I said quickly, embarrassed by the comment. Rikard was standing right next to us and I was sure he spoke English as well as we did.

"Don't worry, Gianni," he said calmly. "I'm used to it. Even in Norway the *hardingfele* isn't properly

15

appreciated. It's regarded as vulgar peasant music, fit only for a bunch of drunken country bumpkins."

"I don't know why you bother with them," Aandahl said. "It's a waste of your time and talent. You could make much more money if you stuck to making proper violins."

"Maybe making money isn't everyone's main object in life," Rikard replied.

He turned away to talk to the other audience members who were still admiring the *hardingfele* and wanted his attention.

"What was that all about?" Guastafeste – whose English was limited – asked me.

"I think you could call it a 'frank cultural exchange'," I replied.

"A few home truths, more like." Serafin corrected me. "I've never heard such a din in my life. If all violins sounded like that, I'd be out of a job. So would you, Gianni."

I resisted the temptation to reprove him for his rudeness. I've known him long enough to know it would make no difference.

"Tell me, Vincenzo," I said. "If it's so awful, why did you come here tonight?"

"That's a stupid question. If I'd known it would be this bad, I wouldn't have come, of course. But I didn't. Besides, Ingvar wanted to do it. Olsen's a man to watch, apparently. Makes terrific violins that a lot of people want to buy. Much better than yours," he couldn't stop himself adding.

He was starting to grate on me – even more than usual. I moved away and joined Margherita in the huddle of people around Rikard, their enthusiasm and welcoming warmth a refreshing contrast with Serafin's unpleasant boorishness.

I took a brief look at the Hardanger fiddle, but then had to pass it on almost immediately to others who were keen to handle it. Meanwhile, Rikard was fielding questions – about the instrument, but also about Norway and Norwegian folk music. Cremona is not an insular city. Its residents are broadminded, accustomed to students from all around the world and to the exchange of ideas from different cultures. They have a thirst for learning, particularly when it comes to music and violins.

It was only when the caretaker came in and began to hover nearby that the crowd took the hint and slowly drifted away. Rikard went to the table at the side of the chapel and put his two violins back in their cases. I noticed that Aandahl and Serafin were still lingering. The Norwegian dealer approached Rikard and they had a short, intense conversation, too far away for me to hear what they were saying – not that I would have understood it, in any case. Rikard shook his head firmly, obviously trying to end the discussion, but Aandahl persisted. Rikard shook his head again, his expression irritated, then he picked up his violin cases and, pushing past the dealer, came across the room to join me and Margherita and Guastafeste by the door.

"Do you have any plans now?" I asked him.

"Not unless you count sitting in my hotel room and staring at a blank television screen as a plan."

"That doesn't sound like the Rikard I remember."

He smiled. "I've mellowed a lot since then."

"We're going for a drink. Would you like to come with us?"

"I'd love to."

He glanced over his shoulder at Aandahl and Serafin. "Shall we go now?"

"Are they bothering you?"

"Dealers, you know what they're like. Pushy, greedy, always making you propositions they like to dress up as mutually advantageous when you know there's only going to be one winner in the deal and it's not you."

I nodded sympathetically. "Sounds like Serafin, too. If there were a Nobel Prize for shiftiness, he'd win it every time."

We went to a bar a couple of streets away and found a table for four at the back. Rikard and Guastafeste excused themselves to go to the Gents and I ordered a bottle of red wine and some snacks from the waiter. Looking back at Margherita, I caught her adjusting her hair in the mirror on the wall next to our table and gave her a lop-sided grin.

"Old enough to be his mother, remember," I said.

If we'd been in a less public place, she'd probably have stuck her tongue out at me, but she contented herself with a look of feigned injury.

"Don't be mean, Gianni. A woman my age needs a bit of excitement now and again."

"That you don't get from me, you mean?"

"You're not a gorgeous, young Norwegian blond."

"He's forty-three."

"That's young to me. And to you."

"You wish I had blond hair?"

"Just hair would do."

"Hey! That hurts."

"It'll teach you to mock me, *tesoro*."

I smiled and filled our glasses with wine. Rikard and Antonio returned and sat down and for a few minutes we talked about the presentation Rikard had just given. Then I asked to see the violins again.

"I didn't get much of a chance in the chapel. There were too many people."

"Which one first?" Rikard wanted to know. "Mine, or the *hardingfele*?"

"Yours."

It was a very fine violin, with a two-piece maple back and a narrow-grained spruce front, the varnish a rich dark brown that glowed in the light from the lamp on the wall behind us.

"Not bad," I said, examining the purfling and f-holes. "You're getting the hang of this."

"I'll take that as a compliment," Rikard said dryly. He glanced at Margherita and Guastafeste. "When I was a student here, Gianni was always the teacher we wanted to please. An approving grunt from him was better than the most effusive praise from another teacher."

"Grunts are one of his specialities," Margherita said.

I took a sip of wine. "I believe in tough love, at least as far as teaching goes. You have to push your students to achieve excellence. And here's the evidence. This is a very good violin. It shows what twenty years of practice can do."

"You taught me well."

"You were a good learner. I always knew you'd make a terrific luthier."

Rikard was one of those challenging students who want to break the rules before they've learnt them. But that's not a bad thing in a young person. Rules can be mastered by even second-rate craftsmen, but you can't learn a unique personal style. That's innate and all the great violin makers have it.

"I appreciate your confidence," Rikard said. "But it didn't feel like that to me. It took me a long time to get established and I kept wondering whether I'd made a mistake in going back to Norway."

"A mistake?" I said.

He nodded. "I missed the life here, all those things you Italians take for granted – the weather, the food, the fact that you can buy a bottle of wine for less than a month's salary. But I think, in the end, it was the right move. There's too much competition here, too many well-established makers. I'm better off in Bergen where my skills are more unusual. You should come and see me there."

"I'd like to." I glanced at Margherita and she nodded eagerly.

"I've always wanted to see Norway," she said. "What's Bergen like?"

"Wet," Rikard replied.

He turned to look directly at her and I could see the effect on her immediately. There was something different about the way Rikard interacted with women, whatever their age. There was a spark in his eyes, a kind of intensity that was flattering, that seemed to say, 'I'm interested in you.' I suspect he didn't do it consciously; it was just something that happened and that had no doubt been happening since he was a very young man.

Margherita is an attractive woman, but she's sixty years old and far too sensible and experienced to have any misconceptions about men. Nevertheless, I could sense her reacting to his gaze. It was nothing obvious, but I knew her well enough to detect subtle changes in her manner, to feel that internally she was blushing a little.

"I'm not trying to put you off," Rikard went on. "That's just a warning. It's a beautiful city: the bay, the old wharf – the Bryggen – which has wooden buildings dating back to the Hanseatic League, Mount Fløyen overlooking it all. The best way to arrive is by boat, preferably a sailing boat, so you can feel the wind and the elements. Come in from the west at dusk with the setting sun behind you, the way the founder of the city, King Olaf Kyrre, would have seen it from his Viking longboat a thousand years ago."

"It sounds magical," Margherita said.

"I'm biased, of course. You want to see the *hardingfele* now?"

He took the Hardanger fiddle out of its case and placed it on the table. Close up, it was an even more breathtaking piece of craftsmanship: the mother-of-pearl inlay, the marquetry, the rococo black decoration across the ribs and front and back plates. In my view, it was over the top, a gaudy confection of a violin, but I had to acknowledge and admire the skill that had gone into its construction.

"Who made it?" I asked.

"I don't know. There's no label inside it and the *hardingfele* tradition is notoriously difficult to pin down. There's no Stradivari or Guarneri of the Hardanger fiddle. There are lots of makers, but many of them never put a label or a distinctive mark on their work. I picked this up a couple of months ago and have been trying to trace the maker ever since."

I inspected the inside of the instrument through one of the f-holes.

"Is it old?"

"I've been trying to work that out, too. I'm not sure it is. The strings had all snapped when I acquired it and they were badly rusted, but I don't think it's more than fifty or sixty years old. There's not much wear on the plates or the upper bouts, so I don't believe it was played much."

Guastafeste indicated the scroll. "And the girl? Who is she?"

"I don't know that either.

I held the fiddle up to the light. I'd seen the Powerpoint slide of the scroll during Rikard's talk, but in the flesh – so to speak – the young girl's face was even more beautiful. Her hair, her eyes, the curve of her full lips were so realistically carved that it was easy to imagine her coming to life and speaking to us.

"Look at the end of the pegbox," Rikard said. "There's a tiny cavity under the scroll."

I tilted the fiddle back and saw the opening.

"Put your fingers in," Rikard continued.

It was a tight squeeze, but I could just get the tips of my forefinger and thumb into the slot. I pulled out a small object that was hidden there – a circular silver locket. I opened it. Inside was a lock of blonde hair.

"I found that after I'd bought the fiddle," Rikard said. "I don't think the people who sold it to me had any idea it was there."

"This is her hair, the girl on the scroll?"

"It has to be."

"What a wonderful romantic gesture," Margherita

said. "Putting something like that inside a violin. Was it the maker who did it, or someone else?"

"That's a mystery I haven't solved yet," Rikard replied.

It was nearly eleven o-clock when we left the bar. We parted company with Rikard outside on the pavement. He was walking back to his hotel in the centre of town, Antonio and I had our cars parked near the violin-making school. We shook hands and promised to keep in touch, then went our separate ways.

Margherita came back with me to my house where she'd left her own car. It was too late to contemplate driving back to Milan, so she stayed the night, as she often did these days. We've known each other for two years now. We met in traumatic circumstances after the murder of her uncle in Venice, and grew closer in the months that followed. We lead separate lives, both valuing our own space, but there are signs that our independence is being gently nibbled away around the edges.

Margherita keeps spare make-up and toiletries in my bathroom, a few clothes and bits of underwear in the bedroom. There was never a single point when we decided that might be a good idea; it just sort of happened gradually. It seemed to make sense, a purely practical move given that Margherita was staying over more frequently, but, of course, it was a lot more than that. The perfume next to the shower, the blouses in the wardrobe, they were merely the surface evidence of a deeper change in our relationship. I'd been a widower for eight years and I welcomed that change. I liked having a woman's presence in my home again, liked the thought – unexpressed by either of us – that in time it might become more than temporary.

Margherita padded barefoot into the bedroom in a turquoise silk nightdress with white lace trim. I smiled at her from the bed.

"You looked very beautiful this evening," I said. "Still do."

"Thank you."

"Rikard was quite taken with you."

She laughed and gave me a dry, amused look.

"Now you're being silly."

"No, he was," I said. "And why not?"

"I could give you a very long list why not. Starting with the number sixty."

She threw back the duvet and slid into the bed next to me.

"But I know what you mean," she said. "Women my age get used to being invisible. It's a cliché, but that's because it's true. Men don't look at us any more."

"I do."

"You're different. I'm talking about men, in general. But Rikard has something about him that's very alluring. He makes you feel that he's noticed you. It might be an illusion, but – well – it's a nice illusion."

She curled up against me, her head on my chest.

"I enjoyed this evening. It was a fascinating talk. Have you ever made a Hardanger fiddle?"

"No, there's not exactly much demand for them in Italy."

"They look like a lot of work to me. Wasn't that an amazing carving on the scroll – the young woman's head? And the silver locket in the hidden compartment. I said it was a romantic thing to do, keeping a lock of someone's hair, but it's also a bit weird. Maybe even a little morbid."

"Morbid?"

"Well, you know, hair's dead, isn't it? You're keeping a dead bit of someone as a memento. Would you want a lock of my hair?"

"I don't need it. I've got it all here, where I can touch it." I stroked her hair, the strands thick and soft under my fingers.

"And I wouldn't want yours, either. Not that you've got much to spare."

I poked her in the ribs. "Don't start that again."

"Does anyone do it nowadays? It seems very old-fashioned to me. Like something they did in the nineteenth century, when so many people died young."

"That's the thing about locks of hair in silver lockets," I said. "You don't do it for loved ones you still have. You do it for loved ones you've lost."

We had breakfast together next morning on the terrace at the back of my house, then Margherita headed off to Milan. I went into my workshop and looked through the collection of CDs I keep on some shelves to listen to while I work. I find music a soothing accompaniment, but it also seems to help me concentrate.

I took out a recording of violin pieces by Ole Bull, played by the Norwegian soloist Arve Tellefsen. After Rikard's talk, I was in Bull mode, keen to hear compositions I hadn't listened to in a long time.

Bull was a world-famous violinist – fêted across Europe and America in his lifetime – but he wasn't a great composer. He led a frenetic, disorganised life of almost constant travelling and performing and was careless about his musical creations. Some he never wrote down, but simply played from memory. Others he just lost, left them behind in hotels or stage coaches or concert hall dressing rooms. Those compositions that survived, however, show that he had a gift for melody, for unpretentious, heartwarming tunes that audiences in London, or Boston or Milwaukee could all appreciate with equal enthusiasm.

His *Polacca Guerriera* was on my disc. So, too, was his famous *En Moders Bøn*, A Mother's Prayer, that went down so well with people in the American Midwest. *Saeterjentens Søndag* was also there and I have to say that, with all due respect, Arve Tellefsen played it better than Rikard Olsen.

Rikard was on my mind as I worked – bending some maple ribs around my iron, my nostrils full of the smell of damp rag and heated wood – so it seemed an eerie coincidence when I received a phone call about him from Guastafeste.

He was at police headquarters and his voice had an edge of uneasiness about it.

"Rikard's been found dead in the canal," he said as gently as he could. "And we don't think it was an accident."

TWO

The shock took my breath away. I slumped down heavily onto my stool, my knuckles white on the phone, and was momentarily speechless.

"Gianni? Are you okay?" Guastafeste asked.

I licked my lips. My limbs felt suddenly weak. If I hadn't been sitting down, my legs would have buckled.

"Gianni?"

"Yes, I'm okay," I said softly.

"I'm sorry to have to tell you. But I knew you'd want to know immediately."

"What happened?"

"We don't know for sure. We won't know the exact cause of death until we get the autopsy results, but it doesn't look good. There was bruising on his head, as if he'd been hit before he ended up in the water."

"*Dio*," I breathed. "Someone killed him? Why would anyone do that?"

"I don't know. Look, I have to go. I'll call you when I have more information."

I put the receiver down slowly and realised I'd barely

been breathing throughout the conversation. I took a few deep breaths and stared out of the window of my workshop. My legs still didn't feel strong enough to support me.

Rikard, dead? The initial shock was wearing off now, a sort of puzzled daze taking its place. How could he be dead? I'd been sitting in a bar drinking wine with him not twelve hours ago. Surely it couldn't be true. Surely it must be a mistake. Yet I knew it was real, or Antonio wouldn't have phoned.

Getting up from my stool, I went into the house and drank a glass of cold water. Then I walked out into the garden and down beyond my vegetable patch to the bench under the pergola, the quiet, shady place where I like to go to think. Death touches us in many different ways – from the war-zone killings or African famines we see on television that are so remote from us we feel nothing more than horror and impotence, to the loss of those close to us when the pain can be unbearable.

Rikard Olsen was somewhere in between the two. He wasn't family, he wasn't even a friend. He was a former student I hadn't seen for twenty years. If he'd died in Norway, the news would probably have saddened me fleetingly, but gone no deeper. But he'd been killed in Cremona, and killed just after I'd been with him. That made a difference. It was no longer distant. It meant more to me, it touched me more powerfully. I was involved, and all the more so because Antonio was going to be investigating it.

I sat there for a long time, just gazing out over the fields that border my garden. The sun was already hot, but the thick vine straggling over the pergola kept the worst of the rays off me. Only a few pale beams broke through the canopy, dappling the ground around me with tortoiseshell splashes of light.

The peace of this cool little bower comforted me, gave me the solitude to think about Rikard. At the forefront of my mind were the questions that, for the time being, at least, had no answers. The why and the who and the how that Guastafeste and his colleagues would be trying urgently to clarify and resolve. I could do nothing but ask myself the questions over and over again, my knowledge so incomplete that even wild speculation about the killing was beyond me. I simply had no idea why it had occurred.

After a while, the seclusion of the garden began to seem a disadvantage rather than a blessing. Sitting there alone with my thoughts was depressing me and I felt a strong need to talk to someone. Going into the house, I phoned Margherita, catching her just before she went into a seminar with her economics students. She was stunned by what I had to tell her.

"*Dead*? Who would do that? Why?"

"That's what I've been asking myself. Antonio didn't know any more."

"Are you all right, Gianni? You're taking this badly, aren't you?"

"Yes, I suppose I am. I didn't really know him, but it's upsetting all the same. We were with him only yesterday evening. He was so full of life and yet now he's gone. And gone in such terrible circumstances."

"There's nothing you can do about that."

"I know. Is there someone I should get in touch with? Family, next of kin?"

"That's not your responsibility."

"He said he had a sister in Bergen, didn't he? And an ex-partner and a daughter. They'll have to be told."

"Leave all that to the police. Let Antonio deal with it, that's his job."

"Yes, you're right."

"My students are waiting. I'll call you later, okay?"

I went back into my workshop and distracted myself with the violin I was making – finishing the bending of the ribs, then fitting them to the mould and gluing and clamping them to the blocks. I had a sandwich at my bench for lunch and continued working into the afternoon. Shortly after four o'clock, Guastafeste called.

"Are you busy?" he asked.

"No."

"Can you come into town? I'll meet you at Lorenzo's in an hour."

We sat on the café terrace under the shade of an umbrella. I had an iced tea, Antonio a coffee and a cheese panini which he bolted down hungrily, as if it was the first food he'd had all day. He'd taken off his jacket and loosened his tie, but his posture was tense, his eyes troubled.

"This is a strange one," he said, spooning sugar into his coffee and stirring it round.

I didn't say anything. He'd tell me in his own time.

"Rikard went back to his hotel after we left him last night," he continued. "He went up to his room, then half an hour later, at around half-past eleven, he went out again. The receptionist saw him go, but she went off duty at midnight so no one was aware that he didn't come back. Guests are given their own key to let themselves in after midnight."

"He went over to the canal at half-past eleven at night?" I asked.

"We don't know exactly where he went at that point. All we know is that at seven o-clock this morning, a jogger out for a run saw a body floating in the canal and called us. His wallet was still in his trouser pocket. Credit cards, driving licence, it was easy to identify him as Rikard."

"Have you got the autopsy results?"

Guastafeste nodded. "Cause of death was drowning. But the pathologist says the bruising to the head happened before that. It looks as if he was unconscious when he went into the water."

I grimaced. "You said on the phone this morning that you didn't think it was an accident. But couldn't he somehow have banged his head and then toppled into the canal?"

"Banged his head on what?"

"I don't know. Which bit of the canal was it? A wall, a pole? Could he have run into something and knocked himself out?"

"The bruising was to the back of the head. No, we're pretty sure he was hit with some kind of blunt object. Not a hammer or an iron bar or anything that leaves a distinctive mark on the skull, but maybe a piece of wood. Something flat and heavy."

I blew air out between my teeth. "This is nasty, Antonio. Why would anyone want to kill Rikard?"

Guastafeste took a sip of coffee before he answered.

"The receptionist says that when he left the hotel, he was carrying a violin case."

I stared at him. "You know which one?"

31

"The Hardanger fiddle. The other violin, the ordinary one, is still in his hotel room."

"You think the fiddle has something to do with his murder?"

"Well, it's disappeared. We've searched the area around the canal, but there's no sign of it. We even sent down a diver to look for it in the water – in case it had sunk – but there was nothing there."

"Why would anyone kill him for a Hardanger fiddle?" I said.

"You're a violin expert. I wondered whether you might have any ideas."

I raised my shoulders and spread my hands in bewilderment. "I know nothing about Hardanger fiddles."

"Was it valuable? Could it be sold for a lot of money?"

"I doubt it. The violins that make the headlines – the Stradivaris and so on – are worth a fortune because they make a sublime sound and there are so few of them. It's supply and demand. But there's no market for Hardanger fiddles. At least, that's what Ingvar Aandahl told me last night."

"Was he interested in it?"

"He didn't seem to be. He expressed nothing but contempt for them."

"Maybe that was only a pretence."

"You suspect Aandahl was involved?"

"We're keeping an open mind about everything. He's a Norwegian violin dealer, after all, and Hardanger fiddles are uniquely Norwegian. Aren't you always telling me what crooks violin dealers are?"

"Well, yes," I conceded. "They're unscrupulous rogues, but I wouldn't go so far as to call them murderers."

"Even for something they really want?"

"There are other, less violent, ways to get things. I know nothing about Aandahl, but Serafin, for example, would never need to kill to acquire a violin. He just negotiates his adversaries into the grave. Have you spoken to Aandahl?"

"He flew back to Norway this morning. But he's on the list of people we want to talk to."

"Anyone else on the list?"

"That's hard to say. It depends how wide we want to cast the net."

"What do you mean?"

"Well, there were fifty or sixty people at Rikard's talk last night who saw the Hardanger fiddle. Maybe one of them decided they had to have it. On the other hand, it's possible the fiddle is a red herring. Maybe Rikard was killed for some other reason."

"Like what?"

"We don't know. But we think he may have known his killer. Why else would he have left his hotel at that time of night? He was obviously going out to meet someone. There's no record of any phone calls on his hotel landline, but his mobile phone wasn't on his body and we haven't found it anywhere else. He must've known other people in Cremona?"

"I'm sure he did," I said. "He was a student here. He may well have kept in touch with friends from the past, but I wouldn't know who they were."

"We're getting a list of his contemporaries from the violin-making school. Some of them will still be in the city. They might be able to help us. And didn't you say he was a bit of a womaniser? Maybe some of his old girlfriends are still around."

"You think he might have gone to meet an old flame?"

"It's one theory."

"And she killed him?"

"We have to consider all the possibilities. Some abandoned woman nursing a grudge."

"For twenty years?"

Guastafeste shrugged. "Women have long memories. Maybe Rikard coming back opened old wounds, maybe they had an argument that turned violent. Who knows? We're floundering around in the dark, Gianni. It could be an Italian, it could be a Norwegian who knew Rikard back in his own country. We're checking all the hotel registration records for Norwegian passport holders, checking the passenger lists of recent flights from Norway. It's going to take a lot of time."

I drank some of my iced tea, glancing away for a moment to watch the traffic crawling by, the flow impeded by roadworks at the junction fifty metres up the street. There was a tang of exhaust fumes in the air, the occasional burst of noise from a pneumatic drill. I looked back at Guastafeste.

"You have no idea at all where he went when he left the hotel?"

Guastafeste shook his head. "It's a long walk to the canal, so we assume someone picked him up. Rikard didn't have his own car. He came to Cremona by public transport – shuttle bus from Malpensa to Milan, then train from there."

"No one saw the car?"

"No. We can only speculate about what happened. Maybe they drove around the city, maybe they went to an apartment or a house where the killer knocked Rikard out, then took his body to the canal and threw it into the water."

I winced as I pictured the actions Antonio was describing so prosaically. He didn't intend to be insensitive. Rikard meant nothing to him except as a murder victim, a case number to be investigated, solved and filed away in a basement somewhere. But that wasn't how I saw it. I'd known Rikard as a young, gifted student just starting out on life and now that life had been taken away from him. I couldn't look on any of it with a policeman's professional detachment. This was personal, and it hurt.

"You've got nothing on CCTV?" I asked.

"There are no cameras outside the hotel or near that particular section of the canal. We're appealing for witnesses, but so far no one's come forward."

I sat back in my chair. There was a lot to take in. Murders in Cremona are rare and I knew from my years of friendship with Antonio that the few killings that do take place are usually relatively straightforward to deal with. There are exceptions, notably the murders of my old friend Tomaso Rainaldi and a Parisian fine-arts dealer named François Villeneuve that caused problems for the police. But in general the killings are things like underworld shootings, domestic violence and drug-related homicides – mostly localised crimes where someone has witnessed the event or where the pool of suspects is small and easy to identify.

But Rikard's case wasn't like that. He was a foreign national with few connections in the city. No one seemed to know where he'd gone on the night he was killed, let alone seen what happened. The strain was showing in Guastafeste's face. This was one case that wasn't going to be simple to solve.

"I have to get back to the *questura*," he said, reaching for his jacket.

"Has Rikard's family been told?" I asked.

"It's in progress. There are language barriers to get round, diplomatic protocols to be observed. 'Official channels', you know how slow and tortuous they can be."

He pushed back his chair and stood up. "Will you do something for me, Gianni? You know violins better than anyone. Will you look into Hardanger fiddles, particularly the one Rikard had, and see what you can find out?"

"Of course," I said. "I'll do whatever I can to help."

"Thank you."

Guastafeste nodded and walked away along the street, his jacket slung casually over his shoulder.

I heard nothing more from Antonio for the next couple of days and I didn't try to get in touch with him. I knew he'd be snowed under with work, preoccupied with the Olsen case, and pestering phone calls from me would not be welcome. I spent some time online, doing research into Hardanger fiddles, then went into the violin school for my weekly class, as usual, but I found it difficult to concentrate on teaching. Looking around at my students hunched over their workbenches, I couldn't help but think of Rikard, remembering him crafting his first violin all those years ago, his blond hair falling over his face as he carved and shaped his wood.

I couldn't recall what that first instrument was like – my memory isn't *that* good – but I'm pretty sure it was nothing special, if only because most people's first attempts, my own included, are generally poor. Violin making, after all, is a skill that has to be learnt, and a skill that has a set of demanding specifications to accommodate, from the thickness of the plates to the length of the bass bar and the dimensions of the pegbox. Most of them were worked out centuries ago and have yet to be improved on, which is sometimes difficult for students to accept. They are young, keen, often brash, and have dreams – or delusions – of reinventing the wheel. They live in a world where rapid technological change is the norm: a faster computer chip, a smarter phone, a more efficient car. It can be disconcerting for them to realise that the form of the violin was perfected three hundred years ago by a bunch of artisans with pencils and paper and a few chisels and it's not ever going to be surpassed.

The key moment for any luthier, and I remember Rikard struggling with this more than most, is when they come to terms with their own essential inferiority. They are never going to be the greatest in history, for those honours have already gone, but that doesn't mean they can't strive to be the best they can, and find satisfaction in that effort.

I was back home in my kitchen, making pumpkin ravioli in butter sauce for my dinner, when Guastafeste called.

"I want to ask you a favour," he said.

"Go ahead."

"Rikard Olsen's sister, Aina, is flying in from Norway tomorrow, to formally identify his body and make arrangements to take it back home for the funeral. Will you come to the airport with me to meet her?"

"Come *with* you?"

"It's going to be a traumatic experience for her. I don't want it to be too cold and detached. You knew Rikard, you taught him. I think it will make things more personal, easier for her, if someone like you is present. There's also the language issue. She speaks English, but not Italian. You can act as an interpreter, if I need you."

"Well..." I considered the proposal. "I don't see why not. If it will help."

"Thanks, Gianni. I'll pick you up at ten."

We drove north-west on the A1, then skirted round Milan and took the A8 out to Malpensa. On the journey, Antonio filled me in on the progress they were making in the Olsen case. Or, rather, the lack of progress.

"We're getting nowhere," he said, his shoulders rising in a brief shrug of frustration. "We still don't know why Rikard went out that evening or where he went. He must have had a good reason, but what was it? Put yourself in his place. You're in your hotel room, you've had a couple of glasses of wine, you're getting ready to go to bed when someone rings you on your mobile and asks you to meet them."

"It could've been arranged earlier," I said.

"True. But the same questions apply regardless of the timing. Who did he go to meet? What would motivate him to go out that late at night? He was a man, and with men I always feel I'm on safe ground when I think money or sex. One or the other, or both, if you get lucky."

"Is this your old flame theory?"

"It's persuasive, don't you think?"

"As a reason for going out, maybe. As a reason for killing him, I'm not so sure. Yes, Rikard was a bit of a philanderer when he was a student, yes, he probably hurt a lot of women, but twenty years on, would any of them still feel strongly enough to kill him? I can't see it. Women can do vengeful things when they're rejected, but it's usually stuff like vandalising the man's car or cutting up his suits. If they all turned to murder, well, there wouldn't be many men left alive in the world, would there?"

Guastafeste smiled. The traffic was heavy on the Milan ring road, but it was moving steadily. He tailgated a Fiat Punto that was holding us up, then accelerated past as the Fiat pulled over. We were in an unmarked police car, but he resisted the temptation to switch on the siren and flashing lights.

"A man, then," he said. "Rikard goes to meet one of his former lovers and her husband, or current partner, catches them *in flagrante* and explodes. He attacks Rikard, smashes him over the head with something, then panics and dumps his body in the canal."

"You have any evidence to support that?"

"Not a shred. But then there's no evidence to support any other theory, either."

"What about the Hardanger fiddle? Why take that to an assignation with a woman?"

Guastasfeste sighed. "I know. That would indicate the other motivation – money. Someone wanted to buy it from him, but they couldn't agree a price, so the killer took it by force."

"You'd have to want it pretty badly to do that," I said.

"Rikard's dead, the fiddle's missing. It's logical to think there might be a link. Did you get anywhere

39

with Hardanger fiddles?"

"Not far. They really are pretty much a niche interest, even in Norway. Not many people make them and not many people play them."

"What kind of prices do they go for?"

"I couldn't find many auction prices, and those I did find were very low – no more than a couple of thousand euros, which isn't much when you consider how difficult they are to make. A British auction house had one in a sale a few years ago, one with an interesting pedigree. Made in 1905, it's known as 'The Rohan Fiddle' because it was used in the score for the *Lord of the Rings* films. It had an estimate of between three and six thousand pounds – that's not a large amount for an instrument with that kind of movie connection, but it still didn't sell. I think Ingvar Aandahl was right. Hardanger fiddles aren't very valuable."

"Someone obviously wanted Rikard's," Antonio said. "People's ideas about what's valuable aren't always the same. You can't necessarily put a monetary price on something."

"True."

"I remember a case, back at the beginning of my career. This man, he'd been collecting kites since he was a kid. He had a huge collection of them, maybe two hundred kites. He didn't even fly them any more. He just acquired them and stored them in his house. Drove his wife mad. She couldn't bear them cluttering up the place, so one day she got rid of them. Took them to the dump. The man blew his top when he found out, beat his wife to death. None of us could understand it. He killed his wife for some *kites* that were virtually worthless. But it made sense to him. He loved those kites. Love, hate, greed, fear, those are my guideposts in a murder investigation. You want a motive for a killing, it's usually one of those four."

He pulled out to overtake a line of slow-moving lorries.

"Did you find out anything more about Rikard's fiddle? Who made it, where he got it from?"

"No. The only mention of it I could find was on Rikard's own website. He had a photograph of the fiddle and was appealing for help in identifying its maker. I don't know whether he had any response."

"Hmm." Antonio went quiet, lost in his own thoughts.

"Have you managed to speak to Aandahl?" I asked.

Antonio nodded. "Not personally, but we've been in email communication with him. He says he drove straight back to Milan with Vincenzo Serafin after Rikard's talk and went to bed at his hotel."

"Do you believe him?"

"I've no reason not to. Serafin's confirmed that he gave Aandahl a lift, and the hotel's records – the time data on Aandahl's keycard – show that he was in his room from just after half-past ten. He looks to be in the clear."

I turned away to watch the scenery rolling past outside the car, the ugly sprawl of warehouses, offices and industrial enclaves that have colonised the land all around Milan. Nestling incongruously amid the concrete and plastic were a few isolated fields of maize and potatoes and terracotta-roofed farmhouses from another era. I wondered how long it would be before they, too, were swallowed up by the city's insatiable appetite.

"We've hit a brick wall, I'm afraid," Guastafeste said.

"Not a credible suspect in sight."

"What about your suspicion that another Norwegian might be involved?"

"That's going nowhere, too. There are a couple of Norwegian students at the violin making school, a girl in her first year, a boy in his third. We've interviewed them both. They went to the earlier talk Rikard gave for the students only, but we've ruled them out as possible suspects. They're just a couple of really nice kids. I can't imagine them swatting a fly, let alone killing a man."

"What about other Norwegians?"

"We're working our way through the hotel records and airline passenger manifests, but there don't appear to be any leads. There were a handful of Norwegian nationals staying in Cremona that night, but none of them has any obvious links to Rikard and, in any case, all of them have alibis for the time he was killed."

"Which was? You never told me."

"Some time between midnight and three."

"So he could've been killed very soon after he left the hotel?"

"Or three hours after that. The timings aren't very helpful."

We were silent for a few kilometres, Guastafeste driving with an atypical restraint.

"What time does Aina's flight get in?" I asked.

"Thirteen thirty."

I looked at my watch. It was just coming up to noon. It wasn't like Antonio to allow so much leeway in his schedule. He normally does everything at the last minute, leaves only tiny margins before appointments.

"I want to make a small detour before we pick her up," he said, reading my mind.

"A detour?"

"Something about the airline passenger manifests caught my eye. Ingvar Aandahl wasn't on any of them."

I frowned. "I thought you told me he flew back to Norway the morning after Rikard was killed."

"He did. That puzzled me for a moment, until I realised we hadn't obtained the records of private flights in and out of Italy."

"He has his own plane?"

"I'm not sure it's his. The Gulfstream jet he used is registered to a Norwegian company called Aksør Tjenester AS. I want to know a little bit more about that flight and Signor Aandahl."

"You said he was in the clear."

"In that he wasn't in Cremona when Rikard was killed. But he interests me all the same. Did you get the impression they didn't like each other?"

"It was pretty obvious."

"And did you notice them talking to each other just before we left the chapel?"

"Yes."

"It looked to me as if Aandahl was proposing something and Rikard was rejecting it."

I nodded. I'd forgotten how quietly observant Antonio was. All those years a police officer, he didn't miss much.

"I'd say that was a fair guess from their body language."

"I wonder what that proposition was. Something to do with the Hardanger fiddle, maybe? I know Aandahl claims not to be interested in Hardanger fiddles, but that raises a question that's been bothering me for the past few days. If he's not interested in them, why did he come to Cremona to hear Rikard's talk?"

Guastafeste slowed and turned off the motorway onto the approach road to Malpensa. We parked in the short-stay carpark and went into the terminal building, picking our way through the crowded concourse to the VIP lounge that was guarded by two armed security men. Antonio showed his police ID card and said he was expected, but the security guards didn't take his word for it. One of them picked up a phone on the wall and checked before they let us through the door.

After the bustle of the concourse – the long queues at the check-in desks, the streams of travellers moving to and fro with wheeled suitcases, the constant grating announcements over the PA system – the VIP lounge was an oasis of peace and quiet. There was hardly a sound to be heard, not even the bland, intrusive background music that has become unavoidable in most of our public places. But, of course, this wasn't a public place. It was private, and private in a particularly exclusive way.

There were no queues in here, no rows of hard, uncomfortable seats, no chain restaurants selling overpriced food to a captive market. Instead, there were deep armchairs and sofas arranged around low tables in small, intimate clusters, to give the impression of an opulent living room, rather than an airport lounge.

A bar at one side was manned by a young, personable *barista* who was dispensing free tea and coffee and champagne, the last the preferred option if the current occupants of the room were anything to go by. There were eight of them: a lone, middle-aged man with the suit, laptop, mobile phone and characterless uniformity of the international businessman; another middle-aged man with a suntan and a paunch who was sitting on a sofa beside an elegant brunette young enough to be his daughter but who, judging by the man's roving hand on her silkily-clad leg, was more likely a wife or mistress; and an Oriental-looking family consisting of mother, father, two children and a young woman who could only be the nanny, who were occupying one corner of the room, the carpet around them almost submerged by a small sea of shopping bags from Milan's most expensive stores.

Through the large, floor-to-ceiling window that filled one wall, the ceaseless activity of the airport could be viewed – tankers and ancillary vehicles speeding across the apron, planes taxiing to and from their gates, others taking off or landing on the runway over towards the horizon – but not heard. The atmosphere inside the lounge had the silence and serenity of a monastery, though chastity and poverty were conspicuous by their absence and the only gods on show had names like Gucci, Versace and Armani.

A young man in a smart black suit approached the family group and whispered something in a low, deferential voice. Then he waved over two uniformed porters who gathered up the rash of shopping bags and carried them away, the family following them out to their waiting jet.

"Detective Guastafeste?"

We turned and saw a slim young woman in a navy blue jacket, matching pencil skirt and high heels.

"Signora Vasari?" Antonio said.

The young woman nodded. "This way, please."'

She led us across the room and through a door into a neat little office that had no external window but a small glass panel through which the lounge and its occupants could be observed. She gestured at two chairs and sat down behind the desk.

"Do you have some identification on you?"

Guastafeste passed her his police ID card and she studied it carefully.

"This is my colleague, Giovanni Castiglione," he said.

Signora Vasari didn't ask to see my police department credentials, which was perhaps as well. She merely glanced at me and, no doubt seeing a rather handsome, distinguished-looking gentleman of clearly impeccable virtue, moved on to her next question.

"How can I help?"

"We're interested in a passenger who came through here a few days ago, a Norwegian national named Ingvar Aandahl," Guastafeste said.

"Ingvar Aandahl," Signora Vasari repeated, typing the name into the computer on the desk.

"Mid-fifties, or thereabouts, silver hair, suntan."

"Yes, I remember him well. A charming man." She peered at the computer screen. "He arrived on the seventh, left the next day."

"On a jet registered to a Norwegian company, I understand."

"That's correct. Aksør Tjenester AS."

"Do you know anything about that company?"

"I'm afraid not. Our system doesn't give us that kind of information."

"And the jet? Has it been to Milan before?"

She moved the mouse and clicked. "Yes, it comes four or five times a year."

"Always with Signor Aandahl on board?"

"I don't think so. I recognise most of our regulars and I hadn't seen him before." She checked the screen. "Yes, this was his first time in the lounge."

"Was he alone on the plane?"

"His is the only name on the manifest."

"Did you speak to him at all?"

"Of course. As the lounge supervisor I speak to all our visitors. That's what the service is all about, the personal touch. I welcome everyone, make sure they're well looked after, that all their needs are being met. Then I see them off at the end of their stay."

"You must meet a lot of interesting people."

"I do." She flashed an apologetic smile. "Though my duty of confidentiality prohibits me from discussing them, except in extraordinary circumstances, like today. We're always happy to help the police."

"We appreciate that, signora. Tell me, how does all this work? Are private flights subject to the same regulations as commercial airlines?"

"Oh, yes, VIPs are treated no differently from anyone else," she said with a straight face. "The names of all passengers must be listed on the manifest, their luggage goes through exactly the same customs checks and security screenings, the X-rays and searches and so on."

"You have your own machines here?"

"Yes. We are just as thorough as the staff in the main part of the terminal."

She glanced up from the computer and through the glass panel in the wall.

47

"Excuse me a moment."

She went back out into the lounge. Guastafeste and I swivelled round in our seats and saw her greeting a thick-set, portly man of Middle-Eastern appearance, who was accompanied by an entourage of three young men and two women. Signora Vasari fussed around them obsequiously, seeing them to the seating area then supervising the service of drinks and *hors d'oeuvres*.

"Remind me never to fly Alitalia again," Antonio said dryly.

Ten minutes elapsed before the supervisor returned to the office.

"I'm sorry, that couldn't wait," she said without sitting down again. "Was there anything else you needed?"

"I don't think so," Guastafeste said. "You have a difficult job, signora. I imagine you must get some demanding visitors."

"Well, some are easier than others," she replied diplomatically.

"Was Signor Aandahl easy?"

She nodded. "He was very friendly, very chatty. Some visitors can be a little, well, reticent, but Signor Aandahl was quite happy to talk about his business. I suppose it was obvious from his hand luggage."

"His hand luggage?"

"The violin case he had with him."

I saw Antonio stiffen. The room was so quiet I could hear the soft purr of the air conditioning.

"I noticed it at once," Signora Vasari went on, "because it was so unusual. We get used to all kinds of baggage – lots of shopping, of course, but we also have guests who've bought paintings or sculpture in Italy, or who have pets with them. You know, mostly dogs and cats, though we do have one regular visitor from the Far East who always brings his python with him. But we don't see many violin cases. I wondered whether Signor Aandahl was an international soloist, but he said he was a dealer."

"What kind of violin case?" Guastafeste asked.

Signora Vasari was bemused by the question. "Just an ordinary one, I suppose."

"Can you describe it? The shape, the colour?"

"Well, violin-shaped. I don't remember the colour. Is it important?"

"You didn't see inside it?"

"Oh, no. We don't search guests' hand luggage, though it went through the X-ray machine, of course."

"Do you keep records of those X-rays?"

"No, the images aren't stored. The purpose of the scan is to pick up immediate security threats. There's no need to retain the information."

"Thank you, signora. You've been most helpful."

Guastafeste waited until we'd left the VIP lounge and were heading over to the arrivals hall before he said, "Interesting."

"Don't get too excited," I said. "He's a dealer, after all. He was here doing business with Vincenzo Serafin. Why wouldn't he have a violin case with him?"

"Hmm," Antonio murmured. "But all the same, I'd like to know a bit more about what was inside it."

THREE

The arrivals hall was crowded with people, all waiting to greet someone from an incoming flight – husbands, wives, partners, friends, grandparents, families with children and the usual collection of taxi drivers holding up white cards with the names of their clients written on them in large capital letters. Guastafeste had brought a card with him, too, with Aina Olsen's name on it.

We waited to one side of the polished steel railing that funnelled the arriving passengers out into the hall, slightly away from the throng where we had a clear view of the sliding glass doors and where Aina would easily spot us when she came through. We could see from the electronic display board on the wall that her flight had landed, but so too had planes from London and Frankfurt. We watched as the doors slid back at intervals and bursts of new arrivals emerged. The British and Germans were easy to single out, but then we caught glimpses of blond hair and distinctive Scandinavian faces and knew that the passengers from

51

Bergen were here.

I identified Aina almost immediately because of her resemblance to Rikard. The shape of her eyes and her mouth were the same. So, too, was her blonde hair, which was cut shorter than her brother's, in a spiky, neo-punk style that might have looked a bit masculine on a less attractive woman. She was very pretty, but everything about her seemed designed to play down her looks. She wore no make-up, no jewellery except a couple of silver studs in her ears and she was wearing a loose T-shirt, baggy cotton trousers and flat white pumps. Slung over one shoulder was a small, black holdall. She saw Guastafeste's sign and changed course towards us.

"Signora Olsen? I am Detective Antonio Guastafeste of the Cremona police," Antonio said in English.

"*Ciao*," Aina said.

They shook hands, then there was an awkward silence.

"You have a good flight?" Antonio asked, digging deep into his reserves of English. He's better at the language than he likes to claim, but still a little uncomfortable speaking it.

"Yes, thank you."

"Good. Good."

Antonio glanced at me, appealing for help, and I stepped into my role as interpreter. I explained in English who I was and why I was there, then offered my condolences for her loss.

"I'm sorry we're meeting in such sad circumstances. It must have been a terrible shock for you."

"Yes, it was."

"It's a difficult time for you to come here, but

Antonio and I will do our best to help you through it."

"Thank you."

I gestured towards the exit. "Our car is outside."

"Please, I carry your bag," Antonio said.

Aina shook her head. "It's not heavy."

"Okay. Good."

We went out to the car and had another small stand-off when I attempted to let her have the front seat and she insisted on going in the back, keeping her holdall beside her. We drove away from the airport and I twisted round to talk to her over my shoulder. The difficult introductions were over and I sensed it might be a good moment to distract her with some conversation that wasn't about her brother.

"Is this your first time in Italy?" I asked.

She seemed glad to change the subject. "No, I've been a couple of times before. To Venice and Florence on one trip, to the *Cinque Terre* on another."

"Did you walk the *Cinque Terre*?"

She nodded. "That was the best bit. The towns themselves were so crowded they weren't much fun. But out on the hiking trails it was beautiful."

I could see her on the rough paths that link the "Five Lands", the ancient clifftop villages on the Ligurian coast that attract thousands of tourists each summer. She had the lithe, springy build of a hiker.

"I'm afraid it's got worse over there in recent years," I said. "I remember doing the walk a long time ago when my children were young. We stayed overnight in Riomaggiore and Vernazza and they were quite peaceful in the evenings. The kids have never forgiven me for the blisters on their feet. After that, it was the beach or nothing every August."

Aina gave a weak smile. I knew she was three or four years younger than Rikard, so that put her in her late thirties, though you wouldn't have known it from her appearance. Her face was almost unlined, the skin smooth and pale, but with a hint of the sun in her cheeks.

"So you haven't been to Cremona before?" I said.

"No... well, yes," she corrected herself. "I did come once, but I don't remember much about it. It was when Rikard was a student. He'd just started at the violin-making school. My parents and I came to see how he was getting on. I was a bit bored, I think. I wanted to be at home with my friends."

She looked away thoughtfully for a moment. "Rikard loved Italy, loved Cremona, loved his time at the school. For this to happen..." Her voice trailed off. "I don't understand it. Why? Why did it happen?"

"We don't know why," I said gently. "But the police are doing their best to find out. Antonio will tell you about it later."

We didn't talk much for the rest of the journey. Rikard's death was too sensitive a subject, and everything else seemed trivial in comparison. When we reached Cremona, Guastafeste drove us straight to the mortuary and I waited in an ante-room while he and Aina went through into the back to formally identify Rikard's body.

Aina looked ashen when they came out. Her eyes were moist, her face and mouth tight with shock. A close friend or relative would probably have given her the comforting hug she needed, but I was neither, so I merely touched her sympathetically on the arm and ushered her towards the exit. Lingering in such a grim place was not going to be good for her.

A café, or one of Cremona's excellent ice cream parlours, might have been a welcome antidote to the ordeal Aina had just had to go through, but it was hardly appropriate in the situation, so we went to the *questura* instead and shut ourselves away in a private little office behind the main squadroom.

In halting English, occasionally using me as an intermediary, Guastafeste told Aina what he knew about her brother's death. The information could have been upsetting, but she took it well. She seemed relieved to be moving on from the mortuary and getting down to the facts of what had occurred. It still didn't make any sense to her, though.

"Rikard was a wonderful guy. Why would anyone want to kill him?" she said with a perplexed frown.

"We don't understand either," Guastafeste replied. "He was a visitor to Cremona, though of course he had lived here as a student. What we try to work out is what happened before he die. Does he say anything to you about his trip before he leaves Norway?"

Aina thought for a second, then shrugged. "Not much. I knew he was coming to do a talk, but that was about it."

"You both live in Bergen, don't you?"

"Yes."

"Did you see much of each other?"

"A fair bit. We led separate, busy lives, but we managed to meet up, maybe, once a month."

"You have other family?"

"Only distant relatives. Our parents are both dead and we don't have any other brothers or sisters."

"Rikard was not married, was he?"

"No, he had an ex-partner, but they were never married."

"What is her name?"

"Kamilla. Kamilla Nygaard."

"He had a daughter, too? He told us when we went out with him after his talk."

"Elin."

"And she is how old?"

"Twelve."

"She live with Rikard?"

Aina shook her head. "She lives with Kamilla, but she used to see Rikard every other weekend, and sometimes during the week."

Antonio made a few notes on a pad, then looked up, his expression serious, but supportive.

"I'm sorry to ask you so many questions. But I try to build a... a picture of Rikard's life, to work out who might have reason to kill him. Did he know anyone in Cremona, maybe friends from the past?"

Aina considered her response.

"I suppose he must have had friends here, but he never mentioned anyone in particular."

"Old girlfriends?"

She let out a soft exclamation that seemed tinged with a kind of wry resignation.

"Well, there are probably a few of those. There certainly are in Norway."

"He was popular with women, no?"

"You could say that."

"But he never give you names?"

"I'm his sister. We didn't discuss our love lives in much detail."

Guastafeste turned over a page of his notepad and

wrote down the reply. Beyond the door, in the squadroom, I could hear phones ringing, voices, the scrape of chairs on the floor.

"Nearly finish," Antonio said. "Your brother bring a violin with him from Norway, a Hardanger fiddle. Do you know anything about it?"

"No. He showed it to me, let me play it a little, but that's all."

"You play the fiddle?"

"In my spare time."

"He take the fiddle with him when he leave his hotel the night he was killed. We have not found it since."

"You think that was the motive for the murder?"

"Is possible."

Aina squinted at him incredulously. "Who would kill for a flimsy reason like that?"

"I do not know, signora," Guastafeste replied. "But murder is complicated. It very rarely makes sense."

Aina was going to be in Cremona for a few days, at least. There were procedures that had to be followed before her brother's body could be released and flown home to Norway, procedures that, like everything else in Italy, are inextricably tied up with our enduring love affair with bureaucracy.

The Romans started it all. They conquered the world with their swords, then kept it subjugated with their filing cabinets. If something could be written down and stored, it was. If it could be subject to a litany of regulations and edicts, all as obscure and complex as possible, then so much the better. If it resulted in endless squabbles over jurisdiction and meaning, well, how else were the lawyers going to pay for their villas by the sea? In the ancient world, the emperor and the generals were not king, the clerks were.

Little has changed since. We live in the age of the computer, but unfortunately no one has told the authorities, who still have a voracious craving for paperwork, preferably in triplicate and only between the hours of nine and twelve, except on Wednesdays. It was a tricky obstacle course for even our native countrymen to negotiate, but for a foreigner like Aina, who spoke almost no Italian, it was like navigating the globe with no map, no compass and no boat. Fortunately, she had both Guastafeste and me on hand to assist her. I claim no special expertise in this area for myself – other than sixty-five years of cynical experience – but Antonio is a true master of the system. Being a police officer, he enforces the rules, but also knows exactly how to bend them to his own advantage. We have a name for this in Italian. We call it public service.

"Leave all to me," he said gallantly. "I fill out the forms and then all you do is sign them."

"Thank you, that's very kind."

"This must be very painful for you. If I can help, I will."

We left Antonio to his duties and walked over to the small hotel near the cathedral that Aina had booked for her stay. It was a good hotel, but it had no restaurant or dining room, just a few tables off the foyer where breakfast was served. The thought of Aina spending the evening alone in her room, or wandering the streets looking for somewhere to eat, troubled me.

We'd met only a few hours earlier, but I felt somehow responsible for her well being, partly because I'd known her brother, partly because she was a guest in my home city and I wanted to be hospitable.

"Would you like to come to dinner at my house this evening?" I asked.

Aina hesitated. "Dinner?"

"It won't just be me," I said, trying to allay any fears she might have about dining with a complete stranger. "I have a friend, Margherita, who will be there. And perhaps Antonio will also join us. Please say no, if you have other plans, but I thought you might like company. It can be very lonely on your own in a new city."

"That's good of you," Aina replied. "Yes, I'd like that. Thank you."

"I'll let you settle in now. Then come back later and pick you up."

The nature of my work is necessarily solitary – making instruments on my own in my workshop – but I am not a recluse. I enjoy those hours at my bench, just me and my wood and my tools, but I also enjoy the company of others. By temperament I am a sociable, gregarious man. That's why I love my teaching, the interaction with students and colleagues at the violin-making school, that's why I get involved with committees and community affairs and why I like to have guests over to my home for meals.

When my wife was alive, we had regular gatherings at the house, though Caterina was always less comfortable with the role of host than I was. She enjoyed the conviviality of the occasions, particularly with close friends, but with new acquaintances or strangers she would often escape to the sanctuary of the kitchen and the preparation of food, leaving me to do the entertaining.

After her death, I retreated into my shell a little. Friends still invited me out and I kept up my teaching, but I stopped having people to the house. It just wasn't the same without Caterina by my side. It's perhaps not a fashionable view, but I feel that dinner parties need two people at the helm to be successful. The stresses and the pleasures have to be shared, which is why I am more inclined to be sociable now Margherita is becoming a greater part of my life. She's shy in many ways and has been understandably tentative about moving into my circle of friends, but she's generally good with people. She's interested in them, relaxed in company and can make conversation with even the most difficult guests. Having her there at the house when I arrived with Aina was immensely reassuring for all of us.

Margherita's English is excellent, which helped, but she also has a natural welcoming manner that puts people at ease. I poured them both glasses of wine and left them together in the living room while I went into the kitchen to finish making dinner – a corn-fed chicken stuffed with herbs that I was going to serve with roast potatoes and green beans from my garden. I was preparing an *antipasto misto* as a starter when Margherita came in to see if I needed any help.

I shook my head. "I'm fine. How are you getting on?"

"Very well. She's a delightful young woman. Very interesting."

"Yes?"

"She works as a graphic designer for a small website development company in Bergen, but plays and sings in a folk band in the evenings. She's thirty-nine years old, has never been married but has two children – a seventeen-year-old girl and a fourteen-year-old boy – by two different fathers."

I stared at her. "You found that all out in fifteen minutes?"

"I'm nosey," Margherita said. "You know how I work. I treat everyone like my students. Put them on the spot and ask them questions, probing them until they give me an answer."

"Did she mind?"

"No one minds talking about themselves. It's everyone's favourite topic of conversation. Besides, it goes two ways. She knows a lot about me now, as well. And you."

"You told her about me?"

"Only the juicy bits. We women need a bit of good gossip."

I sliced some tomatoes and arranged them on a plate with black olives, salami, ham and artichoke hearts.

"How is she emotionally?" I asked. "She had to identify her brother's body earlier. That must have been harrowing."

"We haven't talked about Rikard. I've stuck to safe subjects, tried to take her mind off what's happened. She's having a look around the garden. Why don't you come out and join us?"

"Give me five minutes."

I finished the starter before moving on to topping

and tailing the green beans and putting them in the steamer, ready to cook later. Then, a glass of wine in my hand, I wandered out onto the terrace at the back of the house. It was a fine evening, the sun dipping towards the horizon beyond the fields, bathing the garden in a soft, golden light. Margherita and Aina were strolling on the lawn, talking and inspecting my flower beds.

"You have a beautiful garden," Aina said as I approached. "How do you find the time to look after it?"

"Mostly by employing someone else to do it," I replied. "Well, the boring bits. I have a young lad who mows the lawn, cuts the hedges and does his best to keep on top of the weeds. That means I can concentrate on the fun stuff – the plants, the vegetables, the lounging in a chair just doing nothing. That's my favourite bit."

"I envy you. All this space you've got, the fresh air, the view. Not to mention the weather."

"Do you garden?"

"If only. I live in a first-floor apartment with a balcony that could fit, maybe, two plant pots. No one really gardens in Norway – like this, I mean. All these flowers and fruit bushes and vegetables. The growing season just isn't long enough."

"But you have compensations," I said. "All that stunning scenery, the mountains, the fjords."

"Unfortunately, not in my back garden," Aina said dryly.

She'd changed her clothes since the afternoon – taken off the baggy trousers and shapeless T-shirt and replaced them with a smarter pair of black trousers and a tailored sky-blue cotton blouse. Around her neck was a silver chain with a rainbow-pattern enamelled pendant dangling from it.

"Is that your workshop over there?" she asked, looking towards the old brick smithy at the side of the garden. I nodded. "Could I see it?"

"If you'd like to."

"I like seeing where people work, particularly craftsmen."

I opened the door and we went inside the workshop. I'm so used to it now that I can't see anything of interest about it. It's simply the place where I work. But I've noticed that visitors are often keen to find out more about what I do there. They like to see the templates and moulds I use, the tools hanging from the racks, the violins in all their different stages of construction, from the rough-cut plates to the finished instruments. I suppose it's a novelty for them. Violin making is such a specialised, arcane craft that most people know very little about it. Aina, however, had had a brother who'd been a luthier.

"It's like Rikard's workshop," she said, gazing around the room. "The same in some ways, different in others."

"We all put our individual stamps on our work places," I said.

"This is bigger than Rikard's. His is quite cramped, tucked away off a dark, damp alley. He finds it quite hard to get the varnish on his violins to dry properly. He has an ultra-violet light box that he hangs them in for a few weeks. Have you seen one of those? It's like a dustbin. The violin goes round and round inside it so it dries evenly."

"I know what you mean," I said. "But fortunately for me, I have no need of help like that. I just let the sun do its work."

Aina nodded. "I guess there's a reason why Stradivari didn't come from Bergen."

She lingered by my bench, studying the maple back plate I was in the process of hollowing out.

"You must have made a lot of violins."

"Quite a few, yes."

"I wanted Rikard to make one for me, but he was always too busy on other commissions. Now I'll never have one, never have something to remind me of him."

She ran her fingers along the edge of the bench, feeling the smooth, worn timber, and I knew she was thinking of a different bench in a different workshop. Her face was pensive, her clear blue eyes touched with melancholy. I tried to divert what I could sense were upsetting thoughts.

"Margherita tells me you play and sing in a folk group."

She turned away from the bench to look at me.

"Yes. A Hardanger fiddle for the folk music, but I do play the ordinary violin, too. I still love classical music and Beethoven sonatas sound rather weird on a Hardanger fiddle."

I smiled. "I can imagine."

She took a final look around the workshop, then we went back out into the garden. Margherita and Aina set the table on the terrace and we ate outside, the dusk turning to night. I lit a couple of candles on the table and served the *antipasti* in the flickering light. It was quiet, barely a breath of wind. The air was warm and soft, suffused with the scent of the candles.

We'd finished the starter and were having a short break before the main course when Guastafeste showed up. I hadn't seriously expected him to come, given the pressures of the murder investigation, but I was delighted to see him.

Like Aina, he'd changed his clothes from earlier, replaced his rather worn work suit and tie with a smarter jacket and casual trousers, his white shirt open at the neck. He'd shaved again, too, got rid of the five o'clock shadow that he normally had by this time of the day, and his black hair was combed and neatly parted. I'd rarely seen him looking so well groomed.

I poured him a glass of wine and insisted he had some *antipasti*. I knew he wouldn't have eaten much, if anything, all day; that's how he is when he's engrossed in his work.

Then we ate the roast chicken and chatted, our conversation that strange, haphazard mixture you get when different nationalities are together and everyone is having to speak a *lingua franca* – in this case, English – in which they have differing degrees of proficiency. But it worked well, even for Antonio who, I think, surprised himself with his fluency. The topics ranged widely – music and violins through to politics and Norwegian culture – but the one subject we didn't touch on was Rikard. He was the ghost at the meal, but we all sensed instinctively that his presence shouldn't be acknowledged for fear of the emotions it would arouse. Aina was grieving, but for a few hours, at least, we could try to ease her pain.

For dessert, I produced my own special home-made concoction of sliced fresh strawberries, ice cream and amaretti biscuits crushed and soaked in wine, arranged in layers like a sort of sweet, fruity lasagne and topped with chopped hazelnuts and chocolate sauce – my "diet-buster", I call it because a single serving contains about the recommended calorie intake for a grown man for a month.

Afterwards, Guastafeste and I left the women on the terrace, enjoying one of my many liqueurs, and went inside to the kitchen. Antonio – at my insistence – sat on a chair while I did the washing up, for it is one of the inviolable rules of my dinner parties that my guests do not assist with the chores.

Aina wasn't present, so he had no qualms about updating me on his inquiries.

"I've been in touch with Ingvar Aandahl," he said. "He admits he had a violin with him when he left Italy. You were right, it was one he bought from Vincenzo Serafin. A Gasparo da Salò, he says, and Serafin has confirmed it."

"Are you disappointed?" I asked.

Antonio pulled a wry face. "Maybe. It would have made things nice and simple if Aandahl had been our man. The *questore* is pushing us for a quick solution, but I don't think he's going to get it."

I washed and rinsed a couple of plates and slotted them into the rack on the draining board to dry.

"You have no one else in the frame?"

He shook his head. "No one even close to the frame. The picture's just a blur at the moment. We still have no idea where Rikard went that night, or how he ended up in the canal."

"What about your theory it was someone from his past?"

"It's still just a theory. There's nothing to support it,

well, except common sense. Why would he have gone out to meet a complete stranger? Why would a complete stranger have taken the Hardanger fiddle? This wasn't a random killing. Someone planned it."

"Have you tracked down any of his contemporaries at the violin-making school? Or his old girlfriends?"

"We're working through a list. But, so far, we're getting nowhere. I'm worried. With murder, the first few days are always critical. You usually get a feel for a case, start to get a clearer idea of what happened, maybe identify some possible suspects who can be investigated further, but with Rikard there's none of that. We're blundering around in the dark."

He got up from his chair and walked about aimlessly, going to the door and looking out onto the terrace, then coming back and pacing around the kitchen table. I could feel his frustration and restlessness.

"I have to go, Gianni," he said. "Thanks for dinner."

He paused, gazing out at the terrace again. Aina's beautiful face and blonde hair were illuminated in the candlelight. Antonio watched her pensively for a moment.

"How did she get here?" he asked.

"I picked her up from her hotel."

"Let me give her a lift back."

FOUR

Three days later, Aina flew back to Bergen, her brother's body following on a separate flight. Before she left, we exchanged email addresses and she promised to let me know when Rikard's funeral was to be held. I'd grown very fond of her during her short stay in Cremona. She'd spent quite a bit of time with Antonio, sorting out all the paperwork, but she'd also come out to the house once more for dinner with me and Margherita and we'd met for lunch in town and I'd shown her the cathedral and the violin museum. Her parents were dead. Now her brother had gone too. I felt a fatherly concern for her and wanted to do all I could to support her at this horrendous time.

Going to Rikard's funeral wasn't something I would normally have considered. I hadn't known him well and Norway is a long way away, but I wanted to do it for Aina – and for me, too, if I'm honest, for Margherita and I had discussed the matter and decided to combine it with a holiday. Neither of us had been to Norway and we both had a long-held desire to see the country.

When I told Guastafeste of our plans, he stunned me by saying he might come too.

"Not for a holiday," he said. "I'll leave that to you and Margherita. But on business."

"Business?"

"Our investigation is stalled. We have absolutely no leads in Cremona. No potential suspects, no one who might have had a motive to kill Rikard. We obtained his mobile phone records. He received a call at about seven o'clock in the evening, just before he did his talk at the violin-making school, but the caller's number was untraceable, from a pay-as-you-go phone. We don't know who it was or whether it has anything to do with Rikard's murder. We've hit a dead end."

"You think you can find a lead in Bergen?" I asked.

Guastafeste shrugged. "That's where Rikard lived. I think the key to the murder is more likely to be there than in Italy. He has a past in Bergen, maybe enemies with a reason to want him dead. And that's where the Hardanger fiddle came from."

"You still think that's important?"

"Don't you? It has to be. I want to know more about that fiddle, and I won't do that from a desk at the *questura*."

The stumbling block, I knew, would be his superiors in the police force, who have a pathological loathing of spending money, except on themselves, so I was surprised when Antonio called me to say his plan had been approved.

"The *questore*'s in a tight spot," he said. "An unsolved murder – particularly of a foreign visitor – doesn't look good for the city's image, doesn't do much for the tourist industry. He's under pressure from the mayor and the media to clear it up quickly. Sending an officer to Norway looks as if we're making an effort and, you never know, it might be the breakthrough we need."

We took the same flight from Malpensa and descended into Flesland Airport through a thick layer of black cloud that only cleared when we were virtually over the runway. In the baggage reclaim area, waiting by the carousel for our luggage, I looked around for a toilet and saw something quite bizarre. Signs for public lavatories are commonly stylised silhouettes of men and women, the men in trousers, the women in dresses to distinguish them from each other. That was the case here, but what made them different was that both silhouettes had their legs crossed, their bodies slightly bent over, hands pressed to their groins, as if they were desperate for a pee. I pointed it out to Margherita and she let out a vulgar guffaw.

"Norwegian humour?" she said. "I think I'm going to like it here."

We'd been warned that taking taxis in Norway – and many other things, too – would burn up our limited spending money, not to mention give Antonio's accounts department a collective heart attack, so we took the bus into Bergen, a twenty-kilometre journey that might well have been scenic, if we'd been able to see the scenery. It was raining heavily and the landscape was shrouded in white mist that, when it broke apart occasionally, revealed rocky outcrops and stands of dark coniferous trees.

It was still raining when we reached the city. We got off at the bus station and wheeled our suitcases up a steep hill to our hotel, an elegant white three-storey building that I knew from my booking over the internet dated back to the nineteenth century. We'd come prepared, with raincoats and umbrellas, but we were nevertheless a little damp when we walked into the reception area to check in. Our rooms were up on the third floor and there was no lift so Guastafeste carried Margherita's case for her and was breathing heavily when we got to the top of the stairs.

"See you in a bit," he said, going into his room.

Ours was next door, a decent-sized space with a double bed and en-suite bathroom. From the window, we had a view north over the city, though I use the word "view" advisedly. I recalled what Rikard Olsen had told us about arriving in Bergen to see it at its best: from the west by boat, with the setting sun behind you, the wind in your sails. Hmm.

Leaving aside the obvious problem that arriving by boat from Italy isn't easy, there were a number of other flaws in that evocative scenario. For a start, there was no sun, let alone a setting one. It was hidden away somewhere in the clouds. There was a wind, we'd experienced just how strong and icy on our walk up from the bus station, but rather than filling the sails of a boat, it struck me as far more likely to capsize it, drowning the occupants. Worst of all, even if a seaborne entrance to the city had been viable, there wouldn't have been much to see, for the whole place was hidden under the blanket of mist that had been with us since the airport. "Wet" – that was the one-word description Rikard had used about his home town. Right now, I would have added another: "invisible."

We unpacked and dried off a bit, draping clammy

items of clothing over the radiator. The warm bed looked so appealing, and the outside world so not, that I was tempted to suggest we had a lie down and maybe a nap, but I reproved myself for my weakness. We hadn't come to Bergen to doze, we'd come to explore.

"Shall we go?" I said.

Margherita gave me a plaintive look that told me she'd been having exactly the same feeble thoughts as me.

"Do we have to?"

I was hard on her for her own good. "Yes."

"But it's raining out there."

"We have umbrellas."

"And cold."

"We'll walk fast."

"And I'd really like a coffee."

"We'll find a café."

She liked the sound of that. "There might be one downstairs."

"The hotel coffee shop doesn't count," I said firmly. "Come on, put your shoes back on."

In a slow, lethargic way that reminded me of my children getting ready for school when they were very young, Margherita slipped her feet into her damp shoes and stood up. She put her coat back on and shivered.

"Sometimes you can be really mean, Gianni."

I kissed her lightly. "You'll thank me when you see how beautiful Bergen is."

"I'll thank you when I see how beautiful that cup of coffee is."

We knocked on Guastafeste's door on our way to the stairs. He wasn't very keen on coming out either.

"Why don't we wait until it stops raining?" he said.

"I fear that might be never," I replied.

"Resistance is useless," Margherita said. "As I've discovered to my cost."

Guastafeste sighed and got his umbrella. We walked down the hill from the hotel, past the stark glass and concrete Grieghallen, Bergen's concert hall, and out into the garden surrounding the Lille Lungegårdsvann, the lozenge-shaped ornamental lake in the centre of the city. The rain had eased off a little, but it was still falling steadily, pitter-pattering on the tops of our umbrellas and dripping off the sides. There was no mist this low down, but the hillside to the north and the peak of Mount Fløyen were cloaked in low cloud.

We headed west towards the sea and found ourselves in a long, narrow plaza that was dominated by a statue of a man playing the violin on top of a stack of rocks. Beneath the man's feet, a cascade of water poured out over a smaller statue of what looked like an elf playing a harp before spilling down into a shallow pool.

Margherita read the inscription carved into the rock.

"That's Ole Bull," she said. "Didn't Rikard Olsen play some of his music at his talk?"

I nodded. "The Herdgirl's Sunday."

"How did he describe him, the Norwegian Paganini?"

"That's right. Some people even thought he was better than Paganini."

I studied the statue. It depicted Bull as the young, handsome man who had enraptured audiences, particularly the women, of his day with his looks and astonishing prowess on the violin. He was born in Bergen, and is buried there, but is a huge historical figure across the whole of Norway.

They say the world is shrinking, but we still remain largely ignorant about cultures other than our own. In Italy, Giuseppe Garibaldi, for example, is a revered national hero, the general who brought about the reunification of the nation. There is hardly a town in the country that does not have a street or a square named after him, yet my English friends think he was the inventor of a biscuit.

Norwegian history does not command much interest in Italy. Most Italians would be hard pressed to name even three famous Norwegians and if they did, they would probably come up with Grieg, Ibsen and Amundsen, all great men who made a mark on the world beyond their homeland. Yet in Norway, Ole Bull is as venerated as they are, though few people outside the country have ever heard of him.

"I can see that's Bull on the top," Guastafeste said. "But who's the long-haired fellow with the harp?"

"I think it's a *nøkken*," I replied, for I'd read up on Bull and Bergen before we'd left home.

"A what?"

"A water spirit from Scandinavian folklore. They were said to lure people to their deaths with the beauty of their music. I guess it's symbolic of Bull, whose playing was supposed to be equally alluring."

Skirting the statue, we turned right into a large square, closed to traffic and edged with shops. There were more people here, some sheltering beneath umbrellas, some cocooned in raincoats and cagoules, the hoods pulled tight around their faces. They looked sturdy, sensible people, the inhabitants of this city. There was not a sign of high fashion on display, at least, not as recognised by most Italians. Men and women alike, they were dressed as if planning a long walk to the North Pole: stout boots, waterproof trousers, woolly hats and gloves. Yet they appeared surprisingly cheerful. I suppose they're used to the weather. It brought to mind a joke about Bergen in my guidebook, a young local boy being asked by a visitor if it ever stopped raining who replies, "I don't know, sir, I'm only eight."

Beyond the square, we walked down a slight incline, the pavement slick with water, to the Torget, the quayside by the harbour where they have an open-air fish market. We could smell the produce long before we reached the stalls where it was on sale. The rain didn't seem to have deterred customers from coming out, for the area was crowded with people who looked as wet as the fish laid out on the slab – the herring and hake and glistening orange lobsters.

"Isn't that a cafe across the street?" Margherita said.

"So it is," Guastafeste confirmed. "Gianni?"

I could see I was outnumbered, but decided to make a counter suggestion that I hoped would appeal to all of us.

"You see the mountain over there?" I said, nodding towards the houses that were tiered up the lower slopes of a hill.

"No," Guastafeste replied. "I don't see a mountain."

"I only see a café," Margherita said pointedly. "A nice, warm, dry café that probably sells excellent coffee."

"There's a café up the mountain," I said.

"We can't see a mountain, let alone a café."

"It's at the top. In the mist," I explained.

76

Margherita eyed me narrowly. "Is that your idea of an irresistible proposition?"

"The view's supposed to be terrific."

"The view of what, exactly?"

"You want us to climb a mountain to get a cup of coffee?" Guastafeste said. "In the rain?" he added, in case I hadn't noticed.

"There's a funicular up it," I said. "Come on. It won't take long."

I moved off purposefully before they could argue. I wanted a hot drink as much as they did, but I knew that the minute we were settled in a café, we wouldn't venture out again except to go back to the hotel. We had to show some Norwegian spirit, some of that gritty determination that enables them to defy the elements. If Amundsen could conquer Antarctica, then we could manage a railway up Mount Fløyen.

I bought tickets for us all, knowing that Guastafeste would have difficulty charging the trip to his police expenses. We appeared to be the only passengers on the train. When I inadvisedly commented on this, Margherita said with uncharacteristic sarcasm, "I wonder why."

I wasn't put off. I've always been an optimist and I had a feeling that the weather was about to change for the better. The first part of the journey was in a steep tunnel through solid rock where there was absolutely nothing to see. Then we emerged from the tunnel and there was still nothing to see. I avoided Margherita's eye.

Our seats were facing backwards so, in theory, we should have had a view of Bergen below us, but there was nothing but an opaque wall of cloud that seemed to get more impenetrable as the train rattled its way up the mountain. Margherita and Guastafeste stared intently out of the windows, as if entranced by the scenery. Neither said anything, which made me feel even worse about persuading – all right, bullying – them to accompany me.

At the top, more disappointment was waiting for us. Disembarking and walking the short distance to the summit, we discovered that the restaurant was closed to the public, having been fully booked by a tour party from a cruise ship. Fortunately, there was a small kiosk on the terrace outside the restaurant where we managed to buy three coffees and a bar of chocolate.

The terrace was deserted, but the tables and chairs were still set out beneath a canvas awning that was sagging under the weight of rainwater. On the back of each chair, I noticed folded squares of red material that I realised were blankets – a welcome example of Norwegian adaptation to climate. I gathered up a collection of these squares from adjacent tables, then made Margherita and Guastafeste sit down. I draped one blanket over Margherita's legs and wrapped another around her shoulders. Guastafeste and I did the same for ourselves and we sat huddled together, watching the water dripping off the edge of the awning.

"Well, this is a bit different, isn't it?" I said to break the silence.

No one replied.

"How's your coffee?"

Still no reply. I didn't let it deter me.

"Mine's pretty good. Does anyone want another blanket?"

I opened the chocolate bar and distributed the pieces. We sipped our coffee and listened to the rhythmic patter of the rain. You could feel how saturated the air was. It seemed to cling to the skin like a thin film of oil. Behind us, inside the restaurant, the tourists were enjoying their meal. We could hear the scrape of their cutlery on their plates, the excited chatter of their voices. I glanced up at the bulging awning, hoping it wasn't going to split and deluge us with water.

Finally, Guastafeste spoke.

"What did the funicular tickets cost? Seventy kroner each, was it? Then the coffees were forty kroner each and the chocolate thirty. That makes three hundred and sixty kroner. That's, what? About thirty-six euros? So we've just spent thirty-six euros to sit in the mist on the top of a mountain, watching the rain pouring down."

"Never say I don't give you a good time," I said.

Margherita burst out laughing and Antonio gave a grudging smile.

"Actually, it's quite atmospheric," Margherita said. "It feels as if we're floating in the clouds. And I'm very cosy under these blankets. What a clever idea to provide them."

"It's not good for business if all your customers die of hypothermia," Guastafeste growled.

"He's loving it really," I said to Margherita. "He just doesn't like to show it."

Guastafeste gave an exaggerated scowl. "Are we staying long? Only the view's not doing much for me."

"Wait a few minutes," I said.

"For what?"

I didn't reply. I sensed something in the air – a freshness, the hint of a breeze. I looked up at the sky.

Was it my imagination, or were the clouds getting thinner, the light becoming brighter? Then something quite remarkable happened. The mist filling the valley suddenly started to disintegrate. The grey-white blanket broke apart as if giant, invisible hands were tearing it to shreds. And through the drifting skeins, we caught glimpses of the city far below us. The old harbour, its north side fringed by the tall wooden buildings of the Bryggen, the towers of the Mariakirken and beyond that, near the mouth of the port, the ancient Rosenkranz-tårnet and Håkonshallen.

We could see leisure boats moored in the marina near the fish market, bigger commercial vessels tied up further along the quay, and over to the south, the newer ferry terminal where a massive cruise ship, higher than a ten-storey building, had dropped anchor for a few hours – disgorging, I guessed, the visitors who were eating lunch so noisily behind us.

The entire vista was smudged with gloomy shades of grey, like a black and white photograph, but as we watched, the sun broke through the dispersing clouds, the rays like a spotlight that panned across the city, shimmering on the sea and illuminating the buildings with a pale, watery hue.

My intuition about the weather had been correct, but I resisted the temptation to crow about it. The mist had lifted only partially, after all, and it *was* still raining. I sensed I'd be walking on thin ice if I tried to put too much of a rosy gloss on our trip up the mountain.

The changing conditions had not gone unnoticed inside the restaurant either. The main doors opened and a flood of tourists poured out, all clutching mobile phones and bright orange umbrellas marked with the name of the cruise ship they'd come on. It was a scene an anthropologist would have relished, for in one seething mass – and there must have been more than a hundred of them – they hurried down the path to the viewing area just below the terrace and lined up along the railing, their backs to the valley, and took selfies of themselves.

Margherita, Guastafeste and I watched open mouthed as they shoved and jostled to get the best positions, then posed and grinned for their cameras. Not one of them actually looked at the view with their eyes. Then, as quickly as they'd appeared, they all dashed back up the path into the warmth of the restaurant.

Guastafeste glanced over his shoulder through one of the dining room windows.

"They've finished their meal," he said. "Shall we get to the funicular before they leave?"

"Good idea," I replied.

Not without a trace of reluctance, we pulled off the blankets and exposed our bodies to the cold, damp air. We shivered in unison. The wind was gusting across the mountain, blowing the mist away, but also cutting through our clothes and chilling the skin of our faces.

We walked down to the funicular station and saw from the timetable that the train wasn't due for another five minutes. Sheltering out of the wind by the station wall, we heard a clamour of voices above us. We'd mistimed our departure. The tour party was coming to catch the same train. We'd had the upward journey to ourselves. I wasn't sure I could face the return trip with so many other people. Guastafeste was obviously thinking the same thing for he said, "Shall we wait for a later one?"

Margherita nodded her agreement, but I had an alternative solution.

"Why don't we walk down?"

"We can walk?" Margherita said.

I nodded and took out my map of Bergen.

"There's a hiking trail that goes all the way back to the city."

"And how long would that take?"

"Not long, forty minutes, maybe. It might be nice. And it'll certainly be warmer than hanging around up here waiting for another train."

That seemed to swing the argument. We were all getting cold doing nothing. A bracing walk, getting the circulation going, had a certain appeal, particularly now the tour group was engulfing the station. Pushing our way through the throng, we climbed back up the path onto the bluff above the funicular and found the trail that was marked on my map.

It was an easy walk. The path was signposted and well worn, and it was all downhill. Even the weather was on our side now. It stopped raining shortly after we started the descent and the sun came out fully from behind the clouds. It was surprisingly warm. You could almost see the ground steaming, the water evaporating. We took off our jackets and carried them as the path switchbacked down the mountain. There were trees on the slopes beside us, sunshine dappling the soil beneath them. There was a smell of pine and soggy earth.

Margherita inhaled deeply and tilted her head so the sun bathed her face.

"This is beautiful, Gianni. I'm so glad we decided to walk."

When we reached the outskirts of the city, the houses and winding streets that clung to the hillside, I made a detour to the east, towards a landmark I'd seen on my map.

"Where are we going?" Margherita asked suspiciously, her sense of direction telling her that this wasn't the most direct route back to our hotel.

"You'll see."

We came out onto a wider main road and I led us through an open gateway onto a strip of land that appeared at first sight to be a garden – until you saw the gravestones scattered among the trees and shrubs.

A cemetery?" Guastafeste said.

"The Assistent kirkegården," I replied. "Let's see if we can find it."

"Find what?"

It wasn't difficult. It was just down the gravel path from the entrance, a tall, green copper urn set on a stone plinth with a circular flower bed around it containing white tulips and blue forget-me-nots. There were no markings on the side facing us, but when we walked round to the other side we saw the inscription on the urn: Ole Bull 1810-1880.

"This is his grave?" Margherita said.

I nodded and told her about the great violinist's death on Lysøen, the island he owned about twenty kilometres down the coast. His body was brought to Bergen by sea, in probably the most spectacular funeral the city has ever seen. The ship bearing his coffin was escorted into the harbour by dozens of other boats, the guns of the fort booming out a solemn tribute. All shops and businesses were closed, all flags flown at half-mast. Flowers and juniper were strewn in front of the cortège as it made its way through the streets. The graveside eulogy was given by Björnstjerne Björnson, then Norway's most respected writer, and Edvard Grieg placed a wreath on the coffin before it was lowered into the ground. Then the local people filed past the grave, covering it with flowers and pine branches.

"All that for someone I'd never heard of until the other day," Guastafeste said. "He really was a big man here, wasn't he?"

A big man, but there was nothing ostentatious about his grave: just an urn on a flower bed. No grand tomb, no mausoleum, no marble pillars or statuary. Even the inscription had been kept to a minimum. His name and dates and nothing more.

It was a quiet, low-key churchyard – no signs to lead a visitor here, no pomp or shallow spectacle when you arrived. A few metres away, behind a stone wall, was the railway line leading to the central station. You could see the catenary wires suspended from gantries, the top of a locomotive in a siding. A train chugged past, its wheels rattling on the track. Ole Bull was long dead, so why would he care about his grave, but even so I couldn't help feeling it was a rather undignified last resting place for so great a man.

We had a light lunch in the hotel – just ham and cheese sandwiches and mineral water – then Guastafeste and I left Margherita reading a book in the lounge and went down the hill into town again, past the Lille Lungegårdsvann and the Rådhus to the central police station on Allehelgens gate.

Antonio had already fixed the appointment from Italy, so all we had to do was show some identification and then we were taken upstairs to an office where a plainclothes inspector was waiting for us.

"Dag Pettersen," he said, shaking our hands.

He was in his late thirties, I guessed, a tall, craggy man with thinning sandy hair and a salt and pepper moustache. His teeth had the yellowish stain of nicotine on them and there was a distinct odour of cigarette smoke about him. He didn't look like a man who took much care with his appearance. His grey suit was old, one of the lapels marked with a brownish stain, his shirt was fraying a little around the collar and his black shoes had gone a long time without a polish.

We exchanged a few pleasantries – speaking in English – then I explained who I was. Pettersen raised one of his thick, straggly eyebrows.

"A violin maker?"

"We believe Rikard Olsen's death may be linked to a violin – a *hardingfele* – he had with him in Cremona," I said. "The fiddle has disappeared. I'm on board as a sort of expert adviser – I've done it before for the police – but I'm also here as an interpreter in case we encounter language difficulties."

Guastafeste nodded. "My English is not good."

"And my Italian is non-existent," Pettersen said. He gave me a wry smile. "We may have need of you, Signor Castiglione."

He opened a thin report on his desk and glanced at the contents.

"There's not much I can tell you about him, I'm

85

afraid. He was forty-three years old, which I'm sure you already knew, unmarried, with a former partner and one daughter. He had a violin making and repairing business off Haugeveien, which is in Strandsiden, the area to the south of the harbour. He seems to have led a quiet, respectable life. His business was solvent and doing well. He paid his taxes, had no criminal record and no criminal associates that we know of." He turned the folder around so we could read it. "I've written it in English for you."

"How did you get this information?" Guastafeste asked.

"Some of it from official records, some of it from talking to people."

"Which people?"

"His neighbours, his friends, his ex-partner."

"Did he have enemies?"

"None that we've been able to identify. He seemed to be well liked, in both his private and his business lives."

"We think he perhaps had a..." Guastafeste paused and said something to me in Italian. I translated for the inspector.

"A complicated love life. Did you speak to any ex-girlfriends? Anyone who might have held a grudge against him."

"Norwegian women are famously independent and assertive, but most of them draw the line at killing their ex-boyfriends," Pettersen said dryly.

"Ask him about business associates," Guastafeste said in Italian. "Did he have feuds with anyone, any disgruntled customers?"

"Not that we can find." Pettersen replied, after I'd

repeated the question in English. He leaned back in his chair and stroked his moustache with his fingertips. "I know nothing about making violins, but it doesn't strike me as a business that usually leads to violent conflict."

That showed his ignorance, but I didn't contradict him. I could understand how he'd got that impression. Gentle, sawdust-covered artisans with no ambition, that was how most people saw luthiers – and many of us *are* like that – but that's not the whole story. Violins are beautiful objects. More importantly, some of them are also valuable objects and, like everything else in this greedy world of ours, once money becomes involved, all scruples, all ideas of civilised behaviour go out of the window. People will fight over violins, they will cheat and lie and in extreme circumstances – as I knew from personal experience – they will kill for them. Whether that was the case here, we had yet to establish, but Guastafeste was certainly keeping an open mind about it.

"Rikard worked alone?" he said. "No partners in his business?"

"Yes, it was just him."

"Did he have any..." Antonio checked the word with me "...debts?"

"A small business loan from the bank that he was paying off in regular instalments. Nothing else. He rented his workshop and apartment."

"Do you know who gets his money?"

"His estate? No, you'd have to ask the family that. But I doubt there's much there, not if his tax returns are anything to go by. He wasn't a wealthy man."

"You found nothing..." Again, I had to translate.

"...shady in his past?"

"Not a thing. Not even any minor misdemeanours. You know, drinking or drug taking. He was absolutely clean."

"Have you heard of a Bergen violin dealer named Ingvar Aandahl?"

Pettersen's brow furrowed. "I don't think so."

"You never have reason to look at him? You know, for anything bad."

"Not personally. But I can check the files, if you like." Pettersen regarded us both thoughtfully. "You've come a long way. I'm sorry I can't be of more help."

"That's okay. Thank you for everything you do," Guastafeste said.

"Keep the file. It's more use to you than to us."

"Is it okay if we talk to people, ask them questions?"

"That's why you're here, isn't it?"

We went back downstairs and out into the street. Guastafeste was silent and withdrawn. I knew he'd hoped for more from the meeting.

"It's early days," I said, trying to cheer him up. "There's plenty of time to find your breakthrough."

"Hmm," he murmured doubtfully. "The omens aren't looking good, Gianni. We've only been here a few hours, I know, but I'm beginning to wonder whether this whole trip is just a complete waste of time."

FIVE

We go to funerals to mark the passing of particular individuals – to mourn them, to celebrate their lives – but the occasions are always about more than just the person who has died, for when we attend, we bring with us our memories.

We think not only of the one whose name and photograph is on the Order of Service, but of all the others we have lost and grieved for. Rikard Olsen was gone, but as his coffin was carried into the church and placed on the catafalque at the front, I thought of my wife, taken from me eight years ago, and I thought of my mother and father and my great friend Tomaso Rainaldi and all the other people I would never see again. None of that diminished the significance of Rikard's death to those close to him. Grief is universal and it's only by knowing how we feel that we can understand how others feel.

There were many people in the church, people who had known Rikard much better than I had. Aina was there on the front row, two teenagers beside her who had to be her children. A dark-haired woman and a young blonde girl in the same row, I guessed, were Rikard's ex-partner and daughter – Kamilla and Elin. They were staring straight ahead so I couldn't see their faces or expressions. The rest of the pews were filled with a mixture of mourners, most the right age to be Rikard's friends and contemporaries. Some were there in couples, some on their own. I wondered whether a group of six women seated together on the same row were former girlfriends.

The only person I recognised, apart from Aina, was Ingvar Aandahl. He was three or four rows from the front, sitting next to a tall, elegant blonde woman in a black coat and black silk scarf. Margherita, Guastafeste and I were at the back of the church – it felt less intrusive to be a little apart from Rikard's family and friends – so we had only a rear view of everyone. They were sitting in respectful silence, some hunched forward as if saying a quiet, private prayer.

The service was conducted by a priest, but as it was in Norwegian I understood none of it, except in the general sense that, drawing on my own experience of funerals, I knew he must be paying tribute to Rikard, expressing the feelings of loss that everyone in the church would be feeling. He spoke in solemn, sombre tones, but then gave way to members of the congregation who came forward one by one to say a few more personal words. They were brief and heartfelt, most quite serious, but one or two lightening the mood by producing laughter, something I feel we don't hear often enough at funerals. If we're celebrating someone's life, after all, then it seems only right that we should mix some humour in with the tragedy.

The last of the contributions was from Kamilla and Elin. They came out from their seats together, holding hands. Kamilla spoke first, calm and composed, then Elin took her turn, her voice choking with so much emotion I thought she was going to break down. I had to admire her bravery, this twelve-year-old girl standing up in public to say goodbye to her father.

Aina, I noticed, didn't take part in any of it. But then, after prayers and a hymn, she stepped forward and paid tribute to her brother in her own special way. In her hands were a bow and a Hardanger fiddle. She didn't say anything, just put the fiddle under her chin and played. I didn't know the piece, but it was in a minor key and acutely poignant, the melody underpinned by the drone strings which made a wailing sound like keening women. The acoustics in the church were superb. The violin rang out around us, filling every corner of the building. I felt my skin tingle, the hairs stand on end. I saw people fumbling for handkerchiefs, pressing them to their eyes, deeply affected by the sound. Words are filtered and analysed by the brain, but music bypasses all that and goes straight to the heart.

It was a touching show of love from sister to brother and perfectly fitting, given how important violins had been in Rikard's life. But Aina didn't leave it at that. She clearly didn't want us to remember him in sorrow and gloom, for when the first piece had finished, she immediately launched into another, this one a bright, happy dance tune that made you want to sing and tap your feet. I could sense the mood changing at once. People glanced at one another, their postures altered, becoming less stiff. I even saw a few smiles. It reminded me of the old African-American tradition in New Orleans, the jazz bands playing a slow funeral march on the walk to the cemetery, but a lively, uplifting number on the way back. We grieve and we pay our respects, but ultimately we need to affirm that life is good, for it would be unbearable if we didn't.

At the end of the service, the coffin was carried out to the waiting hearse to be taken to the crematorium, a final journey that only family and close friends would share. We filed out with the other mourners and paused in the vestibule to offer our condolences to Aina. She was obviously struggling to hold in her emotions. Her face was pale and tense, her eyes moist.

"Thank you for coming," she said, holding my hand in both of hers.

"I'm glad we could be here," I replied. "It was a moving service. Rikard will be missed by a lot of people."

"It was good to see so many of them here."

She took Guastafeste's hands in her own and smiled at him.

"*Ciao*, Antonio."

"*Ciao*. It is a sad day, but you play your music beautifully."

"Thank you. I wasn't sure whether I chose the right pieces."

"It was good, very good. Completely right."

Aina shook hands with Margherita.

"Are you staying in Bergen long?

"A few days."

"It would be nice to see you again – in happier surroundings." She hesitated. "Do you like folk music?"

Margherita glanced at me. "We like all music."

"I'm playing tonight with my group. Are you free?"

"I don't think we have any plans."

"I thought about cancelling. I wasn't sure it was right on a day like today, but then I thought, why not? It will cheer me up. And Rikard would have wanted it."

"Where and when?" I said.

"It's a club called Nomaden, on Engen Vaskerelven, south-west of Øvre Ole Bulls plass. You probably won't know where that is."

"We have a map, we'll find it."

"Come after nine. It doesn't really start to warm up until then."

We moved away across the vestibule, leaving her to the other mourners who were waiting to speak to her. It was raining heavily outside. People were buttoning up coats, unfurling umbrellas before they ventured out into the elements. Guastafeste saw Ingvar Aandahl standing just inside the doors with the tall, blonde woman and gave me a nudge.

"I want to talk to him. Can you come and translate if I need you?"

"What, here?" I said. "Are you sure that's – "

"Not here," Guastafeste interrupted. "I'll fix up a meeting for later."

They'd communicated only by email, so Antonio had to introduce himself. Aandahl gave a start of surprise, his jaw dropping a little.

"You're the police officer from Cremona? What brings you here?"

"I would like to speak to you, sir," Guastafeste replied. "When would be a good time?"

"Speak to me? About what?"

"I'd prefer not to say now. Do you have an office? Perhaps I can come there."

"Is this about... Rikard's death?"

"Would this afternoon be all right?"

"Well, yes, I suppose so." Aandahl peered at us both quizzically. "Haven't we met before?"

"We were at the talk Rikard gave in Cremona," I replied.

"Ah, of course."

"You are investigating Rikard's murder?" the blonde woman asked.

She didn't introduce herself and Aandahl didn't do it for her, so I could only guess who she was. His wife? His mistress? Just a good friend? She was certainly attractive, in her forties now, but in her youth she must have been stunning. She had the willowy build and defined cheekbones of a fashion model. The clothes, too, from her expensive wool coat to the teetering heights of her stiletto-heeled shoes.

"That's right," Guastafeste said.

"And you've come to Bergen?"

Guastafeste smiled at her. "Yes, we come to Bergen."

"No, I mean you've come here for a reason? You think there's something, or someone, here that can help you?"

"Maybe," Antonio replied evasively.

Aandahl took out a business card and handed it to him.

"I'll be there at two o'clock."

We had lunch in a café not far from the church – three sandwiches and three coffees that came to four hundred and twenty kroner, about forty-two euros. Guastafeste stared at the bill and took a few deep breaths to steady his blood pressure. "My boss is going to look at my expenses claim and think I brought a family of ten with me."

Margherita stayed behind in the city centre – to browse in some shops, she said, then admitted that it was really just a way of keeping out of the rain – while Guastafeste and I shook out our umbrellas and went to Aandahl's office. It was on the hillside above Strandgaten, the main street along the south side of the harbour on which both Grieg and Ole Bull had been born.

I've been in many violin dealers' premises and they tend to veer between ultra-modern glass and aluminium and old-fashioned wood and varnish, with a sprinkling of dust to add authenticity. Aandahl's place was towards the latter end of the spectrum, though without the dust. It was an old wooden-framed building, clad in planks that had once been bright yellow but had now weathered to a more subtle honey shade. Inside, in the reception area – the locked front door opened remotely by a stout, formidable matron behind a desk – there was more wood: bare floors stained dark brown and untreated pine panelling halfway up the walls. Through an arch to one side was a showroom containing glass cabinets of violins, the instruments suspended from plaited silk ropes and illuminated by soft lights that brought out the colours and patterns of the grain in the wood without dazzling the eye.

There was a faint scent in the air – a slightly musty smell of pine and varnish that brought to mind an artisan's workshop, though it was clear no instruments were actually made here. It was probably just the natural odour of the wooden building, but violin dealers as a breed are so irredeemably untrustworthy that I wouldn't have put it past Aandahl to be pumping out some kind of artificially produced scent to fool his customers.

He was waiting for us in his office, where the wood theme continued: dark panelling on the walls, a polished mahogany desk with a green leather top, an antique filing chest and a couple of display cases containing violins – the cream of his stock, I guessed, from their location. He gestured perfunctorily at some chairs and sat down behind the desk. He didn't shake hands or offer us any refreshment. I could tell he wanted to get this over with quickly.

"So what's this all about?" he asked curtly.

"Thank you for your time, sir," Guastafeste said politely. "It is good of you to see us."

"Yes, yes," Aandahl said. "Get to the point."

Antonio didn't let Aandahl's manner intimidate him. Far from hurrying, he did the exact opposite and slowed down, pausing to think before he spoke and then taking his time with his delivery.

"As you know, sir, I am investigating the murder of Rikard Olsen, in Cremona."

"What's that got to do with me?"

"You were at the talk he gave."

"So were many other people."

"And, afterwards, you go back to Milan with Vincenzo Serafin. Is that correct?"

"I've told you all this already by email," Aandahl said irritably. "I returned to my hotel and went to bed.

Next morning, I flew back to Bergen. That's all I can tell you."

"How well did you know Rikard?"

"How well?"

"You both live in Bergen. You both..." Guastafeste turned to me. *"Guadagnarsi la vita?"*

"Make your living."

He looked back at Aandahl. "...from violins. You must have known Rikard."

"We knew of each other, yes, but we didn't have much contact."

"No?"

"Rikard made violins. I sell them. But I don't sell his."

"Why not? They are not good instruments?"

"They're very good instruments, but Rikard handled all his sales himself. He didn't need me to sell them for him."

"Was that a problem for you?"

"Why should it have been?"

"You could have earned money from him."

Aandahl gave a peevish snort. "Pah! I've been a dealer for thirty years. I have clients and contacts all over the world. Rikard didn't need me, but I didn't need him either."

"You get on well with him?"

"I just told you, we didn't have much contact."

"But when you do, was it friendly?"

"Yes, we got on fine."

"I ask because, after the talk in Cremona, you seem to have an argument with Rikard."

Aandahl sat back in his chair, momentarily lost for a reply. He picked up a letter opener from the desk – a long, slim blade with a silver hilt shaped like a violin – and toyed with it in his fingers. He looked at me, then at Guastafeste.

"*What?*"

"You stay behind to speak to him," Antonio said.

"What about?"

"I don't remember. I was probably congratulating him on his talk. It was very good, don't you think?"

Guastafeste ignored the question. "That is not how it look to me. It look as if you are having some kind of..." He got the translation from me again "... dispute."

Aandahl's smooth, tanned face broke into a condescending smile.

"You're mistaken, officer. I assure you there was no dispute. Now, is there anything else I can help you with?"

He pushed back his chair and started to get up, but Guastafeste wasn't going to take the hint.

"Yes, there is," he said.

Aandahl slumped back down into his seat. "What now?"

"The Hardanger fiddle Rikard had has disappeared. It is possible that is why he was killed."

Aandahl stared at us incredulously. "Are you kidding me?"

"You think not?"

"A Hardanger fiddle? Who would kill for that?"

"I don't know," Guastafeste said. "But then I am an Italian and a police officer. You are Norwegian and a violin dealer. Was there something special about the fiddle?"

"I have no idea. I know nothing about it."

"You are sure?"

"Look around you," Aandahl said, waving a hand at the glass cases. "Do you see any Hardanger fiddles? I deal in *fine* violins." He emphasised the adjective. "Not rustic wood carving."

"You do not think much of them?"

"I'm a businessman. I buy and sell instruments that customers want, and are prepared to pay well for."

"Like the Gasparo da Salò that you say you brought back from Italy?"

Aandahl didn't like the phrasing of the question. His eyes narrowed, taking on a hard, flinty glint.

"What do you mean 'say' I brought back. I did bring it back. And I believe Vincenzo Serafin has confirmed that fact."

"He has confirmed that you bought the violin from him, not that you took it back to Norway with you."

"You doubt my word?"

Guastafeste was too diplomatic to give the obvious answer.

"You have the instrument here?" he asked.

"I bought it for a client. I've already delivered it to him."

"What is his name?"

"I'm not telling you that, it's confidential."

"Only I have a problem, sir. A man has been killed in Cremona and the violin he has with him disappears. Then next day you fly out of Milan with a violin case. I need to know that the violin inside that case really was a Gasparo da Salò."

Aandahl took a moment to reply. I could tell he was angry, but being careful not to show it too obviously. He was shrewd enough to know when it was in his own interests to cooperate.

"I'll have to check with my client first," he said. "I wouldn't want to reveal his name without his permission."

He got up and went out of the office, closing the door behind him. Presumably, he was using his mobile or the phone in the outer office. It seemed unnecessarily cautious, given that neither Guastafeste nor I could understand Norwegian, but it was probably second nature to him to be devious.

I stood up and wandered over to the glass cases to take a closer look at the instruments inside them. They were, indeed, "fine" violins - one looked like a Carlo Giuseppe Testore and the other I was pretty sure was by the eighteenth-century Italian maker Anselmo Bellosio, both worth a great deal of money.

Aandahl wasn't away for long. When he returned, he was brusque and businesslike, making it clear that this was the end of our meeting.

"My client's name is Aksel Sørensen," he said. "He's a very busy man, but he's agreed to see you if you go out to his house now. This is the address."

Guastafeste took the slip of paper he held out and thanked him for his help. Aandahl's response was dismissive.

"I don't know what you're doing here in Norway, or what you hope to find, but if you ask me, you're looking in the wrong place."

"One last thing," Guastafeste said. "If you did not know Rikard Olsen well, and have no interest in Hardanger fiddles, why do you go to his talk?"

Aandahl seemed thrown by the question. He ran a hand through his silvery hair. He wore it long, almost down to his collar, perhaps to give the impression of artistic tendencies, but there's nothing creative about violin dealers except their bills.

"I'm not sure," he said. "I think it might have been Vincenzo's idea."

It was still raining hard when we stepped back out onto the street. We opened our umbrellas and stood for a moment, looking across towards the harbour and the tops of the brightly-painted wooden buildings of the Bryggen, which were just visible over the rooftops.

"I have a feeling that Signor Aandahl isn't telling us the whole truth," Guastafeste said ruminatively.

"He's a dealer," I replied. "He can't help it."

SIX

We took a taxi out to Aksel Sørensen's house. It was much further than we expected. Throughout the journey, Guastafeste kept half an eye on the meter – ticking upwards at an alarming rate – and half an eye on the scenery outside, which was a much more interesting view. Having no worries about expenses, I could focus my attention on the landscape, on the rain-drenched fields and forests, the lakes and stark, glistening crags we passed as we drove west from Bergen.

We crossed a bridge over a narrow inlet, then followed the edge of the ocean for a few kilometres, the road winding between tiny coves where fishing boats were bobbing in the swell, the water around them a dark, threatening grey. I could see land to the north, some of the hundreds of islands that peppered this part of the coast, then a smaller island ahead of us on which a large stone house had been built. It was still raining heavily.

A bridge led to the house. A bridge over a deep cleft

that had sheer sides and a strip of wild, foaming sea at the bottom. A high stone perimeter wall loomed up in front of us, reinforced steel gates blocking the road. The taxi driver leaned out of his window and spoke into an intercom on a post. The steel gates swung open and we drove through and along a drive to a turning circle in front of the house.

It was an imposing building made of the local stone. The windows were big to let in as much light as possible in the gloomy Norwegian winters, the walls a good fifty centimetres thick to withstand the wind and rain. There were outbuildings to one side: a couple of barns and a low stone structure that looked like workers' quarters.

Guastafeste checked the meter and grimaced, as if he'd swallowed a mouthful of vinegar. He paid by credit card – using cash would have just about cleaned out our stock of kroner – and the driver asked if we'd like him to wait. Guastafeste weighed up the options, the remoteness of the location balanced against the inexorable ascent of the meter, and took a chance on the unknown.

"No, thank you," he said. "We'll be okay."

We watched the taxi head back down the drive. I could sense that Guastafeste, like me, was wondering whether this was a big mistake. The land around us was so bleak and – bar the house – devoid of human habitation that getting back to Bergen wasn't going to be an easy task.

The front door of the house was already open. A middle-aged woman in a white blouse and black skirt, who looked like a housekeeper, was waiting on the threshold. She stood back to let us enter, then closed the door behind us. The howl of the wind and the rain cut out immediately and we were enveloped by the quiet warmth of the house.

The housekeeper looked down at our feet.

"Your shoes," she said in English.

"Our shoes?" It took me a moment to realise what she meant. "Oh, yes."

I pulled off my shoes and placed them alongside all the other footwear on one of the shelves on the wall of the porch. Guastafeste did the same.

"This way," the housekeeper said. "Herr Sørensen is expecting you."

She led us along an uncarpeted hall, our stockinged feet sliding a bit on the polished wooden floor, to a large sitting room at the back of the building, then left us alone. The house had clearly been extended quite dramatically. Whilst the front section was nineteenth century in both architecture and building materials, this rear part was very much twenty-first century – a big steel and concrete box with floor-to-ceiling plate glass windows on three sides, which afforded a spectacular view of the scenery outside.

There was a paved patio complete with table and chairs and a stone barbecue area bigger than most people's kitchens and beyond that a patch of land that had obviously been landscaped but was too wild and untamed to be really called a garden. It wasn't much different from the rest of the ground around here – lots of bare rock outcrops with thin soil in between that could support only coarse yellowish grass – but in places an attempt had been made to create flower beds that had been planted with shrubs and bushes hardy enough to withstand the harsh growing conditions.

Even these tough specimens were stunted and bent, their branches twisted out of shape by the fierce coastal winds.

The shoreline was only fifty or sixty metres away, a rugged strip of seaweed-encrusted rocks battered by the crashing waves, the air above them misty with spray. It curved round to a low promontory, in the lee of which was a small harbour. Moored alongside a stone quay was a boat – not the yacht or luxury cabin cruiser that you might have expected to see near a rich man's house, but a sturdy working boat, like a tug, painted red and yellow with a name – Aksør Tjenester AS – stencilled on the side. The name was familiar to me, but I couldn't work out why.

The sitting room was so big that it took us a few seconds to realise it was already occupied. At the far end, two teenage boys were perched on the edge of a sofa, engrossed in a console game that was being projected onto a huge screen on the wall. I'd seen my grandchildren play similar games, every one ostensibly different, but all basically a bunch of heavily-armed men shooting or blowing up everything in sight. The boys didn't look round, weren't even aware we'd walked in.

Guastafeste and I wandered over to the windows. The rain was lashing against the glass, the wind rattling the panes. The sky, already grey and overcast, was starting to disappear behind a wall of mist that was drifting in from the sea. I wondered why anyone would have built a house in such an inhospitable spot. This was early June. What was it like in January?

"I'm sorry to keep you waiting," a voice said behind us in English.

We turned and saw a stocky, broad-shouldered man entering the room. He wasn't particularly tall. Both Antonio and I were taller, but he was a bigger man in every other respect. Thick legs and arms, a chest and stomach as solid as a tree trunk and all of it hard muscle. His dark-brown hair was cropped short to the scalp and his face had the leathery, weathered look of an outdoors man. He was wearing a checked shirt, faded blue jeans and – somewhat incongruously – a pair of soft suede moccasins on his feet.

"Aksel Sørensen," he said, holding out his hand.

His grip was pipe-wrench firm. We introduced ourselves and Sørensen glanced at the two boys on the sofa, the noise of gunfire and explosions a distraction we could do without. He said something to them in Norwegian. They didn't respond. He repeated it and one of the boys waved his hand over his shoulder in a gesture familiar to parents all over the world. "Leave us alone."

Sørensen shook his head and reverted to English. "I have more than three hundred employees, and every one of them does as I say, but my kids take no notice of me. Let's go somewhere quieter."

We followed him back out into the hall.

"When I was their age," he said, "I was taking apart every machine I could find to see how it worked. Televisions, radios, record players. I stripped down a lawn mower engine once, then put it back together and built myself a go-kart that my friends and I raced around the woods outside Bergen. Now my sons just sit around all day playing stupid computer games. They don't care how they work, just how many aliens or terrorists they can shoot."

I nodded sympathetically. "My grandchildren are the same. In *their* home, at least. When they come to mine, I won't let them bring a console. I even confiscate their mobile phones or they'd be on them all the time."

Sørensen gave me an incredulous look. "Really? My kids would probably kill me if I tried. You know, a doctor friend tells me there's now a recognised medical condition for people who spend too much time hunched over their phones. 'Turtle neck', they call it. It's becoming increasingly common apparently, causes all sorts of neck, back and shoulder problems. My kids are headed that way and there's nothing I can do about it."

He pushed open a door and we went into a room that was obviously devoted to music. The centrepiece was a grand piano, and not a baby grand but a full-size Steinway concert piano. The walls were lined with shelves bearing books of sheet music and around the edges of the room were tables on which violin cases had been placed.

"Do you mind if I ask what line of work you're in?" I said.

"The oil business," Sørensen replied. "Not extraction – I leave that to the big boys – but engineering services for the rigs out in the North Sea. I have a fleet of supply boats and helicopters, too. Most based in Stavanger – that's the centre of the Norwegian oil industry – but also a few in Bergen. I like to work up here whenever I can, mainly because my sons go to school in Bergen and their mother lives there."

"Is that one of your boats in the harbour at the back of the house?"

He nodded. "I usually take a helicopter to the Aksør Tjenester offices in Stavanger, but sometimes I hitch a lift on a company boat. It reminds me of my time on the rigs, stops me getting too deskbound."

"Aksør Tjenester?" I suddenly remembered where I'd heard that name before. "Wasn't it an Aksør Tjenester jet that took Ingvar Aandahl to Milan?"

"That's right. He was going to pick up a violin for me. The least I could do was get him there in comfort."

His mobile phone started ringing. He pulled it out of his pocket, glanced at the screen, then swiped to cut off the call.

"Sorry, I have to leave it on. I'm expecting an important call."

Guastafeste joined in our conversation, getting straight down to business.

"This Gasparo da Salò violin you buy from Vincenzo Serafin," he said.

"You want to see it?"

Sørensen opened a case to reveal a violin nestling in the navy blue velvet interior. He lifted it out.

"Do you know anything about violins?"

"It's my business," I replied.

Sørensen handed me the violin. I knew from the first glance that it was a Gasparo. The arching of the plates, the rather elongated sound holes, the carving of the scroll and the double rows of purfling told me that. The label inside looked genuine, too, though labels are notoriously unreliable proof of a maker's identity. *"Gasparo da Salò, In Brescia – 1586."*

Gasparo would have been forty-three or forty-four in that year, well established as the finest luthier of his time. Whisper it quietly in Cremona, but Brescia was then the centre of the string instrument making craft and Gasparo has a good claim to be the "inventor" of the violin, if such a thing exists. Certainly he did a lot to develop it from the viols that preceded it and his instruments – and fewer than a hundred survive – have always been sought after by both players and collectors.

Which category did Aksel Sørensen fit into, I wondered. I've met enough collectors to know that they are not all of a type. Their motives and passions and methods can vary considerably. Some are hoarders, greedy and acquisitive, who want only to possess something and are more concerned about the value of their violins than the sound they make. Others are more selective, building up a small group of particularly fine instruments for their personal pleasure and one or two are philanthropically-minded enough to lend them out to young, gifted players who can't afford to buy the violins their talents deserve.

The collector buying purely for investment purposes may hide his trophies away in a bank vault. Those more vain or self-aggrandising might have them on display in cabinets to admire in private or show off to friends. Sørensen seemed to fit neither of those groups. His violins were here in his music room, but they weren't on show, they were in their cases where most players keep them.

Was he a player then? They, too, are a varied bunch, though Sørensen didn't fit the common stereotype of a musician. He said he'd spent his youth taking apart machines and now he ran a successful engineering business. He had the tough, robust look of an oilman. It was easier to picture him on a drilling rig than in a concert hall or salon, but I knew better than to judge someone by their appearance alone. He was a hefty man, but his hands were small for his build, with broad palms and a long little finger that can be conducive to violin playing. There was a simple way to satisfy my curiosity, of course.

"Do you play the violin?" I asked, putting the Gasparo back in its case.

"Since I was ten years old," Sørensen replied. "I've always loved it. When I was a teenager, it was a big dilemma for me whether to go the music route or the engineering. I went for engineering and I think it was the right decision. I wasn't good enough to make it as a professional player. But now I've made a bit of money, I can indulge my passion for the violin."

I glanced at the cases around the room. There were five. "You collect them?"

"No, I wouldn't call myself a collector. Almost the opposite, in fact."

"What do you mean?"

"Well, collectors buy lots of instruments and hang on to them, don't they? They accumulate. I don't do that. I buy one or two, play them for a while, then sell them and buy something different."

"Really?"

"I'm easily bored. I like to try new things, try new sounds. That's why I bought that Gasparo da Salò. I've wanted to try one since I was a kid and I went to the Kunst Museum in Bergen. There's a Gasparo on display there that used to belong to Ole Bull, a fantastic instrument with a carved cherub's face on the front of the scroll and a mermaid on the back and another on the tailpiece that were supposedly sculpted by Benvenuto Cellini. I used to stare at it in its glass case and wonder what it might sound like. Now I can get an idea from my own Gasparo da Salò."

"You have other valuable violins?" Guastafeste asked.

"A couple, I suppose. I have a seventeen forty-two Guadagnini and an eighteen-oh-eight Giovanni Gagliano. I'll probably sell one of them, maybe both, now I've got the Gasparo. I don't see the point of having lots of violins when you can only play one at a time."

"You don't get attached to them then?" I said. "Most players would find it hard to part with a Guadagnini."

Sørensen shrugged. "They're pieces of wood, not people. I'm not sentimental about them. I've had violins by most of the great makers. I had a Nicolò Amati for a few years and sold it. I had a Stradivari, too, but got bored with it."

I tried to keep the disbelief from my voice. "You got *bored* with a Stradivari?"

Sørensen grinned ironically. "I know, it sounds crazy, but it's true. I just got tired of the sound and wanted a change. The only great I haven't tried is a Guarneri del Gesù. They just don't come on the market very often. But it's my next target, after I've had my fill of the Gasparo."

"Are you interested in Hardanger fiddles?" Guastafeste asked.

The question took Sørensen by surprise. He stiffened, then gave another shrug – this one with his face rather than his shoulders.

"I've never given them much thought, to be honest. They're a folk instrument really. You see them on May the seventeenth. That's our national day, when people dress up in traditional costumes and parade through the streets. But musically, well, they're pretty much a fringe interest. I've never played one, never wanted to own one."

Guastafeste nodded. "Did you know Rikard Olsen?"

"A little," Sørensen replied. "He re-haired bows for me, did some work on my violins. You know, maintenance work, new bridges, new strings, that kind of thing. I was very sorry to hear of his death."

He moved across to one of the tables and opened a violin case.

"This is one of his. I bought it ten, fifteen years ago when he was trying to establish himself in Bergen. I suppose I wanted to do my bit to help him. It's not easy for young violin makers. I don't play it much now, but I've never been inclined to sell it."

He lifted the lid of another case. "I said I wasn't sentimental about violins, but this is another one I've never parted with. Never will, either. It's the violin I started on. My father bought it cheaply in a second-hand shop. It has no label, but I'm told it's probably Danish, late nineteenth century. The sound isn't great, but it still means a lot to me."

His phone rang again. He looked at the screen.

"Excuse me, I have to take this."

Guastafeste and I drifted over to the window while Sørensen had what sounded like an intense, not very amicable, conversation with his caller. We were on the side of the house, facing almost due west. There were a few islands out to sea, but beyond them virtually no other land until you reached North America. The waves were rolling in through the mist and breaking

113

over the rocks along the shore. There was no sign of life, not even any seabirds. It was bleak, but strangely beautiful.

"My apologies. I can switch it off now," Sørensen said, putting his phone back in his pocket.

"You must know a lot of people in Bergen," Guastafeste said. "A successful businessman like you."

"Not as many as you might think," Sørensen replied. "I have an apartment in the city, and another in Stavanger, but I like to come out here whenever I can." He nodded towards the window, the rain and mist clouding the panes. "You know, three quarters of Norwegians live within fifteen kilometres of the sea. The rest of the country is mostly too hostile for human habitation, but we go out into it as much as possible – hiking, mountaineering, cross-country skiing. We have a deep and extraordinary connection with our land, which is strange and maybe rather perverse, given that for most of the year it's trying to kill us."

I smiled. "Yes, we had noticed it's a little inclement."

"Can you imagine what it must have been like for the Vikings all those years ago? Putting to sea in a small wooden sailing boat and heading across the Atlantic to Greenland and America. I think I'm pretty daring taking a ship fifty kilometres out to an oil rig, but those guys, they had real guts."

Guastafeste checked a couple of words with me, then asked his next question.

"You have friends in the local community, the arts community in particular?"

"A few," Sørensen said. "I'm a patron of the Bergen Philharmonic, go to concerts at the Grieghallen when my schedule allows it. I give money to the museum and a couple of arts charities, but I don't get involved much beyond that. What I like best is to get three friends out here on a winter's evening, open a few beers and play string quartets."

I tried to imagine that scene. Sørensen was a strong, beefy man. With longer hair, an axe and poorer personal hygiene he could easily have been a Viking raider terrorising the shores of Europe. Picturing him with a violin, playing Mozart or Haydn, was rather more of a stretch.

"Are they talking about Rikard Olsen's death?" Guastafeste asked.

"Not that I'm hearing."

"Nothing?" Guastafeste turned to me again for more translations. "No rumours, no speculation about the murder?"

Sørensen gave him a shrewd glance. "I know you're a police officer and you're only doing your job, but I'm sorry, I can't help you. I didn't know Rikard well. I have no idea why he was killed, no idea who might have done it."

He looked round towards the door, inclining his head to listen. There were faint voices out in the hall, female voices. One of them I recognised as the housekeeper's, the other I thought I'd heard somewhere before, but couldn't identify it.

"My ex-wife, Agnetha, come to pick up the boys," he said. "Talk to her. She knew Rikard much better than I did."

Pulling open the door, Sørensen led us along the hall to the sitting room where a tall, blonde-haired woman – her back to us – was clearly telling the teenage boys to stop their computer game. Or, rather, negotiating with them to stop, for they were obviously reluctant to obey.

She turned and I recognised her as the woman who'd been with Ingvar Aandahl at Rikard's funeral. She seemed equally surprised to see us. Her eyes opened wide, then flicked inquiringly across to Sørensen. She said something in Norwegian that could only have been, "Why are they here?" and Sørensen replied in the same language. Agnetha looked at us and changed to English.

"I'm sorry, I don't mean to be rude. I just didn't expect to see you here."

"We were asking Herr Sørensen about Rikard Olsen," I said.

She frowned. She seemed bemused, but also worried.

"About Rikard? Why?"

It was Sørensen who answered. "I explained that I hardly knew him and suggested they talk to you instead."

"Me?"

"Well, you'll certainly be more help than I can be."

From the sharp glance she fired at her ex-husband, I got the impression that Agnetha didn't appreciate him drawing her in to the discussion, but she quickly smoothed away her annoyance and replaced it with a smile.

"Of course. I'm happy to help, if I can." She turned back to say something to her sons. You didn't have to understand Norwegian to know that she was telling them – again – to finish their game.

Sørensen offered us his hand. "If you'll excuse me, I have work to do." He paused, something occurring to him. "How did you get here?"

"By taxi," I replied.

"It's waiting for you?"

"We sent it away. Perhaps rashly. Can we call for another?"

"Agnetha can take you back to Bergen. Can't you, dear?"

"What?" Agnetha broke off her argument with the boys and squinted at us.

"You have room in the car for our Italian visitors."

"In the car?"

"They need a lift back to town."

There was no way she could politely get out of it.

"Oh... yes, I suppose so. It's out at the front. It's open. We'll be with you in a minute."

Antonio and I thanked Sørensen for his time, then retrieved our shoes, went out through the front door and got into the car parked on the forecourt. Agnetha, I guessed, would probably be having strong words with her ex now we were out of earshot. I felt a bit guilty about the way we'd imposed ourselves on her, but that was outstripped by my feeling of relief that we didn't have to wait for a cab.

Several minutes elapsed before Agnetha emerged with her sons in tow, the teenagers lagging behind deliberately to show their opposition to this adult control over their lives. Agnetha pulled open one of the rear doors and leaned down to look in.

"One of you come in the front. The boys can sit in the back."

I knew it had to me, as I was the interpreter. Slipping out along the seat, I dashed round to the front – not fast enough to avoid a light dampening from the rain – and scrambled into the passenger seat.

The boys got into the back next to Guastafeste and

Agnetha introduced them.

"These are my sons, Rasmus and Johan."

We said hello to them and the boys grunted a reply. Considering they were brothers, they didn't look much like one another. The older one, Rasmus, was slightly built and had flaxen hair, the younger one, Johan, a heavier, more solid body and darker colouring, like his father. They immediately got their own back for the abrupt termination of their console game inside the house by taking out their phones and playing on those instead.

I could sense an irritation in Agnetha as we drove away from the house and tried to soothe her a little.

"Thank you for this. It's very kind of you."

"That's okay, it's no problem," she replied stiffly.

"I'm afraid we're the victims of our own ignorance. When we were given Herr Sørensen's address, we thought it was a suburb of Bergen. We didn't realise it was so far away, or so isolated."

She seemed able to relate to that. She gave a sympathetic nod.

"Yes, it's pretty much in the middle of nowhere, but Aksel likes that. He likes the remoteness, the sea crashing on his doorstep, the wind blasting across the garden. If it's not like a North Sea oil rig, he doesn't really feel at home."

"You lived out here when you were married to him?"

"Not if I could help it. Summer, maybe – it can be quite pleasant in July and August, though the wind never stops – but the winters..." She gave a shudder. "It's horrible in winter, even with triple glazing and central heating. I prefer the city. A nice, modern apartment with a gym downstairs and friends and a good coffee shop around the corner."

"Do you mind if I ask how long you were married?"

"Eight years, divorced for five. I was wife number two. Aksel's on number three now, but he'll probably trade her in for a younger model soon. He gets bored very quickly."

"He mentioned that," I said. "Though he was talking about violins."

"Oh, yes, his precious violins." Agnetha almost rolled her eyes. "He treats them better than he treats his family."

"Ask her about Rikard," Guastafeste said in Italian from the back seat. He couldn't forget the reason he was here.

"Ask me what?" Agnetha replied, also in Italian.

"You speak Italian?" I said.

"A little. My English is much better, but I picked up some Italian when I used to go to Milan as a model. For the fashion shows."

So I'd guessed correctly. "You work as a model now?"

"I got too old, and too fat," she said dryly. "I have a clothing design business now."

"In Bergen?"

She nodded. "We have an office in Oslo, too."

"And Rikard?" I said. "Where did he fit into your life?"

She didn't reply immediately. We were driving through a sudden burst of torrential rain and she concentrated on the road for a few kilometres, the windscreen wipers struggling to cope with the deluge.

Only when the rain eased off a bit did she answer my question, speaking in English again now.

"In recent years, not at all. But at one time we were friends."

"Friends?"

"More than friends. This is before I met Aksel, and before Rikard met Kamilla Nygaard. He'd come back from Cremona and was just starting his business in Bergen. We had mutual friends who got us together. For a few years, at any rate. It didn't last. Rikard wasn't – how can I put it? – a one-woman man."

"That must have been hard for you."

She shrugged. "I'm a realist. You have to accept people the way they are, not the way you'd wish them to be."

"That's a very pragmatic approach."

"What other approach is there? I'm not a schoolgirl any more. You deal with things and then get on with your life."

"Is that how everyone viewed Rikard? All his women, I mean."

"I can only speak for myself. It was a long time ago."

"Did you stay in touch with him?"

"Not really. We both found new partners. Our paths didn't cross that often afterwards."

"Did he have enemies?" Guastafeste asked.

"Not the way I think you mean," Agnetha replied. "Don't get me wrong. I'm not bitter about what happened. Rikard was a lovely guy. Everyone who knew him liked him. He didn't make enemies. Not ones who'd want to kill him, anyway."

"But, nevertheless," I said, "he *was* killed by someone."

120

"Why do you think it was someone he knew here? Why not simply a stranger in Italy?"

"Because of the circumstances. They point towards him knowing his killer."

"Did he not know people in Cremona? He studied there, after all."

"That was twenty years ago."

"So what are you saying?" Agnetha said. "That someone from Norway went all the way to Italy to kill Rikard? Why would they do that? Why not kill him here where he lived?"

They were very good questions. I glanced round at Antonio, the boys beside him hunched over their phones in the turtle pose their father had described to us. Very good questions that neither Guastafeste nor I could answer.

SEVEN

Margherita was waiting for me at the hotel. She was tucked up under the duvet in bed, reading a book, and looked enviably cosy. I took a shower, more to warm myself up than because I felt dirty, and put on some fresh clothes. The radiator in the room, I noticed, was already covered with damp socks. Margherita's shoes were underneath it, drying off.

"Are you hungry?" I asked. Margherita nodded. "Shall we go and find somewhere to eat?"

She glanced towards the window. "It's still raining, isn't it?"

"I'm afraid so."

"Is the hotel coffee shop open?"

"Yes, but it doesn't do meals, only light snacks."

"So we'll have to go... *out there* again?"

She said it as if we were in one of those sci-fi films, crash landed on some hostile planet with "things" lurking beyond our spaceship.

"It's unavoidable, if you want to eat," I said.

She murmured doubtfully and pulled the duvet up

123

around her neck.

"I've only just dried off."

"We'll find a nice warm restaurant for you."

"And my legs are worn out."

"Bergen's not a big place. We won't have to walk far. Come on, Antonio will be waiting for us."

Margherita sighed and threw back the duvet, shivering involuntarily, though the room wasn't cold. She put her raincoat back on and her soggy shoes, then, umbrellas in hand, we went to find Guastafeste.

There was a restaurant just down the hill from the hotel that looked perfectly acceptable, but it seemed pitifully unadventurous to choose the first place we saw, so we kept walking. The second restaurant we came across was Italian. We hadn't come to Norway to eat the same food as we had at home, so that was out of the question. The third place was a pizzeria.

"I'd like to try Norwegian cuisine," Margherita said, though we had only a vague idea of what that was.

We found an inviting-looking restaurant that appeared to serve Norwegian food and studied the menu on the wall outside that was helpfully translated into English. The prices, however, when translated into euros, were much less attractive. We walked on to another Norwegian restaurant. That was also way outside our budget.

We were in the centre of town now and the rain hadn't let up for even a second. They say that global warming is going to cause sea levels to rise and cities to flood, but in Bergen the sea is the least of their problems. The floods already come from the sky.

The next restaurant was an Indian, but it seemed bizarre to eat curry in Bergen, so that was a no. Ditto the Thai restaurant next door. And the Chinese round the corner. A Norwegian restaurant near the Torget was a possible, but I ruled it out because it was empty and thus broke one of my cardinal rules of dining out: only eat somewhere other people have also chosen to eat.

Two more Norwegian restaurants were rejected by Guastafeste on cost grounds and a hamburger place because the food on offer looked as plastic as the tables and chairs. Margherita was starting to get fed up.

"Look," she said. "We're tired and wet. This is an expensive city. We have to accept that eating out isn't going to be cheap. The next restaurant we find that looks even halfway passable, we go into it, all right?"

"Provided it's not empty," I said.

"Gianni!"

"Okay, we go into it."

We turned left up a side street, went round the block and found ourselves back at the first Norwegian restaurant we'd passed. Margherita walked straight through the door. Antonio and I had no choice but to follow her.

There was a metal rack just inside, where we deposited our dripping umbrellas. They lay there like a trio of bedraggled bats. A waitress showed us to a table. We couldn't afford a starter, so I went through the main courses, translating for Antonio.

"Fish pie, baked cod, hake fillet, fish casserole, haddock stew, fish balls, whatever they are..."

"Is there anything other than fish," Antonio asked.

"Whale steak."

"I know it's a mammal, but it still sounds a bit fishy to me."

"We can't eat whale."

Margherita was appalled by the idea and I was inclined to agree. I usually enjoy new experiences, particularly new food. I'm like the famous wit who said – and I've seen this quote attributed to several different people – he wanted to try everything in life once except incest and folk dancing. Only I would add eating whale to the list.

"Or there's reindeer steak with a lingonberry sauce," I continued.

"What's a lingonberry?" Guastafeste asked.

"I have no idea."

"The baked cod sounds good. How much is it?"

"Three hundred and thirty kroner."

Guastafeste gaped at me. "Thirty-three euros for a bit of cod? We could charter a boat and catch our own for that."

He took the menu and scanned the list of prices. "What's this one here at two hundred and seventy kroner?"

"That's the fish pie."

"I'll have that."

I ordered the food. We didn't even look at the drinks menu, but simply asked for a jug of tap water. Margherita had the baked cod and I had the fish casserole. When Guastafeste's fish pie arrived, it came with a pile of thin, buttered crispbread of the type that, in Italy, only women trying to lose weight would contemplate eating. He stared perplexedly at his plate.

"Have they given me the diet version, or what?"

"You can have some of my potatoes," Margherita offered. "I can't eat them all."

We took our time over the meal, eking out our

single course for as long as possible and thereby delaying the awful moment when we would have to venture back out into the elements. At quarter past nine, when we'd turned down dessert and coffee and were starting to feel the disapproving gaze of the restaurant manager, we paid the bill – Antonio settling his separately for his expenses claim – and left.

It hadn't got any better outside. The rain was still hurling down, the wind funnelling through the narrows streets with enough force to crumple an umbrella. We sheltered for a moment under the restaurant entrance canopy while I consulted my map, then with the route committed to memory, we walked swiftly away and found the Nomaden bar on Engen Vasterelven.

It had a discreet, inset door that would have been easy to miss, then a steep flight of wooden steps leading down into a dimly-lit basement. We could hear the sound of music as we descended, a woman's voice singing to an electronic keyboard accompaniment, but we didn't see the musicians until we turned through an arch into the main room of the bar. They were on a small stage at one end. Three of them – a man on the keyboard, another on string bass and Aina singing, a Hardanger fiddle and bow dangling from her hand.

It was a small venue, maybe ten or twelve tables spread out on the floor in front of the stage and occupied by a mixture of people, their ages ranging from early twenties to, probably, mid-sixties, but most somewhere in the middle. They were casually dressed, a lot of the men bearded, the women in trousers and knitted tops.

We found a free table and I went to the bar and

bought three bottles of beer – ten euros each, but I wouldn't tell Guastafeste that. He was stressed enough as it was.

I'm too steeped in the classical tradition to know much about folk music, but what I heard was easy on the ear: sometimes purely instrumental, sometimes with vocals, occasionally a bit of both, Aina supporting the violin on her shoulder so she could sing and play at the same time. She had a sweet, expressive voice, deeper than I expected, that was a pleasure to listen to, though the lyrics – all in Norwegian – went over my head.

At a break in the performance, Aina came over and joined us at our table. I started to hold out my hand, but she pre-empted me by kissing me on the cheeks, Italian style, then doing the same to Margherita and Antonio. She smiled warmly at us, her eyes lingering a little on Antonio. We complimented her on the music and I asked if she'd like a beer or a glass of wine. She shook her head.

"Thank you, but no. I don't drink when I'm performing."

"You do it often? You sound as if you do."

"A few times a week. It's only a hobby, really. A bit of extra money."

"But you're very good. You could do it professionally, surely?"

"There's not much of a living in folk music. A few clubs and bars like this, the odd concert, but we all have other jobs. I wouldn't want to do it full time, anyway. It would take away the fun."

"Do you write your own songs?" Margherita asked.

"Mostly. But some are traditional Norwegian folk songs."

"They are very good," Guastafeste said. "Though I don't understand the words. What do you sing about?"

"Oh, the usual," Aina replied. "Life and love and loss. What else is there to sing about?"

I saw a fleeting cloud of sadness in her eyes and reminded myself that her brother's funeral had only been that morning.

"So how are you finding Bergen?" she asked.

"Wet," was the obvious answer, but it seemed rude to say it, so I opted for "interesting" instead.

"In what way?" Aina asked.

"Everything about it is so different from Italy," I replied.

"The weather, you mean?"

"Well, you said it."

"It can be a bit of a shock to outsiders. We have only two seasons in Bergen – winter, and July. And sometimes July doesn't last very long."

We laughed, and I could see from her expression that she appreciated it. She'd said in the church that she wanted to play this evening to cheer herself up, but it couldn't have been easy for her, performing when she was still grieving.

"Have you managed to see much yet?" she went on.

I told her about our trip out to Aksel Sørensen's house and she looked puzzled.

"That's a strange place to go."

"It is part of my investigation," Guastafeste explained. "I needed to talk to him. Do you know him?"

"I know *of* him. He's a well-known local businessman, but we've never met."

"He knew Rikard."

"Really? How?"

"He plays the violin, he has a small collection of instruments. Rikard did work for him."

"I didn't know that."

"And we met his ex-wife, Agnetha, too," I said. "She gave us a lift back into town."

"Now Agnetha, I *do* know," Aina said. "Though I haven't seen her in a long time."

"She was a girlfriend of Rikard's, wasn't she?" Antonio said.

"Yes, they lived together, in fact. She was very glamorous, very beautiful. She was a model, you know."

"Yes, she told us."

"Intelligent, too. And a good businesswoman. She had everything, really. Everyone was mystified when they broke up."

"Why was that?"

Aina shrugged. "I don't know. Why do couples stay together, why do they split up? No one really knows the inside of other people's relationships, do they?"

"What about Kamilla Nygaard?" Antonio asked. "How long were she and Rikard together?"

"Nine, ten years."

"But they never marry?"

"It's not uncommon here. I don't think either of them wanted it."

"And after Kamilla? Did Rikard have a new girlfriend?"

"A lot of casual flings, I think, but no one special."

"I would like to speak to Kamilla. Do you have her number?"

Aina took out her phone and scanned through her list. She gave Antonio the number, then stood up.

"We have to go back on. It was nice to see you. We must meet up again before you leave."

She smiled at us and walked back to the stage. I glanced at Antonio. He was watching her with a strange, far away look in his eyes.

EIGHT

After breakfast next morning, I called Kamilla Nygaard. She was already at work, but agreed to see us if we came to her apartment in the late afternoon. That left us most of the day to play with. None of us was keen on traipsing around Bergen in the rain again – and, inevitably, it *was* raining – so I suggested we went out to Grieg's house at Troldhaugen, a place I'd always wanted to visit.

The mere thought of taking a taxi brought Antonio out in a cold sweat, so we went by public transport, walking down into town and taking the light railway to Hop, then doing the last couple of kilometres on foot. It wasn't an enjoyable walk. The route was mainly along roads, quite busy roads, and the rain seemed to defy the laws of physics, falling vertically from the sky, but then somehow managing to turn horizontal and sneak in under our umbrellas. By the time we reached our destination, our lower halves were decidedly damp.

Unrealistic expectations are the curse of every

traveller's life, probably the curse of most people's lives. Troldhaugen was a disappointment to me, at least at first sight. The discrepancy between how I'd imagined it would be and how it actually was was just too great. I'd pictured a striking, rocky hill, wild and isolated and pierced with caves and tunnels in which trolls might plausibly have lurked, but it was more of a low promontory and so hemmed in by the nearby houses that any atmosphere it might once have had was now gone. It was hard to imagine a rabbit living there beneath the earth, let alone a troll.

When Grieg first built it, of course, back in the nineteenth century, it was an undeveloped spur overlooking Lake Nordås and surrounded by fields and woods. It must have been an idyllic, inspiring place for a musician seeking peace and solitude in which to compose. Bergen and its satellite towns have expanded vastly since then so Troldhaugen is no longer isolated and the site itself has been developed to include a visitor centre and concert hall. Turning it into a museum and shrine to Grieg, however laudable the aims, have destroyed our understanding of why he chose to live there.

Going into the visitor centre, we paid our admission fees, then spent some time looking at the biographical display boards and artefacts from the composer's life. I'm not generally interested in this kind of ephemera. Grieg's concert suit and his travelling trunk and a lock of his hair in a silver frame left me cold, but the stuffed toy frog he kept in his pocket and rubbed for good luck before he went on stage to perform was more appealing. It told me something about the man: that he was superstitious, maybe fun, that he had a sense of humour. He owned other lucky mascots, too, a red troll and a pig with a four-leaf clover in its mouth – the kind of things a child might have, but the adult felt a need of too. I found that rather endearing.

Margherita and Guastafeste were studying an unfinished portrait of Grieg by the artist Franz von Lenbach.

"How old was he when this was done?" Margherita asked.

I checked the date on the label. "Eighteen eighty-four. He'd have been in his early forties."

"He looks so ill."

"He *was* ill," I said. "He got pleurisy when he was sixteen and his left lung collapsed, leaving him sickly for the rest of his life."

"It's a sad picture. Look at his eyes. There's something haunting about them. Yet his music is so happy."

"'A pink bon-bon stuffed with snow', that's how Debussy described Grieg's music."

"He obviously never came to Bergen," Guastafeste said dryly. "A pink bon-bon saturated with rain would've been more apt."

We don't hear very much of Grieg's music in Italy. His fame – as it is in most countries outside Norway – is based almost entirely on two pieces: his piano concerto and the incidental music to *Peer Gynt*. But I've always been fond of some of his other compositions. The violin sonatas are fine works, as are the many lyric pieces for piano that my wife used to play for me. Debussy's cheap, and unworthy, sneer at him is both unfair and inaccurate. There's more depth, and sometimes more darkness, in Grieg's music than many people like to think.

I followed the timeline along the wall that picked

out significant events in the composer's life, from his birth in 1843 to his death in 1907. The family originally came from Scotland – spelling their name Greig – but emigrated to Norway in the eighteenth century where Edvard's great grandfather, Alexander, changed his surname and set up a successful fishing business, eventually owning a fleet of boats.

According to legend – or perhaps more accurately, gossip – the older Grieg men were in the habit of calling in on the wives of their employees when the husbands were away at sea and this tender solicitude for their well-being resulted in a number of unfortunate pregnancies. The young Edvard, it's said, was wary of setting foot in the alleys near the quayside in Bergen for fear of bumping into his illegitimate relatives.

True or not, Edvard had an affluent upbringing and showed an early talent for music, impressing family friend Ole Bull so much that the violinist recommended they send him to study at the Leipzig Conservatory, an experience that Grieg later dismissed as a waste of time, but which undoubtedly gave him a sound grounding in harmony and composition.

Most aspects of a great musician's career are rather dull – just lists of concerts and performances in various venues or months spent at a desk scribbling notes on manuscript paper – so we identify more with the private sides of their lives. With Grieg, two events stood out for me: his marriage to his cousin Nina in 1867, a love match which both their families opposed, and the death of their first, and only, child, Alexandra, from meningitis less than two years later. That must have been a devastating blow. The couple never really recovered from it. The child's death left a hollow at the heart of the marriage and it took a great deal of strength and patience – nearly all on Nina's side, it has to be said – to hold the relationship together for the next thirty-eight years. Grieg's music may often seem light and joyful, but his life was not without its difficulties.

"This is boring," Guastafeste said bluntly. "Shall we move on?"

I glanced at Margherita and she nodded. We'd all had enough of the museum, a building erected in only 1995. It was time to see the house that Grieg, more than anywhere, regarded as his home.

Leaving the visitor centre, we crossed a bridge edged with juniper railings and found ourselves outside a distinctive two-storey wooden building with a square tower at one side on top of which a Norwegian flag fluttered in the breeze. Several other people were already waiting on the forecourt and with our arrival we were admitted to the house.

I was disappointed to discover that we would not be allowed to wander around the interior on our own, but had to take a guided tour, which I hate. I don't want to be talked at by a guide, fed reams of facts and information. I want to explore by myself, linger where I wish, move on as I please and make discoveries for myself, not have them pointed out to me by some official escort. But we had no choice: a slight, mousy-haired, middle-aged woman, who introduced herself as Inge, was going to herd us around the place and tell us exactly what we needed to know.

The house was begun in 1884 and completed the following year, Inge explained, speaking in English because all of our small tour group were foreign visitors. It cost twelve and a half thousand crowns to build, a considerable sum at the time, but Grieg was a relatively rich man. His piano concerto, written when he was twenty-five, had made him famous across Europe and he'd built a lucrative career as both conductor and performer. His solo piano music was also much in demand from the public because not only was it lyrical and pleasant to listen to, but it was also well within the technical capabilities of the average middle-class pianist. Accomplished young ladies in their salons might have struggled with Brahms and Chopin, but Grieg enabled them to shine.

Successful though he was, Grieg had not built himself some vast hideous mansion like many wealthy men of the time did. Troldhaugen was modest in scale, reflecting the unassuming nature of the man and his wife. It had only a few rooms, with plain wooden floors and wood panelling on the walls, and all simply furnished, the most ostentatious item being the grand piano in the sitting room on which Edvard and Nina liked to play four-handed duets. Water had to be pumped up from underground and there was no internal toilet – that was housed in a separate little shed in the garden.

Photographs and pictures of friends lined the walls and there were now glass cabinets containing mementos of the composer's life, including his fishing rod and umbrella – "the only two things you need to survive in Bergen," Inge said.

"Well, she's fifty per cent right," Margherita whispered in my ear.

I wondered what life had been like here for the Griegs, living in this thin-walled wooden house, sub-zero temperatures outside, snow and wind and rain hammering on the windows – and that was just the summer. The summer, in fact, was generally the only time they spent here, but even that must have been pretty grim, particularly for Nina. Edvard had his composing to occupy him, but what did his wife do all day, cut off from friends and neighbours on this bleak, exposed promontory?

Inge was still talking, telling us some inconsequential facts about a piece of silver given to Grieg by an admirer, but I'd switched off. So had others in the group. There were eight of us in total – Guastafeste, Margherita and me, plus a French couple, a German couple and a man on his own who, from his accent when he asked the guide questions, sounded American.

He must have been in his mid-forties, a short, rotund man with black-framed spectacles and hair receding faster than an alpine glacier. He looked at me and rolled his eyes discreetly as Inge droned on in the background.

Guastafeste, too, was bored. Some of the English was too difficult for him to understand and there was a limit on how much I could translate into Italian without annoying everyone else. A limit, as well, to how much Antonio actually wanted to know, as he made clear when the tour finally came to an end and we went back out into the drizzle.

"Well, that was gripping stuff," he said sarcastically. "Who knew that armchairs and a couple of chipped vases could be so fascinating."

"Don't be unfair," Margherita chided him gently. "Inge was doing her best, and I found a lot of it very interesting."

139

"Mmm," Guastafeste said non-committally. "Shall we go and have a coffee in the visitor centre?"

"I want to see Grieg's composing hut first," I said.

"He had a hut?"

I nodded. "Away from the house where he wouldn't be disturbed."

I checked the plan of the site I'd picked up in the museum and led them away from the house and down a path past the concert hall to the shore of Lake Nordås. A few metres away from the lapping water was a small wooden hut, about the size of a standard garden shed. It wasn't open to the public, but we could look through the glass pane in the door. Inside, the hut contained a chair and desk at which Edvard would work each day, the window beyond the desk giving him an excellent view of the lake – an inspiration, he always said, but also a distraction for the boats out on the water were often more interesting than a blank sheet of manuscript paper.

Against the right wall was a chaise-longue for him to rest on when the rigours of composition and, probably, a good lunch overcame him with fatigue. On the left wall was an upright piano. The stool in front of it had a thick book of Beethoven's thirty-two piano sonatas on the seat – not to play, but to sit on so the diminutive composer was the right height for the keyboard.

"It's a bit austere, isn't it?" Margherita said.

"You don't need much luxury to compose," I replied.

"It must have been a bit cold."

"It was. Did you read the information about it in the visitor centre?"

"No."

"Apparently, the first summer after the hut was built, it rained every day and it was freezing cold."

"No?" Guastafeste said. "Who'd have guessed it?"

"So Grieg had a wood stove installed and the floor insulated."

"Is there much to see?" a voice said behind us.

I turned and saw the portly, balding man with glasses who'd been on the house tour with us.

"Take a look," I said, moving aside to let him get to the hut.

He peered through the window for half a minute or less, then backed away.

"Nothing special," he said laconically.

"You hoped for more?"

He shrugged. "I guess so. You always do, don't you? You like to see where those great men worked. Maybe you're hoping you'll see what made them tick. You know, where their creativity came from. But, of course, it didn't come from their hut or the pen they used, it came from inside their heads."

He held out his hand. "Michael C. Berg. From Appleton, Wisconsin. Nice to meet you."

We all shook hands and introduced ourselves, though, by European standards, it seemed a little premature and unnecessary. We'd been on a short guided tour with this man. We didn't really need to know anything more about him. But that isn't the American way. They have an openness, a genuine curiosity about other people that I generally find refreshing. It's an attractive trait, but sometimes it can be a little unnerving.

"You guys are Italian, right?" Berg went on. "I don't

141

speak Italian. Don't speak Norwegian either, although my ancestors came from here."

"Oh, yes?"

"Emigrated to the States back in the mid-nineteenth century. They came from a small farming community up north, but couldn't make a living, could barely survive, in fact. My grandfather spoke Norwegian, but it's kind of died out in the family since. My dad didn't have much and my siblings and I have none. I brought a Norwegian phrase book with me and have tried speaking it a bit, but the locals look at me like I'm crazy and just reply in English."

I sensed Margherita and Guastafeste edging away. The rain and the cold down here by the lake weren't conducive to lengthy open-air conversations.

"Well, it's been a pleasure," I said to the American. "I hope you enjoy the rest of your stay."

"Can I ask you a favour?" he said. "Will you take a photograph of me in front of the hut?"

"Of course."

He passed me his phone and posed, grinning inanely, by the door while I took a couple of snaps of him. Then we started to walk back up the path. Berg came with us, falling in beside me.

"So which part of Italy do you come from?" he asked.

"Cremona."

"That's the violin place, isn't it?"

"Yes."

"Never been there. What's it like?"

"Well, very pleasant, I suppose."

"I've been to Florence and Rome. Loved them both, though the crowds, boy, you couldn't move for people.

Had to stand in line for three hours to get into the Uffizi. I guess Cremona's not that busy."

"No, it's not like Florence. But it's very beautiful."

"Yeah? I'll have to go some day. I love coming to Europe, love the cities, the culture. Norway's stunning, isn't it? You been to the fjords?"

"No."

"You should, they're out of this world. I took a tour up the Sognerfjord last week. It's two hundred kilometres long, you know, the longest fjord in Norway. That's like, what, a hundred and twenty miles? And it's, like, I don't know how deep. The tour guide told us, but I forget what she said. You do, don't you? I've only just been around the house up there, but already I've forgotten most of what the guide told us. It just goes in one ear and out the other. You know, all the dates and facts. Who can remember that? I didn't know much about Grieg." He chuckled. "Actually, still don't know much about Grieg. Are you into classical music?"

"Well – "

"I'm not really. It doesn't do much for me. I'm more of a country and western kinda guy. But what I've heard of Grieg, I like. He could write a tune, couldn't he? But his life was pretty dull. Sitting in that poky little hut all day composing, that would drive me nuts. I like to get out, meet people, talk to them, don't you? What do you do for a living? I'm a high school English teacher. I love teaching, love the interaction with my kids. The school kids, I mean. I don't have kids of my own. We tried for a bit, my wife and I, but then we got divorced and, well, it's getting a bit late for me now, isn't it? But the kids in my classes, they're like, you know, surrogates. I can watch them grow and develop, pass on my love of literature to them. That's incredibly rewarding."

We'd reached the top of the path now and paused on the small terrace outside the Troldsalen, the concert hall tucked discreetly away in the ravine next to Grieg's villa, its turf roof and low profile helping it blend seamlessly into the landscape. Berg looked at the statue of Grieg that stands at the side of the terrace, the composer's face dominated by his unruly hair and luxuriant moustache, and said, "He looks just like Mark Twain, don't you think?"

"I was going to say Albert Einstein," Margherita replied. "There's an uncanny similarity."

"Why didn't they make it life-size?" Guastafeste wanted to know.

"That *is* life-size," I said. "He was a very small man."

"You're not kidding. His moustache is almost as big as he is."

"Are you going to the concert?" Berg asked.

I hesitated. I could feel Margherita and Antonio's eyes on me, sense their desire to get away from this over-friendly intruder. But I couldn't lie. He would certainly see us going into the Troldsalen.

"Yes," I said.

"Me, too. We can sit together. That would be nice."

I sighed inwardly. Berg was a little overbearing, but he meant well. It would be churlish to reject his company. We went into the concert hall and sat down on one of the rows in the middle. It was an impressive building, the wood-lined auditorium small and intimate, seating maybe two hundred people. It raked quite steeply down to a stage designed for soloists or chamber ensembles – nothing bigger like a symphony orchestra. At the back of the stage were large windows giving a view down the ravine to Grieg's composing hut and the lake.

I could see from the brochure I'd picked up earlier that there were regular concerts throughout the summer: solo piano recitals, duets and larger groups, all playing Grieg. Today, a string quartet was performing. The usher at the entrance had handed us a programme on our way in, just a single sheet of paper giving the names of the players and some notes on the music we would be hearing: not either of the two string quartets Grieg wrote, but an arrangement of the two *Peer Gynt* suites.

"Good, I like *Peer Gynt*," Berg said. "My high school orchestra plays it all the time. The Hall of the Mountain King, I love that."

He began to hum the well-known tune. I saw Guastafeste stiffen and look away. The hall was filling up around us with other visitors. I skimmed through the programme notes, then passed the sheet to Margherita. I've never seen the play for which the music was written, but it's very different from the socio-realism of Ibsen's other works – a fantastical, rather silly drama about the incredible adventures of a lying, selfish, drunken ne-er do well who seduces and abandons women, makes up preposterous stories and dreams of marrying the troll king's daughter.

I heard Margherita making soft, sniffy-snorty noises, like a small whale exhaling, and waited for her to erupt.

"What a load of rubbish!" she exclaimed, looking up from the notes.

I smiled at her. "I thought you'd enjoy it."

145

"I didn't know *Peer Gynt* was such a stupid story. Kidnapped brides, trolls, seductive Arab girls, Peer doing whatever he pleases while the faithful Solveig waits patiently by the hearth for him to return. I know what I'd have done if I'd been her – given him a thick ear, or worse, and sent him packing."

"That's not what romantic poetry's all about," I said.

"Not as written by men, no," she retorted. "And it could only have been written by a man, of course. What you like to claim is about love is really about lust and promiscuity. About a man's desires, his freedom to use women and avoid responsibility for the damage he causes."

"That's true," I admitted. "But there's something rather touching about Solveig, old and nearly blind, welcoming Peer home despite his betrayals. And when he asks her where his true self has been for all those years since they last met, she replies, 'In my faith, in my hope, in my love.' It's what you women are so good at – forgiveness."

"Don't give me that tosh, Gianni. You don't believe that for a minute. Peer is just a despicable wastrel and Solveig is an idiot."

I laughed. "Well, that puts Ibsen and Grieg in their place."

The musicians were coming out onto the platform, all young players in their mid-twenties. The audience fell silent. The auditorium lights dimmed and spotlights came on above the stage, illuminating the four players. They started with Morning Mood from the first suite, the first violin taking the melody that in the full orchestral version Grieg gives to the flute. It's a bright, joyful tune, but it seemed poignant to me as I remembered that the last time I'd heard it was when Rikard Olsen played it on the drone strings of his Hardanger fiddle in Cremona. It gave me a jolt. For a moment, I'd forgotten the reason why we'd come to Norway.

As the movement came to an end, the audience responded in predictable fashion, and not just by clapping. The Austrian pianist Artur Schnabel once said that he knew only two kinds of audiences – one coughing, one not coughing. This was undoubtedly a congregation of coughers. The cold, wet weather outside had virtually guaranteed it.

The final notes had not even died away before the eructions began. This wasn't morning over a tranquil fjord, it was dawn breaking over a coalmine, a bunch of miners with chronic emphysema emerging noisily into the daylight. The occasional muted splutter or suppressed cough we'd heard during the music now turned into full-throated explosions as the audience felt free to let rip.

This happens in concert halls everywhere, of course, and it's always contagious. Once one person goes, everyone goes. The auditorium resounded with the noise of laryngeal laissez-faire, the coughs at different pitches and volumes like a well-honed choir. If I was so minded, I could write a piece of avant-garde music, not for performers on a stage, but for the audience out in the hall, a four-part ensemble work comprised of soprano, alto, tenor and bass coughing, the passages interspersed with extended bouts of sweet-wrapper rustling. Perhaps some young composer has already beaten me to it.

The quartet moved on through the other movements of

the suite, including The Hall of the Mountain King which, I was relieved to see, didn't spark off more embarrassing humming from Michael Berg. Then we got to Solveig's Song, the heart of the play, in which she sings that she will wait for the faithless Peer throughout her life and, if he has already died, will be reunited with him in heaven. The words were printed in the programme notes, in both Norwegian and English. I read them as the musicians played the haunting melody and felt a sting of tears in my eyes because it reminded me of my wife, gone these eight long years but perhaps waiting for me somewhere.

It had stopped raining when we emerged from the Troldsalen. We managed to shake off Berg in the crush to leave the hall and went back up to the villa and stood on the top of the troll hill, looking out over Lake Nordås. They call it a lake, but it's really the sea, the western end opening out into the ocean.

Almost everything around the house has changed in the last hundred or so years, but not this view. This is what Grieg would have seen when he went out into his small rocky garden: the changeless grey expanse of the water, the horizon where sky and sea were almost indistinguishable from one another, the sun breaking through the lowering clouds and gleaming on the rain-soaked grass.

I pictured him standing where I was standing, maybe pondering over his next composition, maybe imagining trolls skulking beneath his feet and drawing inspiration from them. Then I saw him turning and going back inside the warm, welcoming house where Nina was waiting by the piano to play duets with him.

NINE

Kamilla Nygaard lived in an apartment in the eastern suburbs of Bergen, a modern six-storey block with small balconies outside each apartment and a patch of grass and a few benches near the main entrance where the residents could congregate when the weather was fine enough. It didn't look as if it got much use.

We took the lift to the fifth floor, just Antonio and I; Margherita had stayed behind at the hotel. I'd seen Kamilla at Rikard's funeral, but only from a distance and in the dim light of the church. Close to, she was an attractive, auburn-haired woman in her early forties, with warm, brown eyes and the figure of someone who took plenty of exercise – from the numerous photographs of snowy landscapes on the walls of her apartment, I guessed that probably meant cross-country skiing.

She made us coffee and we sat at the kitchen table and talked – in English, naturally. Antonio had asked me to do most of the initial work, to relieve him of the stress of communicating in a foreign language and make things easier for Kamilla.

"We still haven't got over the shock," she said. "It hit us hard. Elin was devastated, though she doesn't show it. She was very close to Rikard."

"She saw a lot of him?" I asked.

Kamilla nodded. "She stayed at his place every other weekend. And sometimes during the week, too. The arrangements were very flexible."

"You sound as if you were on good terms with him."

"We were."

"Was that always the case? I mean, couples splitting up, it can be difficult for everyone, can't it?"

"It wasn't so good at the beginning. Just after the split. I was angry with Rikard. So was Elin. She didn't understand why it was happening."

"And why was it?"

Kamilla shrugged. "He walked out. Just packed his stuff and left."

"No warning?"

"Not that I noticed. But Rikard was like that. Difficult to read, reserved. You could never tell what was going on inside his head and he wouldn't talk about it."

"Was there anyone else involved?"

"Another woman, you mean?" She gave a sigh of resignation. "With Rikard, there were always other women."

She hesitated. This was obviously very personal territory for her, and we were two strangers she'd only just met, one of us a police officer.

"I'm sorry to ask you these questions," I said. "You don't have to answer them."

"He's dead," Kamilla said. It sounded harsh, putting it

so bluntly, but I think it was her way of dealing with the emotions his death aroused. "What difference does it make now? Rikard didn't believe in exclusive relationships. I'd say monogamy, but we weren't married. He didn't believe in marriage either. It was boring, stultifying, a barrier to freedom, by which he meant his own freedom to do as he pleased."

The words sounded bitter, but there was no bitterness in her tone, just a sort of quiet acceptance. That was how things had been. Why wish it otherwise? Agnetha Sørensen had had pretty much the same attitude.

"How long were you together?"

"Ten years." She gave a wry smile. "It's a wonder we lasted so long. I suppose I'm a tolerant woman, or maybe I hoped he'd change. Would you like some more coffee?"

"No, thank you."

Kamilla went to the pot by the stove and refilled her mug. I glanced out of the window. We were facing north, towards Mount Fløyen. I could see a train chugging slowly up the hill, but the funicular station and restaurant on the summit were hidden in mist.

"He was a funny mixture," Kamilla said as she sat down again. "He could put up with the tedium of making violins, the repetitive nature of the work, all that cutting and scraping and gouging, but he couldn't put up with it in his private life. He had to keep straying, turning things upside down."

"That must have been difficult for you."

"It was. But I didn't want things to end. When he walked out, I was stunned. I didn't see it coming. He had me, and he had his freedom. Why wasn't that enough? I went through all the stages everyone goes through when they split up. Bewilderment, hurt, that anger I mentioned just now. I was really angry with him for a long time."

"But it didn't last?"

She shook her head. "I had Elin to think of. I didn't want her to grow up alienated from her father. For her sake, Rikard and I had to find a way of patching things up."

"Was he with someone in recent months?"

"I don't know. We didn't talk about things like that. I never saw a woman at his apartment when I dropped off or collected Elin."

"Did Elin?"

"I don't think so. Rikard was careful not to upset her. In some areas he could be very sensitive."

"So the woman you think he left you for? That didn't last?"

"No, that was over very quickly. I thought he might come back to me, but he didn't."

I glanced at Guastafeste and he gave a nod and joined in the conversation.

"Please excuse my English," he said apologetically. "I must ask you some questions about Rikard."

"Of course," Kamilla replied. "Go ahead."

"Did he have enemies? People who wanted him dead."

It was an abrupt way of putting it, giving the misleading impression that Antonio is an insensitive man when, in fact, he's the exact opposite, but he simply didn't have the English to make a more nuanced approach. Kamilla took it well.

"You think whoever killed him was Norwegian?"

"It is possible. Is there anyone?"

"Not that I know of."

"You are sure?" Antonio gave me some questions in Italian and I put them to Kamilla in English.

"He didn't fall out with anyone, didn't upset anyone in particular? Clients? Rivals in the violin making trade?"

"I don't think he had any rivals," Kamilla replied. "There aren't many violin makers in Bergen and those there are seem to get along fine."

"They wouldn't have wished to harm him?"

"No, absolutely not. They were Rikard's friends. They were at the funeral yesterday. They're distressed by his death and as mystified by it as everyone else. Rikard wasn't an angel, but he didn't make enemies. I can't think of any reason why someone might have killed him."

"He had a Hardanger fiddle," Guastafeste said. "With a woman's face on it. Do you know where he got it?"

Kamilla lifted a hand and swept her long hair back behind her ears. "I'm afraid not. Since the split, I've rarely been to his workshop, almost never asked him anything about his business. Do you want me to ask Elin?"

"Is she here?"

"She's in her room."

Kamilla left the kitchen and returned a minute later with her daughter. Elin was a tall girl, with the skinny, still-developing build of an adolescent. Facially, she was like her mother, but her striking blonde hair had definitely come from her father. She was listening to music on her phone, but pulled the earpiece out to speak to us – in fluent English.

"Yes, I know the fiddle you mean. I was with *pappa* when he bought it."

Guastafeste's eyes lit up. "When was this?" he asked excitedly.

"Oh, a couple of months ago. I was staying with him for the weekend and we drove out of Bergen to look at it."

"Drove where?"

"To Osterøy."

"Where is that?"

"It's an island north of here," Kamilla said.

"Can you remember where on the island?"

"Not well. It was somewhere beyond Valestrand. A little village on the main road. Just a few houses. Someone had died and they were selling off all the contents of a house."

"Including the fiddle?"

"Yes."

Antonio paused, obviously struggling with his English.

"Ask her if she remembers anything else," he said to me in Italian. "The name of the person he bought it from? The name of the village?"

I repeated the questions in English and Elin shook her head. "No. But I remember the house was painted yellow. And there was a farm nearby with horses grazing in a field."

"Did your father tell you anything about the fiddle?" I went on.

"He showed it to me a lot, kept on pointing out how well it had been made – all the decoration on it, and the woman's face. She was very beautiful, but I wasn't really interested. It was just a violin to me and I'm not into violins."

"He didn't say any more about it?"

"I don't think he knew any more. He bought it, then spent lots of time trying to find out who'd made it and who the woman on the scroll was."

"Did he succeed?"

"No. He posted a piece on the internet. You know, with a photo of the fiddle, asking if anyone knew anything about it. He got some replies, I think, but they didn't help. It was a bit of a... I don't know the word in English." She said something in Norwegian to her mother and Kamilla gave us the translation.

"Obsession. Rikard was obsessed with the fiddle."

"Every time I went to stay with him – in the past few weeks, I mean – he was on his laptop," Elin continued. "Searching for stuff about the fiddle. It got a bit boring. He wasn't so interested in me. It was all about that violin. And then..." She paused. "Then he went to Italy and..."

Her voice cracked. She wasn't as composed as she appeared. Kamilla stood up and put her arm around her daughter.

"I think that's enough now."

I nodded, looking at Elin. Her eyes were moist.

"I'm sorry. We didn't intend to upset you. Thank you for your help."

Kamilla led Elin from the room. Antonio and I exchanged rueful looks, but didn't say anything. When Kamilla returned, I apologised again for intruding.

"That's all right," she replied. "I'm happy to help the police, if I can. So is Elin. But she's only twelve. She thinks she's more grown up than she really is. I didn't want her to speak at the funeral, but she insisted. She felt it was the right thing to do, but it's taken a lot out of her. This is a difficult time for her."

"We understand," I said. "I hope she's all right."

We took the lift back down to the ground floor and walked out into a light drizzle. The top of Mount Fløyen was still cloaked in mist. The air had a chill, damp edge to it.

"I wonder if the shops are still open," Guastafeste said. "I want to buy a map."

We ate out again that evening – unless we wanted to eat sandwiches in our hotel, we had no choice. Margherita put a ban on any more exhausting wandering around the city in a search for a cheap restaurant that we knew would be as fruitless as looking for the pot of gold at the end of the rainbow that was currently arching over the waterfront. But, nevertheless, we had to be sensible about where we went or our budgets, already creaking at the seams, were likely to explode in our faces.

Somewhat reluctantly, we decided to try the pizzeria we'd passed the previous evening, on the grounds that pizza, even in Norway, surely couldn't be too expensive. We were wrong.

"Two hundred and fifty kroner," I said, looking at the menu by the door.

"For three pizzas, that's not too bad," Guastafeste said.

"Per pizza."

"*What*! Twenty-five euros for a pizza? What's the topping, caviare and diamonds?"

"It's still cheaper than reindeer and whale," Margherita said, heading inside.

Pizza, of course, is the world's universal food, Italy's greatest cultural export after opera and the Mafia. Wherever you go around the globe, you will find it available: in cities, in the countryside, on beaches and in the mountains. It's so ubiquitous that I wouldn't be surprised if explorers, venturing deep into the Amazon rainforest, came across some hitherto unknown tribe who sat them down for dinner and presented them with a *Capricciosa,* a *Quattro Stagioni* and a couple of thin-crust *Margheritas* with extra cheese.

It's pretty difficult to make a truly revolting pizza – though the supermarkets are having a good go – and this particular pizzeria's offerings, a few suspiciously fishy toppings aside, were quite acceptable. They should've been, of course, given the price.

Afterwards, back out on the pavement, Antonio told Margherita and me to go back to the hotel without him.

"I think I'll stretch my legs," he said. "I fancy a bit of fresh air."

We watched him stride away along the street.

"Didn't he get enough fresh air at Troldhaugen?" I said incredulously.

"It's not fresh air he fancies," Margherita replied.

I looked at her. She was smiling, with that slightly smug, superior air women affect when their intuitions are glowing red hot and we poor Neanderthal men are floundering around in the dark.

"You know where he's going?" I said.

"Don't you?"

TEN

I knocked on Guastafeste's door next morning, on our way down for breakfast, but there was no answer. I knocked again, louder, in case he was in the bathroom, but there was still no response.

"He must've gone down already," I said.

Margherita said nothing.

But he wasn't in the dining room, either. I looked at Margherita.

"You don't think..."

She didn't reply, just gave me an enigmatic smile and picked up a plate and cutlery. Breakfast was help-yourself-buffet-style, the food laid out on a long table: bread rolls, pastries, the cheese and yoghurt and hardboiled eggs the north Europeans like and – just for the Norwegians – a big bowl of pickled herring. I took a roll and filled a cup from the coffee pot and followed Margherita to a table which, by chance not design, gave us a view out into the hotel foyer.

We'd been there only a few minutes when I saw Antonio come in through the front door. He was unshaven and looked damp and rather dishevelled. He walked across the foyer towards the stairs and stopped dead as he noticed us in the dining room. He hesitated, his body language an awkward mixture of guilt and embarrassment, then he changed course and came over to our table.

"You're up early," I said. "Have you been for another walk?"

He mumbled something incoherent in reply and shuffled off to the buffet to get a cup of coffee. Margherita and I exchanged looks.

"Is it still raining?" I asked, when he returned to the table and sat down, more to make conversation than because I was interested in the answer. I could see from his clothes and hair that it was another wet day in Bergen.

"Mmm," he replied, taking a sip of his coffee.

I ate some of my bread roll. Margherita took a spoonful of her fruit salad. We waited. Antonio cleared his throat, then sat up and thrust his shoulders back, not quite making full eye contact with us.

"Last night," he said, with the resolve of a man getting something off his chest, "I went back to Nomaden."

He stopped.

"Oh, yes?" I said.

"After our talk with Kamilla and Elin, I felt we needed the help of a local. Someone who knows the area, who speaks Norwegian."

"Did you have someone in mind?"

"Well, Aina. She was performing again, so I had a chat with her when she'd finished. She's taking the day off and is going to try to help us find the place where Rikard bought the Hardanger fiddle."

"That's very good of her."

"She's picking us up at half-nine." He glanced at his watch. "I've just time for a shower." He downed the rest of his coffee and hurried out of the room.

I deliberately waited a few seconds before turning my gaze on Margherita.

"I know," I conceded. "You're always right."

"I could see it in his face when we were watching her play," she said. "Then afterwards, when she came to our table. It was obvious he was smitten, and she was equally interested in him."

"Maybe the club's open all night. Maybe that's where he's been."

She gave me a withering look, as if to say, "get real."

"If that was the case, he would have told us. It's what he's not saying that counts."

"It's a bit quick, isn't it?"

"Not really. They saw quite a bit of each other in Cremona, remember. And they're twenty years younger than us. They don't hang around the way we used to, they just get on with it."

We finished our breakfast, then returned to our room to get ready. We picked up our umbrellas and were back down in the foyer with Antonio when Aina arrived to collect us. She was dressed in what we had come to realise was the unofficial Bergen uniform: waterproof shoes, the kind of thin walking trousers that dry out quickly when wet, and a cagoule. Her spiky blonde hair was hidden beneath a peaked cap.

She kissed us on the cheeks again, perhaps taking more time with Antonio. They smiled at each other – trying to be discreet, I think, but the warmth in their eyes giving away the game.

161

We drove north out of Bergen, Guastafeste in the front next to Aina, Margherita and me in the back. The road followed the coast to begin with. The sea was to our left, the offshore islands hazy in the mist and rain. The car windows were steamed up, but I wiped a hole with my fingers and peered out, seeing a boat in the channel, a tourist excursion vessel I guessed from the glassed-in observation deck. I felt sorry for the people on board. They weren't going to see much on a day like today. We stayed alongside the boat for a short time, then began to pull ahead. Aina was driving fast, the wipers slicing back and forth across the windscreen.

After a few kilometres, we turned inland, the road going through a tunnel, then past the outskirts of a town before we reached a stretch of open countryside where the land was broken up by lakes and craggy hills whose summits were veiled in low cloud. Before long, the road came to an abrupt end at a channel of water about two kilometres wide. We joined a queue of vehicles and were directed across a metal ramp onto the deck of a ferry.

It was only a short crossing to the island of Osterøy, then we were quickly through the first settlement, Valestrand, and back out on the open road. A yellow house, a farm with horses in a field; those were the only things Elin could remember about the place she'd visited with her father. We kept our eyes peeled, scanning the edges of the road and the land beyond. It was Guastafeste who saw it first.

"There," he said, pointing ahead through the windscreen. "That must be it."

I leaned forward to get a better view. In the

distance, maybe half a kilometre away, was a two-storey wooden house painted yellow. Aina slowed down. Guastafeste had a map open on his lap.

"There is a track off to the left," he said.

We nearly missed the junction, the visibility was so poor, but Aina braked just in time and we turned off through a narrow opening between stone gateposts and onto a rough, unmade track that was pitted with ruts and holes, all of them filled with rainwater.

We bumped along the track for a couple of hundred metres and emerged onto a dirt forecourt outside the yellow lapboard house. Something about the building, probably the lack of curtains or blinds in the window, told me immediately that it was unoccupied. Umbrellas ready to unfurl, we climbed out of the car and went to take a closer look.

The house had a double frontage, large windows on either side of a central door, which was accessed via a short flight of steps. The windows were high off the ground, but I was tall enough to see in. Both the front rooms were empty – no furniture, nothing on the walls or floors. We went round to the back and checked the windows there. It was the same: the house had been stripped bare.

"Just as Elin said," I said to Guastafeste. "It was a house clearance sale. There's nothing left."

"Damn," he said, looking around the back yard.

There were several small outbuildings, little more than wooden sheds that didn't look habitable, but we inspected them anyway, peering through the grimy windows into dark, empty interiors.

"What now?" Margherita asked.

The house was isolated, surrounded by fields, some

planted with potatoes, others pastureland for grazing animals. The nearest other buildings were several hundred metres away, a group comprised of a house and barns that had to be a farm.

"Let's go and see the neighbours," Guastafeste said.

We drove back to the road and kept going until we reached the turn-off to the farm, another unmade track leading to a muddy yard behind a farmhouse whose wooden walls were weathered to a silvery-grey colour, like birch bark. Enclosing the yard on the other side was a stable block, the top parts of the doors pegged open to reveal horses inside, and a couple of shabby wooden barns containing bales of hay, a tractor and other agricultural equipment.

As we got out of the car, we saw a man in rubber boots and a waterproof jacket appear in the entrance to one of the barns. He was in his forties, a short, wiry man with engine oil on his hands and smudges of grease on his face. He didn't seem inclined to come out into the rain so we walked across and joined him in the barn. We left all the talking to Aina. She had a short conversation with the man, then gave us a summary of it in English.

"The house belonged to his uncle, a man named Knut Karlsen who died back in February. An agent handled the sale of the contents, but he remembers the Hardanger fiddle."

"Does he know where it came from?" Guastafeste asked.

"No," Aina replied. "He says they didn't even know his uncle had it until after he died and they went through all his possessions."

"He did not play it?"

"No, they'd never seen it before. It was hidden away in the back of a cupboard. The uncle had never shown it to them, never mentioned it while he was alive."

"Can he guess where his uncle got it?"

Aina put the question to the farmer and he shrugged, so we knew the answer was in the negative.

"He knows absolutely nothing about it, I'm afraid," Aina said. "His uncle didn't inherit it, as far as they know, or get it as a gift. And there are no violin makers round here he could've bought it from."

"Maybe the agent who handled the sale would know more about it," Margherita suggested.

"He says not. All the agent did was catalogue the house contents and publicise the sale."

"It was an auction?"

"Yes, but some items, including the fiddle, were sold in advance. Rikard came out to look at the instrument and made an offer on the spot."

"How much did he pay?" I asked.

"The farmer doesn't remember the exact figure, but he thinks it was something like fifty thousand kroner."

Antonio looked at me. "About five thousand euros. Is that a lot?"

"Based on my internet research, I'd say it was pretty high for a Hardanger fiddle," I replied.

"Were other people interested in it?" Guastafeste asked and Aina relayed the question to the farmer.

"There were a few inquiries," came the reply. "But by then it had already been sold to Rikard. He made a good offer that the agent was happy to accept. The estimate on the fiddle was less than half what Rikard was prepared to pay."

"Does he know who made those other inquiries?" I said.

"No. The agent handled all that."

"Could he give us the name and number of the agent?"

"The number's somewhere in the house, but he doesn't know where. His name was Snorre Svensen. I can find him online."

Guastafeste nodded. It was obvious that the farmer was getting irritated by all these questions.

"Would anyone else know where the fiddle came from? Other family members, perhaps?"

The farmer shook his head as Aina passed on the query, then they had a longer exchange in Norwegian.

"Karlsen didn't have any other living relatives," Aina explained. "He never married and had no children. He didn't have many friends, either. Not locally, or even from his youth, apparently. No one from his home village came to the funeral."

"His home village? Where's that?"

"Budal. Above Aurlandsfjord."

"Is that far away?"

"Aurlandsfjord is north-east of here," Aina said. "About a hundred and twenty kilometres. I've never heard of Budal."

The farmer said something in Norwegian that we three Italians couldn't understand, but we got the meaning from his facial and body language and it said clearly, "Can I get back to work now? I've had enough of this."

We thanked him for his help and walked back to the car. Aina got out her phone, found a number for Snorre Svensen and called him. I listened to her conversation with the agent, thinking how alien a language Norwegian was. I tried to pick out words whose meaning I could guess from my knowledge of English and German, but there were almost none. It was just an incomprehensible sequence of strange sounds, like listening to someone gargling with mouthwash.

Aina hung up. "He vaguely remembers a couple of other people being interested in the fiddle, but he can't remember any names and has no written record of them."

Guastafeste grimaced. "We're not getting very far, are we?" he said disconsolately in Italian.

Aina picked up on his mood without any translation.

"Why don't we go to Rikard's workshop?" she said. "See what we can find there."

The workshop was on the south-west side of the harbour in Bergen, a small, one-storey building hidden away off a dark, narrow alley that rose up the hillside in a series of steep steps. This was the old part of the city, dating back to the time of the Hanseatic League, when German seafaring traders dominated the economic life of the area. The buildings seemed to be a mixture of business and residential, mainly two storeys, but some taller and all clad with stout wooden planks painted mostly in muted colours – pale yellow and creams, though one or two had more striking dark red exteriors.

It wasn't difficult to imagine what it must have been like a few hundred years ago, the harbour crammed with fishing boats and whalers, their masts and rigging like a forest sprouting from the water; the streets echoing with the clop of horses' hooves and the rattle of cartwheels; the cramped little alleys crowded with dirty children and fishwives hawking their baskets of herring; the inns and alehouses teeming with raucous seamen, their pockets heavy with the proceeds of the catch; the merchants' warehouses bustling with clerks and porters, the offices at the back quieter, more genteel little havens where the masters gathered to smoke and haggle and share a glass of the Scotch whisky or Polish schnapps that had just come in on one of their ships.

It was quieter now and undoubtedly more salubrious, but the buildings were still the same, though I guessed that their timber cladding must have been replaced and repainted over the years. We followed Aina up the flight of stone steps. A shallow channel beside them guided the rainwater down the slope to the harbour. Buildings towered up on either side, shutting out what little sunlight had managed to penetrate the mantle of cloud over the city. The sky was just a sliver of murky grey above us.

Twenty or thirty steps up, when I was starting to feel the gradient, Aina turned off through an archway into a tiny courtyard. Rikard's workshop was at one side, a low wooden building with windows along its front and skylights in the sloping roof to maximise the amount of light getting in. Aina unlocked the door and led us in. There was room for us all, but only just. We shuffled around, trying to spread out a bit, but there was almost nowhere to go. We ended up in a line between the workbenches that took up three sides of the workshop.

I looked around at the tools hanging on racks, the

violins in various stages of construction, and felt a pang of sorrow as it came home to me that Rikard would never again sit on that stool, never again use the chisels and saws and templates on the walls. Those half-finished instruments would remain forever in that state. I knew I wasn't alone in my thoughts – I could see it in the others' eyes, in the restrained, respectful way they were gazing at Rikard's work. Aina, quite understandably, seemed particularly affected by the place.

"This is the first time I've been here since he died," she said.

She put her hand on the workbench, then ran her fingers over a maple plate that Rikard had been hollowing out, as if touching the wood renewed her connection to her brother.

"This is where I'll always picture him," she went on. "Sitting at the bench with a piece of wood in front of him. He always seemed so happy, so peaceful here, just making his violins. You must feel the same in your workshop."

I nodded. I've always found my work satisfying, found a quiet contentment in the magical process of making wood sing.

Guastafeste touched Aina gently on the arm.

"We do not need to stay long," he said. "What are we looking for?"

Aina opened a drawer and pulled out a laptop computer. "Let's see what he's got here," she said, suddenly businesslike and practical, her reflective mood put aside for the time being. She plugged in the laptop and turned it on.

"We know that he'd put out an appeal on the

internet," I said. "Asking for information about the fiddle."

Aina clicked on an icon, then scrolled down through a list of files and selected one. An image of the fiddle appeared on the screen, reminding us just what a fine piece of craftsmanship it was – the intricate inlay on the body and fingerboard, the exquisitely beautiful face of the young woman on the scroll. Below it was some text in Norwegian that Aina translated for us.

"It's what you said. He's giving a description of the fiddle, saying where and when he acquired it and asking if anyone knows who might have made it."

"Elin said he'd had a few replies, though they weren't much help."

"Those will be in his email folder."

She selected another item and Rikard's inbox came up on the screen, a number of more recent emails unopened. Aina glanced lower down the list of subjects and clicked on one. She read the message, then clicked on two more emails.

"Elin was right. They're just commenting on the fiddle, saying how much they like it, but they don't actually know anything about it."

"Oh," Guastafeste said glumly. "Another dead end."

"What's this?" Aina said and something in her voice made me look more closely at the screen.

She'd opened another email and was reading it intently. I peered over her shoulder at the text, but written Norwegian was as impenetrable to me as the spoken version. We'd just have to wait for the translation.

"This came only the day before yesterday," Aina said. "It's from a woman named Helga Valstad. She recognises the fiddle."

"Really?" I felt a surge of excitement. "What does she say?"

"She thinks it was made by a man called Håkon Halvorsen. The woman on the scroll is his daughter, Laila."

Antonio stepped forward eagerly, automatically doing what I had done – studying the words on the screen more closely, as if his desire to understand them would somehow be enough to make it happen.

"Does she say anything else?" he asked.

"Only that she thinks it was made around the early nineteen sixties."

"Can we email her back?"

"I can do better than that. She's given a phone number. Let's call her."

Aina took out her phone and punched in the number. I glanced at Margherita and Antonio. I don't think any of us were hopeful there'd be an answer, but someone picked up after only a few rings and Aina started speaking.

We listened, trying to detect from Aina's voice, or her face, whether she was being given anything useful. Even when she hung up, it was impossible to tell.

"Well?" Antonio said impatiently.

"She doesn't like talking on the phone," Aina replied. "But she'll happily see you and tell you more."

"Where does she live?"

"Budal."

"Budal?" Margherita said. "You mean..."

Aina nodded. "By coincidence, or maybe not, Knut Karlsen's home village." She turned back to the lap-top. "Let's see if there's anything else."

We watched as she went through the rest of Rikard's inbox, skimming quickly through the messages. Then she stopped. I knew from her expression that she'd found something.

"What is it?

"An email from Ingvar Aandahl. Actually, several emails over the past few weeks. He's wanting to buy the Hardanger fiddle."

"To *buy* it?" I said.

"Offering a lot of money."

Antonio's mouth tightened.

"I think maybe we go to see him again."

ELEVEN

Aandahl wasn't there.

The large, intimidating receptionist declined to tell us where he'd gone, only that he was "out on business" and wouldn't be back before the office closed at five-thirty.

"You'll have to come back tomorrow," she said.

That put us in a difficult situation. What did we do next? Go to Budal to find out more about the missing Hardanger fiddle, or wait around in Bergen to speak to Ingvar Aandahl? It was Guastafeste's call; this was his investigation.

"Aandahl is more important," he said. "We will speak to him tomorrow, then go to Budal."

"I doubt you'd get to Budal today, anyway," Aina said.

"No? Is it a long way?"

"Let me show you."

She took the map from him and pointed out Aurlandsfjord, a small arm at the far eastern end of Sognerfjord, which we already knew from Michael Berg was the longest fjord in Norway, a two-hundred-kilometre-long gash in the landscape from the Atlantic to the high central mountains. Budal was just a tiny dot on the map, a remote little village on the plateau above the fjord.

"How do we get there?" Antonio asked.

Aina gave it a moment's thought, then shrugged. "Well, you could hire a car and drive, I suppose. There's also the boat. You can go up the coast and all the way along Sognerfjord. But probably the best way is by train. You can go here to Myrdal." She traced the route on the map with her finger. "It's one of the most beautiful train journeys you could imagine. Then you change at Myrdal and take the Flåm railway down to Aurlandsfjord. That's another spectacular journey through some stunning scenery."

"I like the sound of that," Margherita said. "We're here in part for a holiday, after all, aren't we?"

There was no trace of resentment in her voice, but I realised I'd been neglecting her. Most of our time in Bergen, the visit to Troldhaugen aside, had been swallowed up by Guastafeste's priorities. I could hardly blame her for feeling a little left out.

"I like it, too," I said. "How long does it take?"

"A few hours," Aina replied.

"Maybe the weather will be better there," Margherita said.

Aina laughed. "It can't really get worse than Bergen."

"That leaves us the rest of the day," I said. "What shall we do?"

"How much of the city have you seen?" Aina asked.

"We've been up Mount Fløyen in the mist," Margherita replied. "And seen Ole Bull's statue and grave."

"Have you been to Lysøen, Ole Bull's island?"

"No."

"It's beautiful, well worth a visit. Why don't I take you there? It's not far."

I looked at Margherita. "Would you like that?"

She smiled at me. "I think we both would."

"Antonio?"

He hesitated, glanced at Aina, then nodded.

"Why not?"

He hadn't come to Bergen to go sightseeing, but there was nothing more he could do until Aandahl returned. In any case, I got the impression he was more than happy to delay the next stage of his investigation if it meant spending more time with Aina.

It wasn't a long drive. We headed south from Bergen, through rolling countryside, the fields beside the road green and cultivated, the low hills in the background daubed with smears of woodland and bare rock. Dotted across the landscape were sheep and cattle grazing in the meadows and small farmsteads with black roofs, white windows and dark red lapboard walls.

After half an hour, we reached Buena Kai, the launch point for the boat trip to Lysøen, which wasn't much more than a car park, a restaurant and a quayside at which a stubby little vessel was moored, its engine idling and ready to go. We boarded and dropped down a short flight of steps into a rear cabin that could accommodate maybe nine or ten passengers sitting on the wooden benches along the sides and a few more standing in between. There were only five or six other people there so we all got a seat and settled down as the boat cast off and chugged out across Lysefjorden.

The rain had stopped as we neared Buena Kai and now the sun came out. Hidden for so long behind cloud, it seemed to want to make up for lost time by shining with an intense brilliance, scintillating on the surface of the sea as if there were shoals of diamonds just below the surface.

It was only a kilometre or so to the island, but we could see very little of it from our position in the cabin until the boat was almost there and it slowed and turned to starboard, giving us a view of a tree-covered hillside and fleeting sight of a house on a low bluff overlooking the water.

Disembarking onto a jetty in the tiny, sheltered harbour, we passed a cluster of three or four cottages before the path turned along the shoreline and began to go gently uphill. Ahead of us, partially hidden by trees, we caught tantalising glimpses of Ole Bull's villa. Only when we came out onto the gravel forecourt in front of the house did we see what an extraordinary building it was. The lower parts were stolidly Norwegian in their stone foundations and lapboard walls painted grey, but above that was an eclectic mix of architecture, part Moorish, like a mini Alhambra, part Russian Orthodox in the onion dome on the tower that dominated the roof.

"What a magnificent house," Margherita said, gazing in awe at the sweeping staircase that led up to the main doors on the first floor, the veranda outside the entrance sheltered by an ornate canopy whose white arches and finials and pillars - like thick, twisted ropes - looked as if they'd been carved from icing sugar.

"Impressive, isn't it?" Aina said.

"This is where Ole Bull lived?"

"When he wasn't travelling the world playing concerts."

"Can we go inside it?"

"Of course."

Annoyingly, for me, at least, you couldn't just go into the house and walk around on your own; you had to go on a guided tour – as we had at Troldhaugen. Even more annoyingly, when we'd bought our tickets and gathered around our guide, we saw a familiar face in the group – Michael Berg.

"This is a coincidence," he said, manoeuvring himself to stand next to me. "Or maybe not. Troldhaugen, Lysøen, they're probably on most tourists' itinerary, aren't they? You just arrived?"

"Yes."

"I came on an earlier boat, but had to wait till now to look inside the house. They only do a tour every hour. Are you interested in Ole Bull? I guess you are or you wouldn't be here. I'm *very* interested in him."

"He was a great man."

"That depends on your point of view," Berg said cryptically, but didn't explain further, for the guide was introducing himself.

"My name is Erik Rasmussen," he said in English. He was medium height, with short fair hair and pale blue eyes behind rimless glasses. "Please follow me. And take care on the steps."

The main entrance was out of bounds to tourists so we went into the house through the much less grand side door, also up a flight of steps to the first floor. Immediately inside, we had to put blue plastic bags over our shoes to stop them dirtying the polished

177

wooden floors, then we followed the guide into a reception room that contained three glass cabinets.

My attention was aroused at once as two of the cabinets contained a violin each, both instruments that Ole Bull had owned and played in his lifetime. One was by the great French luthier, Jean-Baptiste Vuillaume, an elegant, golden-varnished instrument which, according to the label in the cabinet, had been made when Bull was in Paris during the revolution of 1848. Bull and Vuillaume were great friends and Ole, when his work took him to the French capital, would spend hours with Vuillaume, inspecting, taking apart and reassembling violins. The second fiddle was more eye-catching, and much more valuable – a Guarneri del Gesù of 1733.

In between the two violins was a third glass cabinet in which various smaller items were displayed, including jewellery given to Bull by the tsar of Russia and king of Sweden and – somewhat bizarrely – a small bottle of smelling salts that were a standard requisite of the virtuoso's concerts, to revive the many women who swooned over his playing – and his Norwegian good looks.

I peered closer at the Guarneri, trying to examine it from every angle to fully appreciate the maker's remarkable craftsmanship, but after only a few minutes the guide was moving on into the next room and instructing us to follow him. I tried to hang back, but Rasmussen wasn't going to allow anyone to escape from the flock. He waited in the doorway, glaring at me impatiently until I dragged myself away from the cabinet and rejoined the group.

"Please stay together," he said, staring pointedly

at me. "We don't want to lose anyone."

"Are you being a bad boy, Gianni?" Margherita murmured.

"I *hate* guided tours," I murmured back. "Why can't I just go where I want?"

"This way, please," Rasmussen called out. "Gather round."

The group shuffled into a semi-circle around the guide. Guastafeste and Aina were together to my left. I saw them touch hands, then entwine their fingers. Margherita saw it, too, and gave me a "told-you-so" look.

"Ole Bull knew Lysøen well when he was a boy," Rasmussen said. "He used to row out in a boat and explore the island. A few local people lived here, but only along the shore. They didn't dare go into the interior for fear of the evil spirits they believed were lurking there. That might sound a bit silly, but I live here on the island and it can be very spooky, particularly in winter. Then, in eighteen seventy-two, when he was in his early sixties, Bull managed to buy the island, paying the equivalent of two of his concert fees for the seventy hectares of land. He then spent one concert fee on building this house."

The guide paused for a second, letting us reflect on just how fabulously well remunerated the violinist had been if one fee could build a villa like this. Or, alternatively, how badly paid the workers had been, but he didn't mention that; it would spoil the myth.

"The centrepiece of the villa," Rasmussen continued, "is this large drawing room, which takes up almost the entire first floor. Bull intended it to be a performance space for his recitals, and it's still used for concerts today."

The guide kept talking, but it was only a background drone to me. My eyes were roving over the room, taking in the rows of chairs, the sparkling crystal chandeliers and the carved ceiling which was the most extravagantly ornate piece of woodwork I'd ever seen. It reminded me of the gingerbread house in Hansel and Gretel, only more extreme, as if the creator had gone mad with a pastry cutter.

Every part of the high vaulted ceiling was covered with golden pine, carved away into stars and semi-circles and flowers and other geometric designs, giving the feeling that the interior of a sultan's palace had been transported to the Norwegian coast.

I could see Ole Bull here. He was an exotic creature who travelled widely across Europe, North Africa and America. It was quite in keeping with his cosmopolitan character to import influences from other cultures into his island home.

Rasmussen was pointing out some of the objects in the room: the huge mirrors, the unusual Norwegian flag which had the stars and stripes in its upper left quarter – a relic of Bull's failed attempt to create a Norwegian colony in the United States – and a massive wooden sideboard that was the result of another of his eccentric schemes that didn't come to fruition: an experimental piano that would never need tuning. It didn't work so he had the instrument cut down and converted into a piece of furniture. That was Bull all over: an unworldly dreamer, full of ideas and schemes that he couldn't always realise.

He sounded a fascinating, if fallible, man. Like many people who go on to achieve great things, he had an immense belief in himself, a confidence that was not always matched by his competence. He was also selfish, wilful and arrogant, but those characteristics were offset by his musical talents and a real warmth and genuineness that seemed to charm everyone who met him.

He was certainly a precociously gifted violinist, a passionate Norwegian nationalist with a deep attachment to his home country and to the folk music that formed the basis of many of his compositions. But Norway was never going to be big enough for an ambitious young man like Ole. He had to make his mark on a wider audience.

That meant travelling, the exhausting life of a wandering musician that would continue until he died. Germany first, then Paris, where he met Chopin, Rossini and a fourteen-year-old girl named Félicie Villeminot who, four years later, would become his wife and, probably, the most unfortunate casualty of his restless nature.

He was reputedly a loving man, but he wasn't a good husband or father. The domestic stage was far too small and restricted for him; he needed a larger arena for his talents and for the adulation he so craved. Poor Félicie got a week's honeymoon after their marriage in 1836, but then Ole went off on tour without her, setting a pattern that was to last until her death twenty-six years later. Ole, who liked to wax lyrical on the joys of the family hearth, but who was much less enthusiastic about actually experiencing them, would come home for a couple of weeks, then get itchy feet and head off elsewhere, often leaving his wife pregnant and on her own to cope with their growing family. And his absences weren't short; sometimes he was away for years at a time.

Europe was his early stamping ground, but he soon felt the need to conquer America and went across the Atlantic to New York and Boston where audiences were bowled over by his dazzling virtuosity. Women, young and old, were particularly susceptible to his allure as he was young and handsome and cut a striking figure on stage with his long, flowing hair, soulful eyes and tall, straight posture – like a Norwegian pine or an "angel with the violin", as the poet Longfellow later described him.

The professional critics, however, were a little sniffy about his choice of repertoire. By now, Bull had adopted Paganini's practice of playing almost nothing except his own compositions, a decision that opened him up to the accusation that he was all show and no substance, but Ole knew his audiences, particularly in the Mid-west, where he gave hundreds of concerts. The area had been frontier territory only a few years earlier and the miners, farmers and tough Mississippi gamblers were more interested in variations on Yankee Doodle than a Mozart sonata.

Bull, unlike a lot of other visiting artists from Europe, had a genuine affection for the Americans – not just their dollars – and it was his admiration for the country that led him to embark on the project that would break him financially and do serious damage to his reputation in his homeland – the creation of New Norway, a utopian colony for his fellow countrymen in the United States.

He'd long felt that his Norse forbears had been the first Europeans to discover the New World and liked to think of himself as a latter day Leif Ericksson, giving many concerts to raise funds for a statue of the explorer in Boston, but the comparison was hardly accurate. Ole was so chaotic and disorganised that, had he been a Viking sailor, he would probably have got halfway across the Atlantic before he realised he'd left the boat at home.

New Norway was conceived with the best intentions, a new home for emigrant Norwegians where they could escape the arduous struggle of trying to survive in Norway's harsh climate and terrain, but it was a calamity for all concerned. The land Bull bought in Pennsylvania was steep and heavily forested and wholly unsuited to agriculture. Ole had grand plans for his first settlement – called, with characteristic immodesty, Oleana – but he'd given no consideration to the economic soundness of the scheme or the nature of the land he'd bought. The colony survived for less than two years, then collapsed amid acrimony, leaving behind lawsuits that plagued Bull for years afterwards.

His finances recovered, through prodigious effort on the concert stage, but the New Norway settlers were always bitter about their experiences at his ill-fated colony. Ole had lured them there with his name and reputation, and promises of milk and honey, but it had all turned sour. They'd come to America to escape poverty and hardship in Norway, but the cure proved to be worse than the disease.

New Norway had been an expensive disaster, but Bull sailed on, relatively unscathed by the debacle. A child-man in many ways, he had always done what he pleased and left others to pick up the pieces, not least his long-suffering wife. Ole was away on tour again when, in 1862, Félicie died, lonely and unhappy in

Christiania – now Oslo – a city and a country she loathed. She'd stood by her husband and cared for their children for all those years, but Ole had repaid her love and loyalty with neglect and betrayal.

He got married again, eight years later – to Sara Thorp, the daughter of a wealthy Wisconsin lumberman and state senator, the match engineered by Sara's ambitious mother, Amelia, who remained a hovering third-party presence in the union. Sara was twenty years old, Ole sixty, but still attractive to women and still in need of their love.

The marriage was a curious misalliance, partly because of the disparity in age between them, but also because of their differences in temperament; Sara conventional and repressed, the product of her sheltered upbringing and a controlling mother, Ole the exact opposite – wild, ebullient, eccentric and with a careless attitude to money and morals that shocked his new in-laws.

It was probably in part to escape the suffocating clutches of the Thorps that Bull came back to Norway and bought Lysøen. His winters were spent giving concerts in America, but every summer for the rest of his life he came here to his "island of light."

"Gianni? Gianni?"

I turned my head and saw Margherita looking at me.

"Are you all right?" she asked.

"Yes. Why?"

"You seem, well, a little cut off."

"I was thinking about Ole Bull. My own thoughts, that is, not the facts the guide wants to give us." I glanced around. "Has he finished?"

"Yes."

"Thank goodness for that. He was getting on my nerves."

"He's given us a few minutes to look around on our own."

"About time, too."

The group had split apart and the other people were drifting around the room. Michael Berg was examining the flag in the corner, Antonio and Aina were sitting on two of the chairs, still holding hands. I watched them for a moment, feeling glad for them both, but particularly Antonio. He's been a part of my life for more than four decades. I've seen him grow up, from child to adolescent to adult, and I look on him as family rather than friend. He was married once, but it didn't last. The divorce hit him hard and I've sensed a loneliness in him in recent years. It was good to see him falling in love again.

I turned away and joined Margherita, who'd wandered to the end of the room and was gazing up at the ceiling. It was almost a century and a half since the wood had been carved, but there was still a scent of pine in the air.

"It's quite something," Margherita said. "But perhaps a bit over the top for my taste."

"Over the top was an Ole Bull speciality," I replied. "He liked to put on a show, in both his public and his private lives."

"That's him on the wall over there, isn't it?"

We went to look at the framed photograph that hung above the piano-cum-sideboard. It showed Bull in his later years, still straight and erect, his long hair grey, a violin in his hand.

"He's a handsome man. I could've fallen for him,"

185

Margherita said.

"A lot of women did."

"It would've been nice to hear him play. What do you think he sounded like?"

"I don't know. Opinion was divided at the time. Some people raved about his technique and wonderful, sweet tone, others thought he was a charlatan and a humbug. But he managed to sustain a very successful career for fifty-plus years. Audiences aren't stupid. He must have had something special."

I tried to imagine Ole in this ostentatious hall, playing for a group of friends, but no picture would come. It was an overpowering room, quite claustrophobic in some ways. Bull had planned the decoration in detail himself, overseen its installation, but I could feel no trace of his spirit lingering here.

Erik Rasmussen was waving his arms at the other end of the hall.

"That's it, the end of the tour," he called out. "Please follow me."

A little reluctantly, we rejoined the group and went downstairs to the ground floor where there was a small shop selling souvenirs, books and CDs of Bull's music. Some people began to browse the items, but they were of no interest to me. I went out through the exit onto the gravel in front of the house. Margherita, Antonio and Aina were right behind me.

Margherita immediately gave voice to the thought that, I suspect, was in all our minds.

"I could do with a coffee."

We went to the café in the outbuildings next to the villa and bought coffee and sandwiches, then sat down at a table outside on the terrace. The sky was cloudless, the sun still shining. We were all keen to take advantage of the break in the weather before the rain – inevitably – returned. Rasmussen, I noticed, had followed us over from the house, got his own cup of coffee and sat down at the table just behind us, no doubt worn out by all that talking.

"What did you think?" Aina asked. She'd taken off her cap and was letting the sun hit her face.

"Incredible," Margherita replied. "I've never seen anything quite like that drawing room. The carving was out of this world. How did they do it?"

"Skilled carpenters," Aina said. "Norway is full of trees – you may have noticed. We've been working with wood for thousands of years." She looked at me. "You know wood well, Gianni. You probably appreciated it more than anyone."

I nodded. "It was certainly extraordinary work. I wish we'd had more time to take it all in. I particularly wanted to spend longer on the violins, the Vuillaume and the Guarneri."

"You're on holiday," Margherita said. "You can forget about violins for a few days."

"Forget about them?" I said, with mock indignation. "That's the only reason we're here. This villa only exists because of one man and his violin."

A shadow fell over the table. I looked round and saw Michael Berg behind me, a tray in his hands on which were a coffee and a sandwich.

"Do you mind if I join you?" he asked.

We did mind, of course, but we were too polite to say so. I gestured at a chair.

"Please."

Berg sat down and put his tray on the table. There

was an awkward silence, but it didn't last long.

"That's a hell of a house," he said. "Bull certainly knew how to look after himself. It must've cost a fortune. Pity he had my ancestor's blood on his hands."

It was such a strange remark that, against my initial inclinations, I was forced to engage him in conversation.

"Pardon? Blood?"

Berg nodded. He lifted his sandwich off the tray and took a bite, giving his answer with his mouth full, crumbs of bread escaping from the corners of his mouth.

"He killed my great, great, great – I forget how many greats – grandfather."

"Ole Bull killed one of your ancestors?" I said incredulously.

"Yep." Berg chewed on his sandwich.

"How?"

"Oleana."

"What's he talking about?" Margherita whispered to me in Italian.

"Bull's Norwegian colony in the United States. I'll tell you about it later," I replied in Italian, then went back into English.

"Oleana? What do you mean?"

"You know what Oleana was?" Berg asked.

"Yes."

He was surprised. "Really? How come?"

"I'm in the violin trade. I'm interested in Bull and his life."

"So you'll know what a flop it was?"

"Yes."

"It was a disaster from start to finish. A lot of people got hurt, but not Ole Bull."

"He lost a lot of money, didn't he?"

"But he didn't lose his life, like my great, great, whatever, grandfather, Alexander Berg. He came over to America with his family on the *Incognito*. That was a sailing ship that arrived in New York in the fall of eighteen fifty-two. They'd barely docked before Ole Bull came on board and gave a big speech about his new colony in Pennsylvania, telling all these naïve emigrants what a great place it was going to be and how he was going to pay them to clear the land and settle there. Alexander had been planning on heading further west, but Bull's name and his smooth talking persuaded them to go to Pennsylvania instead. A big mistake."

Berg took a gulp of coffee then another bite of his sandwich and went on, "Alexander's wife, Caroline – I'll call her Grandma Caroline to keep things simple – kept a journal of her early years in America. It's written in Norwegian, but I've had it translated into English. It gives a vivid account of their time at Oleana, starting out all bright and hopeful, then deteriorating into misery and despair.

"It all looked so good at the beginning – in New York, I mean. Bull was going to give everyone fifty acres of land at three dollars an acre, but they wouldn't have to pay for it up front or even in cash. They could pay by doing a couple day's work for the community every month and the rest of the time they could clear their land for farming and Bull would pay them fifteen dollars a month with free meals and accommodation. It sounded too good to refuse."

Berg rummaged in his jacket pocket and pulled out his phone.

"Let me show you something."

He turned the phone round, the screen taken up by a photograph of a steep valley with a river in the bottom.

"That's what Oleana looks like now."

"You've been there?" I said.

"It's now Ole Bull State Park. You can camp there and rent cabins and go hiking." He swiped to another photo. "That's the foundations of what they called Bull's 'castle', the big house he was going to live in, but it was never finished."

He went back to the first photograph.

"There are still trees in the valley, but nothing like the dense forest that was there when Alexander and his family arrived. It must have been a big shock for them. Grandma Caroline writes in her journal that she doesn't know how they're going to turn this, 'Black Forest', she calls it, into viable farmland. They never did, of course, but they were optimistic at the start, like all the other settlers. Bull was so confident, so famous, so full of ideas that no one thought it could possibly fail.

"But you can see the mood change as the weeks go by. Grandma Caroline starts to wonder about Bull's plans, about some of the weird things he does. He buys a couple hundred high silk hats in ivory white in New York and brings them to Oleana, hoping that the hats will become the official colony headgear. But these are people who are going to spend their days chopping down trees. What're they going to do with white top hats?"

"He *was* quite eccentric," I said. "From what I've read about him."

"Eccentric?" Berg said. "Crazy more like. And he doesn't keep his word either. The settlers start clearing the valley, but then the money dries up. They don't get their pay. Bull is nowhere to be found. No one knows whether he's given up on the colony or whether his agents are stealing the money. Then winter sets in, snow three feet deep, temperatures well below freezing. They all almost starve or die of the cold. Grandma Caroline says they're living off cow cabbage and nettles and whatever game they can find in the woods."

"And Alexander?" I said. "How exactly did Ole Bull kill him?"

"That comes in the spring. Somehow the family survives the terrible winter, then when the snow thaws they resume clearing the land. Alexander is out in the forest with an axe and a tree falls on him, crushes him to death."

"An accident?" I said. "You can hardly blame Bull for that."

"Not directly, no. But it wouldn't have happened if Bull hadn't persuaded them to go to Oleana. Grandma Caroline certainly felt that Bull should've taken some responsibility for it, paid them compensation. She was left on her own with three children to look after."

"What did she do?"

"What they should've done in the first place. She left Oleana and headed west to Wisconsin, where there were other Norwegians and plenty of good, cheap land that *was* suitable for farming."

Berg finished his sandwich and coffee and wiped his mouth with a paper napkin.

"I still think Bull owes my family for what he did."

191

"He's been dead for a hundred and forty years," I said.

"I don't care. He ruined my ancestors' lives. Grandma Caroline had to raise her family with no husband to support them. The effort exhausted her and she died aged only thirty-eight."

"It's a bit late for compensation now, don't you think?"

"Is it? Bull was a rich man. Look at this house he built. His estate must be loaded."

"I think his family gifted the house to the Norwegians years ago."

"What about those violins in the glass cabinets then? One's a Guarneri. Aren't they worth millions of dollars? They could sell them and give the proceeds to the families who suffered at Oleana – and mine wasn't the only one. I think that would be the right thing to do."

I didn't argue with him. When people have an axe to grind, it's always wise to give them a wide berth in case the axe ends up in the back of your head. I turned to Margherita and said in Italian, "Shall we go for a walk?"

She didn't need to be asked twice. She was on her feet immediately, slipping her shoulder bag around her neck.

I looked at Antonio and Aina. They'd been having their own quiet, private conversation on the other side of the table. I asked if they wanted to come with us and Antonio shook his head.

"You go. We'll be fine here. What time's the last boat?"

"Five o'clock, I think."

"We'll meet you down by the jetty."

I turned back to Berg. It seemed discourteous to just walk off without a word.

"Well, it was nice meeting you again."

"You're going?" Berg said.

"Just to explore some of the island," I replied, then realised what a mistake that was when Berg got to his feet and said, "That's a good idea. I'll come with you."

"No, it's all right. I think we'd rather – " I began, but Berg was already taking out the small map of Lysøen we'd all been given with our tickets for the villa.

"There are lots of paths," he said. "Which way do you want to go?"

I saw the dismay in Margherita's face, her eyes appealing to me to get rid of this irritating little man.

"Don't worry," I said softly in Italian. "We'll shake him off."

We went up the path behind the villa, through the pine forest that covered nearly all the island. The sun broke through the canopy of branches, warming our faces and dancing over the rocky ground.

"I'm thinking of writing a book about it, you know," Berg said, tagging along behind us.

"A book about what?" I said.

"About Oleana. Use Grandma Caroline's journal as the basis for it. She wrote well, considering she was a farmer's wife who probably didn't have much of an education. But her journal's full of superstition – stuff about evil spirits and wood sprites and mumbo-jumbo like that. She says there was a troll on the *Incognito* when they came across the Atlantic. A female troll who was in love with a young man who was emigrating. But because trolls can't cross water, she began ageing as soon as the ship sailed and by the time they arrived at Oleana she was a haggard old woman who died shortly afterwards. She was buried on the far side of

193

the creek so she couldn't come back across the water to bother anyone. I looked for the grave when I visited the area a few years back, but I couldn't find anything."

"You looked for the grave of a troll?" I said and got a disapproving glare from Margherita which said clearly, "Don't encourage him."

Berg chuckled. "Yeah, it does sound a bit weird, I admit. But Grandma Caroline's description of it is so evocative you could easily start to believe in things like that. *They* certainly believed it, the Norwegian emigrants, I mean. And it's still there in their descendants. My dad used to tell me and my sister tales about trolls when we were kids, say they'd come to get us if we didn't behave and do our homework."

We came out onto a ridge and paused. The path divided, one branch dropping down over the ridge, the other heading up the hill towards the centre of Lysøen. I stepped off the path, pulling Margherita with me so Berg walked on ahead of us, taking the route that led down off the ridge. I let him get some distance down the hill before I called out, "We're going to go this way. We'll see you later."

He turned, looking back in surprise, but by then we were walking rapidly up the other path, the trees closing in around us so we were hidden from sight. We kept going for an intense few minutes before the pace and the incline forced us to stop to draw breath. I looked back. I'd feared that Berg might follow us, but I could see no sign of him.

"Well done, Gianni," Margherita said. "That was neatly done."

"I feel bad about it," I replied.

"Why?"

"It seems very rude, and a bit underhand, sneaking away like that."

"We didn't 'sneak' anywhere. We just took a different path, and told him we were. If he wouldn't take a hint, what choice did we have?"

"I know. I just didn't like doing it that way."

We walked on up the path until we reached the summit of the hill, a rocky outcrop with a stone tower on it about four metres high. We climbed up the steps that spiralled around the tower and stood on the platform at the top. Above us, the Norwegian flag hung limply from its pole.

This was the highest part of the island. From where we stood, we had a clear three-hundred-and-sixty degree view of the whole area. To the east was the strip of water across to Buena Kai and the mainland, to the west the Atlantic Ocean. Below us, on the western side, the ground fell away steeply to one of the island's two lakes, Lysevågsvatn, and beyond that was a rocky cove where, according to our map, you could swim in the sea.

I saw a red and yellow boat in the mouth of the cove, a couple of yachts further out in the ocean. Somewhere down in the trees between us and the lake was Michael Berg. My feelings of guilt aside, I was glad we'd escaped from him. I wanted to enjoy the rest of the day with Margherita and no one else.

"What a fantastic view!" Margherita exclaimed. "And what a beautiful island. I can see why Bull built his house here. Was he really as bad as Berg claims?"

"Well, his Oleana colony was certainly a catastrophe for him. His reputation, particularly in

Norway, took a battering, but it recovered and he regained his national hero status. To blame him for a logging accident, like Berg, is a bit extreme. Bull was vain and naïve and a hopeless organiser, but he wasn't a killer. Quite the opposite, in fact. Everyone who met him was struck by how warm hearted he was, how gregarious and fond of people. But he had no staying power. He flitted from one idea to another, one place to another, always looking for something to hold his interest."

"Yet this must have been a very peaceful place to come. Quiet, away from the city and other people."

I nodded. "I guess he sometimes needed somewhere to escape, to recharge his batteries."

We took a last look at the view, then descended the steps to the base of the tower.

"Where next?" Margherita asked.

I showed her the map.

"Why don't we go down this path to the other lake? Then it's not too far to the harbour."

There were other visitors on the island, but I was struck by how empty the interior was. Most people clearly didn't venture much further than the villa and café. We seemed to have the forest to ourselves as we walked down through the trees and came out onto the shore of Heimavatn, the smaller of Lysøen's lakes. We were the only people there, too.

We walked round one side of the lake and came across a wooden bench on the edge of the path.

"Let's stay here a while," Margherita suggested. "We've time before the boat."

We sat down and let the stillness envelop us. There was a narrow strip of shore in front of the bench, sparsely covered with low undergrowth and silver birch trees whose trunks were like gnarled fingers poking up through the earth. Beyond that was a marshy fringe and then the lake itself, the water smooth and limpid, the surface patterned with reflections. The air was warm and damp, the quiet broken only by the drowsy buzz of insects. We breathed in the soft, sweet scents of the forest. It was the most tranquil place I'd ever been.

Neither of us spoke. We knew each other well enough to be comfortable with silence. Words would only break the spell, and that was the right word, for there was something magical about this hidden little lake. I could see why the local people, back in Bull's time, had believed that wood nymphs and water sprites inhabited the island. I could almost believe it myself, looking around at the swampy ground, the moss-encrusted logs and the hollows on the lake shore in which mysterious creatures might be living. There was something timeless and primeval about it.

Ole Bull would have seen just what we were experiencing; the same lake, the same ancient rocks, the same unknowable forest. I hadn't felt his spirit in the grand villa on the coast, but I could feel it here in the peace of the interior. He was a complex man, addicted to the excitement and the acclaim of the concert stage, but also deeply connected to his homeland – in both the sense of the country, Norway, but also, literally, the soil beneath his feet. I could picture him here where we were sitting – not on a bench, but perhaps on one of the many fallen trees brought down by the winter gales – his violin under his chin, his fingers tentatively picking out a melody for one of his compositions. The atmosphere here was perfectly conducive to creativity.

I wish I'd met him. He seemed an immensely likeable man. Fickle and unreliable, undoubtedly, but very human and imperfect, which was why most people found him endearing. His close family and friends, of course, veered more towards exasperation, but that comes with the territory. Ibsen supposedly modelled Peer Gynt on him and there were certainly striking similarities between the two: the dreaming, the unrealistic fantasies, the ceaseless travelling and neglect of loved ones, Félicie playing Ole's Solveig, waiting faithfully by the fire for him to come home.

Bull's behaviour wasn't exceptional for successful men of his era, maybe for successful men of any era for that matter. Men have always been selfish and irresponsible and it's always been the lot of many women to have to put up with them. I've been lucky in many ways to have led a quiet, insignificant life, to have a job that keeps me close to home. I haven't earned great wealth or fame, but I *have* been there for my wife and children, and that's what's made my life worthwhile.

I'm here for Margherita, too, now. Maybe it was the thought of Caterina, or even Solveig. Maybe it was the air in this secluded spot, but I felt a sudden swell of emotion for the woman sitting beside me. On impulse, I leaned over and kissed her softly on the lips.

Margherita looked at me in surprise, but didn't say anything. She just put her arm through mine and leaned in closer and we sat there together for a long while, listening to the gentle rustle of leaves and watching the reflections of the trees in the lake and the sunlight dappling the surface.

But time, as it tends to, soon caught up with us. I looked at my watch and saw that we had to be going.

"Do we have to?" Margherita asked plaintively. "Can't we stay a bit longer?"

"Not unless you want to spend the night here. Or swim back to the mainland."

She sighed. "Okay, I suppose we have no choice."

She slipped her hand into mine as we stood up and kept it there as we walked through the forest to the harbour. Antonio and Aina were waiting for us, basking in the sun on a rock like a couple of contented lizards.

I was bracing myself for another encounter with Michael Berg, but, to my relief, he didn't show up for the boat. He must have taken an earlier one back to Buena Kai.

Aina drove us back to Bergen. We were nearing our hotel when Guastafeste – perhaps feeling guilty that he'd spent the afternoon enjoying himself – suddenly said, "I don't want to wait until tomorrow to speak to Aandahl. Can we go by his office now and see if he's there?"

Aina found a parking space on one of the narrow streets above Strandgaten and she and Margherita stayed in the car while Antonio and I walked the short distance to Aandahl's office.

It was gone half-past six. I wasn't hopeful that the dealer would be there, but then changed my mind as we approached the building and saw that there were lights on inside. The front door was closed, but not locked. Antonio turned the handle and we stepped into a deserted reception area.

"Hello?" Antonio called out. There was no reply.

The door to Aandahl's inner office was ajar. Antonio pushed it open.

"Herr Aandahl?"

The office seemed to be empty too. No sign of either the dealer or his receptionist. We went in, Antonio going first. He stiffened and let out a sharp exclamation.

"Gianni, don't..." he began, but it was too late.

I saw it, too – Ingvar Aandahl's body splayed out on the wooden floor behind the desk. His shirt front was soaked with blood and protruding from his chest, just over his heart, was the violin-shaped hilt of the silver letter opener.

TWELVE

Dag Pettersen came out of the inner office and stood aside to let more of the police team through. The place was filling up quickly – plainclothes detectives, scene-of-crime officers with their white boiler suits and mountains of kit, a middle-aged man with a black bag who had to be the doctor. Outside, uniformed officers had taped off the area and were standing guard to keep curious spectators away. Not that there were many of those; the rain was torrential enough to deter anyone from lingering too long near the building.

"It's getting very crowded in here," Pettersen said. "Let's go outside."

We went out onto the forecourt, unfurling our umbrellas before following the inspector up the street to a corner where a wide overhanging roof provided some shelter from the rain. Pettersen hadn't pulled up the hood on his waterproof jacket and his hair was gleaming wet, slicked down across his head in thin strands. He didn't seem to notice it was raining.

It became apparent immediately that he had an ulterior motive for wanting to get away from Aandahl's office: he needed a cigarette. He took a crumpled packet from the inside pocket of his jacket and held it up.

"You don't mind?"

Antonio and I shook our heads. Pettersen offered us one then, when we refused, lit up his own and inhaled deeply, turning his head to blow the smoke out into the street. He brushed a few droplets of rain off his moustache.

"Okay, so tell me about it," he said.

Guastafeste let me do the talking. Not just about finding Aandahl's body, but also about our earlier encounters with him, at his office and in Cremona. Pettersen took a moment to digest the information, sucking thoughtfully on his cigarette.

"There were emails from him on Rikard Olsen's computer, offering to buy the Hardanger fiddle?" he said, checking the facts I'd given him.

"That's right."

"And yet he'd denied any interest in the instrument?"

"Yes."

"You think he stole the fiddle from Olsen, in Cremona?"

I deferred to Antonio on that one. It was his case; it wasn't up to me to speculate.

"I don't know," he said. "He had a violin case with him when he leaves Italy, but he says it has another instrument inside – a Gasparo da Salò he'd bought for a man here in Bergen, a businessman named Aksel Sørensen."

"Sørensen? The oil man?"

Antonio nodded. "We went to see him. He confirmed Aandahl's story, showed us the Gasparo violin."

"Could Aandahl have also brought the Hardanger fiddle back from Cremona with him? Perhaps in his hold luggage." Pettersen paused to reflect on that, then shook his head. "No, you'd have to be stupid to entrust something fragile like a violin to airport baggage handlers."

"He did not fly commercial," Antonio said. "He uses Sørensen's private jet."

"So it's possible he had the fiddle with him?"

"Yes, it is possible."

"Let's run with that for a moment. Aandahl kills Olsen and takes the Hardanger fiddle, then brings it back to Norway with him. A few days later, he ends up dead. Why? Was he killed for the fiddle? Did someone else also want it?"

Antonio shrugged. "That is possible, too. But we do not think Aandahl killed Rikard Olsen. He has an alibi for the time of the death."

"This seems to be an interesting violin," Pettersen said. "What's so special about it?"

"That is what we are trying to find out," Antonio replied.

The inspector tapped the ash off his cigarette, avoiding the rain that was dripping down from the edge of the overhang above us. Fifty metres away along the street, a white van with a satellite dish on its roof was pulling in behind the line of police vehicles. The television cameras had arrived. Pettersen watched the van for a second, then turned back to us.

"Let's move on to this evening," he said. "You say you came back to speak to Aandahl and just walked into the building?"

"The door was unlocked, the lights were on. He has

a receptionist, but she was not there. She leave earlier, probably."

"You know her name?"

"No, she did not tell us."

"And then?"

"Aandahl's office door was open. We went in and found him on the floor."

"Did you touch him?"

"I check his neck for a pulse, but he is dead. The knife – what do you call it?" He glanced at me for help.

"The letter opener," I said.

"Yes, the letter opener. I think it go into his heart."

I gave an involuntary shudder as I pictured the body again. Guastafeste noticed my reaction.

"Are you all right, Gianni?" he asked in Italian.

"Yes."

"You sure? We just found a man stabbed to death. Do you need a doctor? You might be in shock."

"No, I'm fine."

"Honestly?"

"Yes, I don't need a doctor."

"Is everything okay?" Pettersen said.

"I worry about my friend, that is all," Guastafeste replied in English. "Finding Aandahl dead. The letter opener, the blood. Everything. We are policemen, but it is not easy for Gianni."

"You want to speak to a counsellor?" Pettersen asked me. "They can help in situations like this."

"Thank you, but no," I said. "I'll be all right. Please, go on."

Pettersen hesitated, looking at me with concern, then he shrugged and picked up the thread of our discussion.

"The letter opener," he said. "An unusual choice of weapon. Did the killer bring it with him?"

204

"It was Aandahl's." Antonio replied. "He has it on his desk."

"So the killer snatched it up and stabbed him with it? Sounds like a spur of the moment action, rather than premeditated."

Antonio nodded. "That is what I think, too."

"Did you see anyone near the building when you arrived?" Pettersen went on.

"No."

"Nothing suspicious?"

"No."

"And after you found the body?"

"We called you, then I went outside to look around. But I find nothing."

Rainwater splashed down onto the sleeve of the inspector's jacket and he edged back towards the wall of the building. Along the street, the television crew were unloading their equipment, setting up a camera beneath a large umbrella.

"The murder of Rikard Olsen, now Ingvar Andahl. There has to be a connection between the two," Pettersen said.

"Yes," Antonio agreed.

"The same killer?"

"I don't know."

"And the Hardanger fiddle?"

"We go to Aurlandsfjord tomorrow to see someone about it," Antonio said.

"We need to work together on this. Let me know how you get on and I'll keep you informed about the Aandahl case."

"Of course."

Pettersen dropped his smouldering cigarette to the

ground and crushed it under his shoe. Then, to avoid littering, he picked up the stub and put it away in a small metal tin he took from his pocket.

"I'm afraid I'm going to need formal statements from you, about Aandahl."

"Now?"

"If you don't mind."

Antonio and I went back to Aina and Margherita, who'd been waiting patiently in the car all this time. We drove down the hill to Allehelgens gate and made our statements, then Aina took us back to our hotel. Guastafeste didn't get out of the car.

"I'm going to Aina's," he said. "You don't mind, do you?"

"Of course not," I replied. "We'll see you tomorrow."

After the cold and the wet of the Bergen evening, our room was a warm, comfortable haven. There's something very intimate about hotel bedrooms. Margherita had stayed over at my house in Cremona many times, and I had spent the night at her apartment in Milan, but this was the first time we'd been away together, the first time we'd shared a hotel room, and it felt different. All the distractions, the chores we had at home had been left behind, the outside world had temporarily disappeared and we just had each other.

Margherita came out of the bathroom in her night-dress and sat down on the edge of the bed. We'd talked already about Aandahl's murder, but she was still worried about me.

"You're sure you're okay?" she asked.

"Yes, I'm sure."

"It's not every day you find a dead body."

"No, thank God. But I'm over it now. Let's talk about something else."

She slid into bed beside me. I could hear the rain pattering on the window, footsteps in the room above us.

"How long has Antonio been single?" she asked.

"Too long. It's probably seven, eight years since his divorce."

"There've been women since, I assume?"

"Not many."

"He's a handsome man. They should be queuing up."

"He works too hard. He doesn't have the time for girlfriends."

"Aina will be good for him. They seem very attached."

I nodded. "It's nice to see him happy. He deserves it."

I clicked off the bedside light and Margherita snuggled up against me.

"This afternoon, on Lysøen, wasn't it beautiful?" she said. "Sitting by the lake, watching the sunlight, the reflections on the water. That kiss – it was one of the most romantic things that have ever happened to me."

"Really? You've had a deprived life. We'll have to put that right."

I tilted back her head and kissed her again. Then I put my arms around her, hugging her tight. Ingvar Aandahl was still on my mind. I couldn't erase the image of his dead body, couldn't stop wondering about who had killed him. But I didn't need a counsellor, or a doctor. All I needed was Margherita.

We were having a late breakfast in the hotel dining room when Guastafeste – as he had the morning before – walked in through the front door. He saw us and came straight over to our table. I could see from his face that something had happened.

"What is it? What's the matter?" I asked. "Something to do with Aandahl?"

"Not Aandahl," Antonio replied. "There's been a break-in at Ole Bull's villa on Lysøen. His violins have been stolen."

I stared at him. "*What*?"

"The Guarneri del Gesù and the Vuillaume. They've both gone. I saw it on the TV news with Aina."

"How? What happened?"

"The custodian arrived at the house at seven this morning and found the glass cabinets broken open and the violins missing. The alarms had been disabled and the side door forced."

"My God!" Margherita exclaimed. "This was last night?"

"Or yesterday evening, after they locked up the villa at six o'clock. And guess what... the police want to talk to Michael Berg."

"Berg?" I said incredulously. "Why? Do they think he had something to do with it?"

"They're not saying, but he's obviously significant in some way for his name to have been mentioned in the news reports."

"Berg?" I said again, thinking back to the previous day. Had he stayed on the island and broken into the house? It seemed too far fetched to be believable.

"We should go to the police," Antonio said. "Tell them what we know about him."

"What about Aurlandsfjord?"

"We can catch a later train. Aina's already checked that for us."

I nodded. "Okay. I'll fetch my coat."

Antonio and I went alone to Allehelgens gate and asked

for Dag Pettersen. He was surprised to see us.

"I thought you were going to Aurlandsfjord?"

"We are," Antonio replied, then told him why we were there.

"It's not my case," Pettersen said. "Let me see what's happening."

He went out of his office. Even in his absence, the room smelt faintly of cigarette smoke. The desk was cluttered with papers and files, one of them a grey cardboard folder with Ingvar Aandahl's name written on it in black marker pen. I resisted the urge to take a quick look at it. That would have been a breach of trust and, besides, what would have been the point? It would all be in Norwegian.

Instead, I picked up the framed photograph that was propped up in a corner of the desk. It showed Pettersen on the deck of a sailing boat with a woman about his own age and two young boys who had to be his sons. I was still holding the picture when the inspector returned with a sheet of paper in his hand.

"Is this your boat?" I asked, putting the photo back in its place.

Pettersen sat down and nodded. "Yes. Do you sail?"

"I like the idea, but, unfortunately, Cremona's rather a long way from the sea. I imagine Bergen's an ideal place for it. The wonderful coast, all those islands to explore."

"I don't get out as often as I'd like," Pettersen said ruefully. "My wife hates sailing."

"Really?"

"That photo was taken in the harbour, the boat safely tied up to the quay. Go half a kilometre from the shore and my wife is violently sea sick."

"That's a shame."

"But my boys come with me sometimes. They love it out on the water. We sail to one of the islands. On a windy day, the boat skimming over the sea, it feels as if you're flying. Then we pitch a tent on the shore, go fishing and fry our catch on a primus stove. It's so simple, so different that for a time you can forget about the real world." His mouth curled sardonically at the corners. "Until you have to come back to it, that is."

He glanced at the sheet of paper that he'd placed on the desk top. "Okay, the officer in charge of the Lysøen case is still on the island, but I have a better idea about it now. Why don't you tell me what you know."

He looked at both of us, but Antonio gestured at me to answer. Pettersen made notes on a pad as I told him about Berg.

"So you met him twice, at Troldhaugen and then on Lysøen?" he said.

"Yes."

"And what did you make of him?"

"He just seemed like a tourist, visiting obvious tourist spots around Bergen."

"Did he tell you much about himself?"

"He said he was from Wisconsin, a high school English teacher, divorced with no children."

"Anything else?"

"His family came from Norway, back in the nineteenth century, and were some of the first settlers at Ole Bull's Oleana colony."

"Ah, yes, Oleana." Pettersen referred to the sheet of paper. "I must say, I'm not that familiar with it. It failed, didn't it?"

"Yes, quite badly."

"Berg talked to you about it?"

I nodded. "He said he was thinking of writing a book about it. It was obviously a sore point. He seemed pretty bitter about what his ancestors had had to go through."

Pettersen stroked his thick moustache as if he were petting a caterpillar.

"You say he was in your tour group when you went round Bull's home. Did he show a particular interest in the violins on display?"

"Well, he looked at them. I was probably more interested in them than anyone else. But he *did* talk about them later, when the tour had finished and he joined us for a coffee and a sandwich in the café."

"What did he say?"

He was talking about how Bull's estate ought to pay compensation to the families who'd suffered at Oleana. He said they should sell the violins and distribute the money."

Pettersen didn't seem surprised by the information. He gave a nod, as if I were confirming something he already knew, and made another note on his pad.

"You both heard this?"

"Yes," Guastafeste said. "So did the two friends who were with us."

"And that was when you last saw him?"

"No," I replied. "He came with us on a walk afterwards. With me and my friend, Margherita. But we split up on the hill behind the villa."

"Which way did he go?"

"West, towards the cove on the other side of the island."

"What time was this?"

"I don't remember exactly. Probably around four o'clock."

"Can I ask you something?" Guastafeste interjected. "Why are you so interested in him? Do you think he was involved?"

Pettersen gave an apologetic shrug. "I'm sorry, I don't have all the details of the case to hand. But what I *can* say is that Berg didn't take the regular shuttle boat back to Buena Kai. And he hasn't been back to his hotel since yesterday morning."

"He's disappeared?"

"Yes. That's all I know at the moment, I'm afraid."

"And the violins?"

"We don't know where they are."

"What about Ingvar Aandahl?"

The inspector pulled a face. "No significant progress. We've spoken to his receptionist, Birgit Holm. She left the office at five thirty. Aandahl had just returned from a business meeting and was in his office. You arrived there at half past six, so some time in that hour Aandahl was killed."

"You have no witnesses, no camera pictures to help you?"

"We're still out there interviewing neighbours. There's a CCTV camera further up the street, outside an insurance broker's office, but it's not provided us with anything useful. There's a back entrance to Aandahl's office. The killer may have come through that."

Pettersen stood up. "I'll pass on your information about Michael Berg to the investigating officer. Thank you for coming in. Let's speak again after you've been to Aurlandsfjord."

We shook hands and left the office. Walking back up the hill to our hotel, I said, "This is really quite incredible. It doesn't add up. Is Pettersen holding something back? What sparked their interest in Berg? Do they seriously think he stole the violins? He didn't look, or act, like a thief to me."

Antonio nodded sagely, drawing on his many years of experience. "They rarely do, Gianni."

I don't like to think of myself as an old-fashioned man, although I suppose in many ways I am. My children, even more so my grandchildren, would probably say I'm set in my ways, out of touch with the modern world and often nostalgic for the past. I don't think they're generally right in that assessment.

The young always like to think that they are the only ones who keep pace with progress. It's their way of asserting their independence, and their difference, from the generations that preceded them, particularly their parents. It's a kind of superiority complex that they need to bolster their confidence, to dispel the lurking fear that they are still children and reassure themselves that they are fit to inherit the world. We know things that you don't, we can do things that you can't is their mantra and in some ways they're right. But it's not always the question of competence that they like to claim, sometimes it's simply a question of choice. I can understand technology, I can use its products when it suits me – it's not difficult, after all – but I don't have any need for most social media, not because its complexities are beyond me, but because I've got better things to do with my time.

One area, however, in which I will openly

acknowledge my fondness for the good old days is transport. Driving long distances is no longer a pleasure to me – there are just too many cars on the roads – and flying has become a loathsome ordeal, a pact with rapacious airlines that will get you to your destination quickly but only by making every minute of it as unpleasant as possible.

The railways, though, are different. I like travelling by train. The locomotives and rolling stock have changed over the years, in many cases improved, but the routes are still broadly the same as they were a century ago, the ease and comfort of using them – though, unfortunately, not the price – as good, if not better than in my youth.

It's all so effortless and stress free, which is why I was glad we were taking the train to Aurlandsfjord. We got to the station in Bergen with plenty of time to buy our tickets, then bought coffee and sandwiches and cinnamon buns at the concourse cafe and boarded our train. We settled down in our reserved seats in a quiet, comfortable carriage and that was it: there was nothing more to do except relax and enjoy the journey.

And what a journey it was. We've all seen pictures of the Norwegian landscape, maybe film footage too, but nothing can prepare you for the beauty of the real thing. It was quite simply the most spectacular rail trip I've ever been on, the early stages passing through wooded valleys, past lakes and farms and fast-flowing streams before climbing steadily higher into Alpine pastures, deciduous trees giving way to darker conifers, the skyline framed by snow-capped peaks and precipitous rock faces.

Then slowly the mountains seemed to recede into

the earth and we emerged onto the fringes of the Hardanger Plateau, an area so harsh and inhospitable that polar explorers like Amundsen and Shackleton trained here for their expeditions. It was June, but you wouldn't have known it from the land around us, from the frozen lakes and the vast, limitless plateau on which almost every feature was hidden beneath an undulating carpet of snow.

By now, we'd stopped commenting on the sublime grandeur of the scenery – it was just getting too repetitive. We looked at it, let it take our breath away, but didn't talk about it. Some things are beyond words.

Then we arrived at Myrdal, the junction with the Flåm railway, and disembarked. I'd expected a small town, or maybe a large village, but Myrdal was basically a station with a scattering of houses just beyond the platform, most of which were surely unoccupied for their doors and ground floor windows were half buried in snow.

It was cold. The sky was a steely blue, the platform surface pale and bleached from the winter frosts. All around us were mountains, the lower slopes white with snow, the peaks dark grey rock, too sheer and jagged for the snow to stick to. At the base of one of the mountains was the gaping black mouth of the tunnel through which we'd just come.

I saw Margherita shivering. "Let's go inside."

The waiting room and restaurant were crowded with people, far more than had got off the train from Bergen. I realised they must be passengers who'd come up the line from Flåm and were waiting to go back the same way.

"I can't believe there's so much snow in June," Guastafeste said. "Does it never melt?"

"At least it's not raining," I replied.

I picked up a brochure about the Flåm railway from a stand near the ticket office and skimmed through it, reading how it was the world's steepest railway without cable or rack wheels, a twenty-kilometre-long engineering wonder that descended more than eight hundred metres through twenty tunnels from the Hardanger Plateau to the shores of Aurlandsfjord. One of the top ten scenic rail routes in Europe, it was enjoyed by more than six hundred and fifty thousand passengers every year – to which impressive number Margherita, Guastafeste and I were about to add another three.

A sudden flurry of movement, people heading for the exit, told us the train had arrived. We scrambled on board and managed to find seats together by a window in the rear carriage. The first leg of the journey was through semi-enclosed snow tunnels, metal shelters built over the track to protect it from avalanches, then we emerged into the open and began a long, twisting descent from the plateau.

Halfway down, we stopped at the Kjosfossen waterfall for no other reason than to allow people to get out and take photos of the foaming two-hundred metre cascade. We joined everyone else on the platform and I took a snap of the waterfall with my phone with Antonio and Margherita in the foreground.

"I'll send a copy of it to the *questura*," I said. "To show your boss how hard you're working."

Antonio grimaced. "Don't remind me how little progress I'm making."

"According to this brochure, in summer you can see wood nymphs in the waterfall."

We peered across at the rock face down which the white water was pouring but could see no sign of any nymphs, wood or otherwise. What we did see, however, was a woman coming out of a ruined stone building on the hillside beside the waterfall. She was blonde and clad in a bright red ankle-length dress. As she appeared, the roar of the water was suddenly drowned out by a burst of ethereal violin music being transmitted from hidden speakers. The woman began to twist and turn, waving her arms and dancing over the rocks.

"Is that supposed to be a wood nymph?" Margherita asked.

"I think it's probably Brita Fretheim," I replied, glancing at the text in the brochure.

"Who?"

"She was a local beauty who was bewitched and taken away by the fairy people."

"Really? The *fairy people*?"

"That's what it says here."

Margherita watched the woman cavorting across the hillside, her flimsy dress fluttering in the wind, and her practical nature came to the fore.

"Poor woman, I hope she's wearing plenty of thermal underwear."

"Is that her job?" Guastafeste said in a baffled voice. "Leaping around by a waterfall for a bunch of tourists?"

"So it would seem."

"Who pays her wages? And why? The railway company? The tourist board?"

The brochure was silent on the matter, so we could

217

only speculate. The woman danced around for a few minutes then, as suddenly as she had appeared, she disappeared, ducking into the ruined building as the violin music cut out. Still bemused by the spectacle, we got back on the train and continued our journey to Flåm, which turned out to be a small, non-descript settlement at the head of Aurlandsfjord.

Apparently, it was already a tourist destination back in the nineteenth century, particularly popular with the English aristocracy, who came for the fishing, but the building of the railway in the 1940s had opened it up to the mass market, as you could see from the shops and souvenir stalls piled high with tat.

There was a fine outlook down the fjord, or would have been if the view hadn't been almost totally obscured by a huge cruise ship moored just off the shore – the temporary floating home, I suspected, of many of our fellow passengers on the train.

It was early evening by now. We found rooms in a hotel next to the railway station – and in Flåm nearly everything was next to the station – and had dinner in the hotel restaurant. Afterwards, Margherita and I left Antonio nursing a ten-euro beer and went for a walk down by the shore. To our delight, the intrusive cruise ship had gone and we could now enjoy the magnificent vista of the fjord: the sheer cliffs plummeting down into the dark, fathomless water, the mountains dusted with snow rolling away to the horizon that even this late in the day was still bathed in sunlight.

We walked along the narrow shore road. There was no traffic, no other people around. It was so quiet we could hear the lapping of the water on the pebbles that fringed the edge of the fjord. The surface was slightly choppy, broken up by the breeze. The reflections of the steep sides were distorted, as if a sinuous wave were rippling through the cliffs. It was cool, though not cold. We had light sweaters on, but no coats. Margherita linked arms with me.

"Isn't this beautiful?" she murmured.

I nodded. I live in the countryside, but it's largely a man-made landscape of fields and farms and well-worn tracks. This was different. This was a land that man would never fully tame, that would forever be wild and hostile. You could tinker around the edges, build houses and railways, cultivate tiny patches of it, but the fjords would always belong to nature. You would never conquer those stark rock walls, never know the secrets of the water that was so shallow and crystal clear by your feet but soon plunged down into a chasm deep enough to swallow up the surrounding mountains.

"Is it what you expected?" I asked.

"Better. So many things are an anti-climax, but not this. This is truly impressive. Have you ever seen a view like that? Have you ever breathed in air that felt so clean? This is God's own country, Gianni, and I feel privileged to be sharing in it."

I smiled. "You might not be so keen on a stormy winter's night."

A small open fishing boat came chugging past, the soft purr of its outboard motor almost inaudible in the vast open space of the fjord. It changed course, heading for a wooden boathouse that was built out over the water on stilts. The man reclining in the rear throttled back and let the boat glide silently to its mooring. We watched him unload his fishing rod and net and a bucket that, presumably, contained his catch for the day.

The sun had dipped below the mountains and the light had taken on an eerie quality, as if it were shining through a film of silver. What little warmth still lingered was ebbing away quickly in the dusk.

"Shall we go back?" I said.

We took a last look at the water, the surface daubed with splashes and streaks like the brushstrokes of an impressionist painter whose palette was restricted to sombre shades of grey and black and dark green. Then we turned and strolled slowly back to the hotel.

THIRTEEN

Next morning, we took a taxi along the shore to Aurland, then a smaller, corkscrew road up to the village of Budal, a cluster of houses that were perched so perilously on the steep mountainside it was a wonder they hadn't slid away into the valley below.

As the taxi drew nearer, we could see that some kind of festival was being held in the village. There were Norwegian flags flying from the roofs of the houses, bright blue and red bunting strung across the streets.

The taxi driver pulled in on the outskirts.

"This is as far as I can take you," he said. "The centre of the village is closed to traffic."

"What's going on?" I asked.

"You don't know? I thought that's why you were coming here – for the annual goats' cheese festival."

"Goats' cheese festival?"

"Budal is famous for its goats' cheese. Try some, there are – I'm not sure – maybe fifty or sixty different varieties."

We paid the fare and watched the taxi head back down the hill. Then we walked the final couple of hundred metres into the centre of the village. The main square was festooned with coloured banners and flags and crowded with people – probably only a hundred or so, but it felt like many more because the space was so tiny, hemmed in by wooden houses and a larger, grander building that had to be the village hall.

From stalls set up around the perimeter, local farmers were selling their produce – mostly goats' cheeses, but also freshly-baked bread and eggs and vegetables. In a barbecue pit manned by three large men, burgers and sausages and lamb chops were grilling, the scent of charred meat wafting out across the square. Several children, in what I assumed must be traditional dress – white blouses, black embroidered dresses and red scarves for the girls, breeches and stockings and red waistcoats for the boys – were circulating with trays bearing samples of cheese on small crackers. They homed in on us at once, smiling and offering us a taste of their wares.

We tried a few, then a few more, reluctant to refuse their hospitality. In ten minutes, I must have eaten more goats' cheese than I'd had in years – perhaps even in my entire life, for I'm not generally a fan of it. Some were peppery, some flavoured with herbs or spices, some hard, some soft and creamy. Fifty or sixty varieties the taxi driver had said. Looking round the bustling stalls, that seemed an underestimate.

Somewhere close by, I could hear music playing. I picked out the distinctive sound of a Hardanger fiddle.

"You hear it?" I said to Margherita.

She nodded. "Where's it coming from?"

222

"Over there, I think."

We eased our way through the throng, following the sound of the fiddle, and found ourselves in a smaller, narrower public space off the main square where a covered stage had been erected on which a band was playing: a middle-aged man with plump cheeks and a paunch to match on the *hardingfele*, a woman of a similar age playing a clarinet and four children of different ages playing instruments – two girls on trumpet and clarinet, an older boy on a Hardanger fiddle and a younger boy, maybe ten or eleven years old, playing an accordion that was almost as big as he was. From their facial features, I was pretty sure they were all one family.

The music was a lively dance tune, the same melody repeated over and over, but embellished on each reiteration with ornaments and slight variations. I watched the *spelemann*, fascinated by how he played his fiddle. His left hand rarely moved from first position – the easiest on a violin – but that didn't mean the sound he produced was simple. On the contrary, the rhythms were complex, with a lot of syncopation, and almost every note was double or triple stopped – played on more than one string – the sound made even more polyphonic by the vibrations of the drone strings underneath. He was a very accomplished player, with an equally talented wife and children.

As we listened, a few couples in the crowd began an impromptu performance, linking arms to swing each other round, then changing partners while clapping their hands and stamping their feet in time with the music. One of the couples must have been in their seventies, and borderline creaky, but they threw themselves into the fray with a vigour that belied their years. You could see the pleasure in their faces, the joy of dancing together.

"Are you thinking of Rikard?" Margherita asked me.

I knew how perceptive she was, but even so I was surprised. I stared at her.

"How did you guess?"

"I remember what you said in Cremona. How Hardanger fiddle music was meant to be danced to, not listened to in a concert hall. This is the real thing."

"You want to join in?"

"Are you kidding? I wouldn't know what to do."

"There's nothing to it," I said. "Look at the others. There aren't any rules. If that old fellow and his wife can do it, so can we."

I took her by the hand. She resisted.

"Gianni, I'm not sure – "

"It'll be fun. Come on."

I pulled her out into the group of dancers, feeling her holding back for a second, then giving up and going with the flow. I whirled her round, first one way, then the other before passing her on to the next man in the line and getting a new partner myself – the elderly woman, who linked arms with me and leaned back, letting me spin her in a circle. The dance wasn't difficult to pick up. If you clapped and stamped in the right places, it didn't really matter what else you did, or didn't, do. Technique wasn't the point. Simple enjoyment was.

Four or five more women joined me briefly, then Margherita was back in my arms, slightly breathless, a flush in her cheeks. It was more energetic than it looked. I smiled at her, trying to remember when I had last danced. With Caterina, probably, almost a decade ago now. I'd forgotten how exhilarating it could be.

We did another couple of rounds, the tempo getting faster and faster, the *spelemann*'s bow flying over the strings of his fiddle until, just as we were close to dropping, the music suddenly ended in a flourish of chords. Margherita toppled against me and we held each other up while we recovered our breath.

"That... was... very silly," she panted.

"I know. But what a way to have a heart attack."

Antonio was watching us with amusement from the sidelines. We staggered over to him.

"Have you finished?" he asked dryly.

"What do you think?" I said. "Has this changed your mind about the Hardanger fiddle? Or has Aina already done that for you?"

He gave a sheepish grin. "Maybe. But much as I was enjoying your antics, I think we should get on. We have work to do."

Aina had called Helga Valstad again for us, got directions to her house and established that she spoke English. She lived on the upper edge of the village in a small two-storey cottage. It was built of wood painted bright crimson and had a terraced garden behind it that a mountaineer with ropes and pitons might have struggled to access.

Helga herself looked as sturdy and weatherproof as her house, a strong, stocky woman with thick legs, solid arms and no-nonsense grey hair that clearly had never been anywhere near a stylist, if such a thing existed out here. I put her age as somewhere in her late sixties.

She made us coffee and we sat in her living room, which overlooked the valley. The vertiginous drop

225

from the window made me feel slightly queasy and I helped myself to one of her home-made shortbread biscuits to settle my stomach.

"What a wonderful view you have," I said, sinking down onto the sofa beside Margherita and Antonio. "Have you lived here long?"

Helga took the chair opposite us and folded her hands on where her waist would have been, if she'd had one.

"In this house, only since I retired. But I've lived in the area all my life."

"It's very remote," Margherita said. "What work did you do?"

"Goats."

"Goats?"

"Yes, there are more goats than people around here. We had a farm down the valley, my ex-husband and I. We made cheese. It's very big in Budal. You must have noticed on your way here."

"It was difficult to miss," I said. "We tried some of it. It was very good. Are you not involved in the festival?"

"I'll go down later and do my bit."

"I hope we're not delaying you."

"No, not at all. There are plenty of helpers."

"It's very good of you to see us."

"I don't like the telephone," she said. "I like to see who I'm speaking to. So you're police officers from Italy, are you?"

"*I* am," Guastafeste replied. "A detective with the Cremona police. But Gianni, here, is a violin maker. And Margherita is a university lecturer in Milan."

Helga looked at Margherita, then back at me, sizing

us up. "You're married?"

"No, we're not. We're..." I hesitated. What were we? Friends was an understatement, partners was inaccurate, lovers too personal. But Helga wasn't really interested in the exact nature of our relationship.

"Keep it that way," she said to Margherita. "You marry them, you're stuck with them."

"Thank you," Margherita replied, catching my eye. "I'll bear that in mind."

"You want to know about the Hardanger fiddle, I understand?" Helga went on.

"Yes."

Guastafeste took out the photograph of the violin we'd printed from Rikard Olsen's computer and showed it to her.

"That's the one," she said. "Håkon Halvorsen made it, no question about it. As soon as I saw the picture on the internet I knew it was his work."

"Who was Håkon Halvorsen?" Antonio asked.

"A violin maker who lived near here. I say violin maker, but that wasn't all he did. He made furniture, too. He could turn his hand to anything, tables, chairs, sideboards. If it was made of wood, Halvorsen could do it. He was an exceptional craftsman."

"What makes you so sure he made this fiddle? It's not named."

"As I said in my email to Rikard Olsen, the girl on the scroll is his daughter, Laila. Who else could have made it?"

"How do you know it's Laila?"

"Because I knew her. Everyone knew Laila Halvorsen. She was the most beautiful girl in the valley. Well, not just the valley. Wherever in the world you put her, she'd have been the most beautiful girl."

"This was when?"

"The nineteen fifties and sixties."

"Is she still alive?"

Helga shook her head. "No, she died young. The early sixties, maybe nineteen sixty-two or three. I forget the exact year."

"And her father?"

"He was an old man when he died. That would've been some time around nineteen ninety."

"How did Laila die?"

Helga reached for her coffee and drank some before she replied.

"A car crash. She was a very bright girl, had everything going for her – looks, brains, personality. She was nine or ten years older than me. I used to look on her with awe. All the younger girls in the area did. She was dazzling, so perfect in every way, and nice with it. Of course, the boys were all in love with her. They'd follow her around like sheep, begging her to notice them, but Laila was never going to settle for one of the idiots we get round here."

Helga gave a thin, slightly bitter smile. "She was destined for bigger things. Or so she thought, anyway. Fate, though, thought otherwise. She went away to university in Oslo, to study music and drama. She could play the violin like an angel, sing like one, too. At all the local music festivals she always won first prize. She was in her final year when she was killed. One of those senseless crashes that happen all the time to young people. The driver had been drinking, he lost control and the car skidded off the road."

"How old was she?"

"Twenty-two, twenty-three. Her father, as you can imagine, was heartbroken. Her body was brought back here and buried in the church graveyard."

"And the Hardanger fiddle? Was that made after Laila's death?"

Helga looked again at the photograph. "I don't know. That carving on the scroll, she looks like a young woman, not a girl. Maybe her father made it when she was a student, maybe he made it afterwards as a memento."

"Did she have blonde hair?"

"Yes. Why do you ask?"

"There was a... how do you say it?" Antonio gave me a phrase in Italian and I translated it for Helga.

"A silver locket hidden under the scroll, with a lock of blonde hair in it. We think it must have been Laila's."

"You've seen the fiddle?"

"Rikard showed it to us in Cremona. Then he was killed and the fiddle disappeared. Did Håkon Halvorsen have other children?"

"No, just Laila. His wife died when Laila was very young. Håkon brought her up by himself. That's why her death was so devastating. I don't think he ever got over it."

"Have you ever heard of Knut Karlsen?" Antonio asked.

Helga gave a start. "Knut? My goodness, that's a name from the past."

"You knew him?"

She shrugged. "Not well. He was one of the love-sick boys that used to follow Laila around. He left the area too. Went to Bergen, or Oslo, or somewhere, I believe, but I can't tell you more than that. Has he something to do with this?"

"The fiddle was in his house when he died earlier this year."

Her eyes opened wide. "Knut died? I didn't know. And he had the fiddle?"

"You are surprised?"

"I suppose I am. How would Knut have got hold of it?"

"We hoped you might be able to help us with that."

"I'm sorry, I have no idea."

"Could Halvorsen have given it to him, or sold it to him?"

She mused on that for a time. "It's possible. But Knut hadn't been back here in years. That's what happens. The young all leave and never return. Only the stupid ones get stuck here."

"Maybe he acquired it when Halvorsen died," I said.

"Maybe he did. You could always ask Arne Falk." She paused. "If you can get any sense out of him, that is."

"Arne Falk?"

She hesitated for a moment before she answered. "Perhaps I shouldn't have mentioned him. He bought Halvorsen's house and workshop after his death. Carried on making violins there for a time, though I don't think he's made many recently. He might know something about the fiddle."

"Where do we find him?"

"Go up the hill past the church and keep walking up the valley. It's quite a rough track..." She glanced at our feet "... but you've got the right shoes for it. You can't miss his house. It's the only one up there."

She hesitated again. "But be careful."

"Careful?"

"Arne's a bit, well, odd. You know, a recluse. He lives by himself, almost never comes down to the village except to get a few supplies. God knows what he lives on. Mostly potatoes, I think, and whatever he can shoot. He hunts a lot. He's a bit unpredictable, not quite right in the head. You might catch him on a good day, or you might not."

Guastafeste raised an eyebrow and said to me in Italian, "Did I understand correctly? He hunts. You mean, he has guns?"

"Apparently. What do you think?"

"We've come all this way. We might as well give it a go."

"Does Arne Falk speak English?" I asked Helga.

"I don't know. But most people round here have a bit of English."

We thanked her for her help – and the coffee and biscuits – and made our way up the hill. I could still hear the dance music drifting up from the centre of the village, still smell a faint whiff of barbecued meat. The church was set on a knoll above the houses, a typical Scandinavian construction with white-painted lapboard walls and a wooden tower with a small tiled steeple on the top. It was Margherita who decided to make a diversion into the graveyard, but Guastafeste and I followed her without question.

Laila Halvorsen's grave was near the boundary wall, a simple, well-tended rectangular plot with a headstone inscribed with just her name and dates: 1940 – 1962. It was only fifty or so years old, but already showing signs of weathering – the hard winter frosts and sub-zero temperatures would make sure of that. At the foot of the grave was another, smaller, stone that looked newer and less worn than the headstone. A few words had been carved on it: *Og jeg skal nok vente for det lovte jeg sidst.* We studied the inscription without knowing what it meant, then Antonio pulled out his phone and took a photo of the grave.

"I've got to show the *questore something* for my time here," he said, a little desperately.

"She was so young," Margherita said. "What a waste of a promising life."

She lifted her eyes from the grave and looked around. The sun was shining on the knoll, gleaming on the neat rows of headstones and the white walls of the church. Beyond the perimeter wall, the ground fell away down a grassy bank – to the village on one side, but on the other into a void that seemed to have no bottom.

"It's so quiet, so peaceful," Margherita went on. "I suppose it's not a bad place to be laid to rest."

We had a moment's silence, out of respect, then returned to the path and continued up the valley. Helga was right about the track. It was rough and stony, like the bed of a stream. In places, it *was* a stream, for water was seeping out of the mountainside and trickling down onto the path.

We climbed higher, rounding a spur into a steeper, narrower section where a proper, fast-flowing stream cascaded down a series of small falls before plunging over a cliff in a dramatic waterfall. On the crags beside the waterfall, goats scampered agilely over the rocks.

We paused for a moment to rest and admire the

scenery. There were four seasons in one view. Far below us, we could see Aurlandsfjord sparkling in the summer sunshine, then the lower slopes were washed with the lush green shades of spring. The land immediately around us had an autumnal hue to it and high above were the snow-topped peaks where it was always winter.

"That is some sight," Antonio said, gazing around spellbound.

I nodded in agreement. You could feel the power in this land, something ancient and potent that left you awestruck but also intimidated, chillingly aware of your tiny size and fragile mortality. Out here we had no more significance than a speck of dust in the wind.

The path kept going beside the stream, getting higher and higher until we could no longer see the fjord: it was hidden by the huge bulk of the mountain below us. We'd seen no sign of any house, but as we clambered round the base of a rock buttress, we got the first indication of human habitation – the scent of woodsmoke. The smell got stronger as we followed the path up the slope, then we came over a rise onto a flatter patch of ground and saw a cluster of buildings ahead of us: a wooden house and a couple of smaller outbuildings.

We walked across towards the house, relieved that the arduous climb was finally over. We were all out of breath, our legs aching. We were nearly there when the door of the smaller outbuilding opened and a man emerged, wreathed in a cloud of smoke.

He was the strangest person I'd ever seen – a small, gnome-like figure with long, straggling hair, bushy eyebrows and a luxuriant grey beard that dangled down below his collar bone. The only parts of his face that were visible were the tops of his dirty cheeks and two dark eyes sunk deep into their sockets, like black olives pressed into dough. The door swung open behind him and we saw chunks of what looked like raw meat hanging from racks over a smouldering fire.

The man stopped dead as he saw us, then his eyes narrowed and he started yelling at us – in Norwegian, but we didn't need an interpreter to tell he was angry. He closed the door of the smokehouse and scuttled across to the main house, ducking inside the front door and coming back out with a hunting rifle in his hands. He shouted at us some more, brandishing the rifle threateningly.

My initial instinct was to turn and flee, but Antonio has had years of experience of dealing with difficult customers. He stepped forward, smiling, his arms outstretched, palms down, in a gesture of peace.

"Hello, you must be Arne Falk," he said in English. "My name is Antonio Guastafeste."

Maybe it was his disarming manner, maybe it was the surprise of being spoken to in a foreign language, but Falk seemed to relax a little. The barrel of the rifle dropped a few centimetres and he gaped at Antonio.

"This is Margherita Severini," Antonio went on, "And Giovanni Battista Castiglione. We do not speak Norwegian. Do you speak English?"

"English?" Falk said.

"Yes."

He frowned, his brow sinking down over his eyes. "You are English?"

"Italian. Gianni here is a violin maker, like you."

Falk looked puzzled. I took advantage of his

confusion by holding out my right hand. He glanced at it, then hesitated for an instant before taking his own right hand off his rifle and shaking. His grip was firm, his palm hard and calloused.

"It's a pleasure to meet you," I said, going through the common courtesies to distract him, to take his mind off whatever violent urges were seething beneath that unkempt mass of hair and beard. "How are you? Are you well?"

The simple questions, the standard building blocks of beginners' English wherever you learn it, must have jolted something in his memory, for he said, "Yes, I'm well, thank you." I sensed more cogs turning in his brain and he added, "How are you?"

"I'm very well, thank you."

I stepped aside for Antonio and Margherita, and by the time they'd also shaken hands with him, Falk seemed to have forgotten all about the rifle.

"You are Italians?" he said. That was still perplexing him.

"Yes."

"Why are you here?"

"To talk about violins. Perhaps we could go inside? It will be more comfortable."

I took him by the arm – he didn't seem to mind – and guided him through the door into the house. He reeked of smoke. As we crossed the threshold, Antonio gently removed the rifle from his grasp and put it out of the way against the wall. Falk didn't appear to notice. His belligerence had evaporated and he was quiet and compliant, like an obedient child. I led him across to an armchair and helped him to sit down. It was hard to gauge his age exactly, but he looked to be

235

in his late seventies, or even older.

I backed away and pulled out a wooden dining chair from the table that took up a large part of the room.

"Well done," Margherita murmured to both Antonio and me. "I thought he was going to shoot us."

It wasn't a big house. As far as I could tell, it was just this one living room and maybe a couple of bedrooms and a bathroom beyond the door in the far wall. There wasn't a separate kitchen – a stove and a deep stone sink occupied the space under the back window and there was an old-fashioned range in the hearth that also looked as if it was used for cooking. A wood fire was burning in the grate and its warmth was very welcome, for it was cold this high up the mountain, even in June.

"Violins?" Falk said, sounding bemused.

I nodded. "You make violins, don't you?"

"You are Italians?" he said again.

"Yes."

"But you speak English."

"I don't speak Norwegian. Can we talk in English?"

"I forget my English."

"You seem to be doing okay."

"No, I forget all." He paused, his forehead furrowing. Then he corrected himself. "I *have forgotten*. I learn English in school, but I have forgotten it all."

He spoke slowly, feeling his way through the words as if they were unfamiliar to him. He was clearly out of practice in English. If he was the recluse Helga had described, he was probably out of practice with any form of communication.

"Are you still making violins?" I asked. I wanted to

engage with him, to encourage him to talk.

"Violins?"

"Yes."

I looked around the room. It was full of clutter, the junk that we acquire as we pass through life, but there was no sign of a workbench or any tools. I guessed that the larger outbuilding outside was a workshop.

Falk shook his head. "No violins."

"You don't make them any more? Where's your workshop? Is it outside?" I waved in the general direction of the outbuildings.

"Elk," he said.

Now it was my turn to be bemused. "Pardon?"

"Elk."

I didn't know what he meant. I'd never heard the word before, but Margherita came to my aid. Her English vocabulary was more extensive than mine.

"I think he means *alce*," she said, using the Italian word.

"*Alce*?" Then it dawned on me. Falk had misunderstood my earlier gesture and thought I was asking about the smokehouse. Now I knew what the meat we'd seen hanging there was. "Ah, elk."

"Elk," Falk repeated, the word muffled by his thick beard. "I kill." He mimed the action of lifting a rifle and shooting. "Then I eat."

"Where's this going?" Guastafeste asked me in Italian.

"I have no idea."

"Why are you talking about elk?" He reached into his pocket. "Can I show you something?" he said to Falk, but the old man was looking intently at Margherita.

"We have a woman," he said. "Drink?"

"What?"

"We must drink."

He got up from the armchair, went to the cupboard near the sink and took out four glasses and a bottle containing a clear liquid. He gave each of us a glass and filled them with the liquid, then downed his own in one gulp.

"Is good," he said, refilling his glass. "Drink."

I allowed a drop of the liquid to touch my lips. It burnt like acid. There was no label on the bottle. This was obviously some kind of moonshine he distilled himself. It tasted like industrial ethanol.

Margherita and Guastafeste were trying their own glasses and suppressing grimaces, but Falk didn't notice; he was too busy finishing his second shot and pouring another one.

"Have you seen this before?" Antonio asked, showing him the photograph of the Hardanger fiddle.

Falk glanced at it, then turned away and said something in Norwegian. There was a strange, vacant look in his eyes.

"We think Håkon Halvorsen made it."

"Håkon Halvorsen," Falk said in a dead voice, as if he'd never heard the name before.

"He used to own this house, didn't he?"

"Håkon Halvorsen," Falk chanted.

"We think he made this violin. The young woman on the scroll here." Guastafeste put his finger on the photograph. "Is his daughter, Laila."

"Laila," Falk said. "Laila." He gazed off into the distance again.

"Do you know anything about it?"

Falk emptied his glass and wiped his beard with his

soot-stained fingers.

"Elk," he said.

"What?"

"I kill, I eat."

He did the rifle mime again. Antonio exchanged looks with Margherita and me.

"I don't think we're going to get very far here," he said in Italian, then went back to English. "Do you know anything about this violin?" he asked Falk.

"Laila," the old man said.

"Yes, Laila."

"Håkon Halvorsen."

"Yes, she was Halvorsen's daughter. Did you know Halvorsen?"

"Håkon Halvorsen."

"Did you know him? You bought his house."

"I buy house."

"Did you know him before that?"

"I make violins."

"Where did you make violins?"

"In Oslo."

"Then you moved here?"

"Yes. Move here, make violins."

"Have you seen this violin before?"

Antonio held the picture under his nose to focus his attention on it. Falk touched the paper, running his fingertips over the image of the violin, caressing it gently.

"Laila," he said.

"She died. A long time ago. The violin ended up with a man named Knut Karlsen. Do you know anything about that?"

"Knut Karlsen?"

"Yes. He came from here, from Budal. He's dead, too. Did you know him?"

Falk was still gazing at the photograph. "Laila. Dead," he said.

"Yes, she died in a car crash."

"Dead."

He knocked back his glass and stared into space.

"Dead," he repeated.

"Did you know her?" Antonio asked.

"Dead."

Arne stroked the photograph, his fingers lingering over the scroll. Antonio caught my eye. He shook his head. Falk picked up the bottle of moonshine.

"More drink?"

We walked back down the mountain to Budal and called a taxi to take us to Flåm. A train to Myrdal and a convenient connection and we were back in Bergen by nightfall. It was raining.

Margherita and I were getting ready for bed when there was a knock on the door. Antonio was outside.

"I've just had a phone call from Dag Pettersen," he said. "They've found Michael Berg. There's only one problem – he's dead."

FOURTEEN

"Where was he found?" Antonio asked.

Pettersen didn't answer the question immediately. He turned the wheel of the unmarked police car and sped down a side street, the parked vehicles giving him only a narrow channel to negotiate.

"About ten kilometres south of Lysøen," he said. "A fishing boat saw his body floating in the sea."

"Do you know the cause of death?"

"Drowning."

"How did it happen? How did Berg get into the water?"

Pettersen's reply was cautious, carefully worded. "The location of the body, the prevailing currents along that bit of coast, are consistent with him entering the water off Lysøen."

Entering? That seemed a strange word to use. I leaned forward from the back seat.

"You think he went swimming?" I recalled that the American, when I'd seen him last, had been heading for the cove on the west side of the island. Had he gone for a dip and got into trouble?

"He was fully clothed," Pettersen said.

"So what happened?" Antonio asked. "Did he fall in?"

Pettersen didn't answer. He seemed to be concentrating rather more than necessary on his driving, crossing an intersection and turning into a small carpark outside a two-storey concrete and glass building.

Guastafeste tried a different tack. "How does this affect your investigation into the theft of Ole Bull's violins?"

Pettersen didn't bother with that one either. He pushed open his door and got out. Antonio and I followed him into the building, then down an echoing corridor to the morgue. Guastafeste knew the procedure, knew how disturbing it could be, so he made me wait in the reception area while he went in to identify Berg's body. A relative from the United States was going to be arriving in the next couple of days, but the police wanted an interim identification to speed up their inquiries. A passport, driving licence and credit card had been found on the body, but visual corroboration was still needed to confirm that it was Berg.

It didn't take long. Antonio and Pettersen came back out in less than ten minutes.

"It's him," Antonio said.

I suppose I hadn't really expected anything else, but the confirmation was, nevertheless, upsetting. I'd barely known the man. If I was honest, I hadn't warmed to him. But for him to die, that was a shock.

"What now?" Antonio asked.

"Let's go to my office," Pettersen replied.

He didn't say anything more until we got to Allehelgens gate. He peeled off his outer jacket and hung it on the back of his office door. Underneath, he was wearing the same stained grey suit he'd had on the day we first met.

We sat down around the desk and he remarked dryly, "The bodies seem to be piling up since you arrived in Norway. Ingvar Aandahl and now Michael Berg."

"Is there a connection between them?" Antonio said.

Pettersen mused on that for a time, rubbing the edge of his forefinger to and fro over his moustache – a sort of unconscious, reflex action that seemed to help him think.

"I don't know. I can't see one at the moment."

"Tell us about Berg."

The inspector nodded slowly. "Well, he drowned, as I told you earlier. He'd been in the water for a couple of days so his body was not in a good condition. But there were bruises and cuts on it, small particles of rock embedded in the skin that would seem to indicate that he fell from the rocks on Lysøen."

"So it was an accident?"

Pettersen hesitated. "That is one possibility."

"And the other possibilities?"

"There was a bruise on his forehead that could've been caused by a fall, but it could also have been caused by a blow from a blunt instrument. The pathologist couldn't be certain which it was."

"You are saying he was hit on the head and then pushed into the sea?"

"We're not ruling it out."

243

"And this was when?"

"His body had been in the water too long to give an accurate estimate of the time of death."

Guastafeste squinted quizzically at the inspector.

"Can we start at the beginning? Tell us what you think happened."

"Okay, let's start with what we know for certain," Pettersen said. "The last time Berg was seen alive by anyone was three days ago, around four o'clock in the afternoon, when you..." He glanced at me "...split up with him on Lysøen. As I told you before, he didn't take the boat back to the mainland. We showed his photograph to the shuttle boat captain and his mate and they were absolutely sure he didn't return to Buena Kai. He appears to have remained on the island. The question is, why?

"We think it was part of a plan to steal the violins from the villa. And we don't believe he acted alone. We believe there were others involved. There are signs on the west side of the island that a boat landed in the cove and people got off it. We think Berg was there to meet them. They then went to the villa, disabled the alarm system and CCTV cameras and broke into the building. They forced open the glass cabinets and stole the violins."

"He was a schoolteacher," Antonio said. "You think he could do that? With the alarms, I mean."

"That's one of the reasons why we think he had accomplices. Professionals who *did* have those skills. We do know that Berg was inside the villa that night."

"You do? How?"

"Well, his fingerprints were on the glass cabinets."

"So were mine, probably. So were Gianni's. I'm sure

we all touched the cabinets when we tour the house. Berg, too."

"And there was a credit card receipt on the floor under the cabinets. From Berg's card."

"Maybe he drop that on the tour, as well."

"Except for the time on the receipt," Pettersen said. "It was three fifteen in the afternoon, *after* the tour had finished, and it was itemised. A cup of coffee and a chicken salad sandwich, which he bought from the Lysøen café. You said he joined you for lunch. Is that what he ate?"

"Yes, I think it was."

"We think the receipt must have fallen out of his pocket when he went back into the villa that night. And he didn't notice."

"And then?"

"He and his accomplices returned to the boat in the cove with the violins."

"You are guessing this?"

"Yes."

"And his death?"

"More guesswork. The light would probably have been fading by the time they reached the cove. The cliffs are dangerous around there. He may have slipped and fallen into the sea. Or his accomplices may have decided to get rid of him. One fewer to share in the proceeds of the theft."

Guastafeste pursed his lips. "You think he plan this from America? And his motive?"

"You heard it yourself, and we've had it confirmed by another witness. Berg thought Ole Bull owed his family compensation for Oleana. He thought the violins were the source of that compensation. They must be worth a lot of money."

"Where do you think they are now?"

Pettersen shrugged. "Probably on their way to a dealer or an auction house somewhere in the world. Maybe London, or New York." He looked at me. "This is your area. What do you think?"

I shook my head. "The thieves will never sell the instruments on the open market. They're too well known – a Guarneri del Gesù and Jean-Baptiste Vuillaume. Any reputable dealer or auction house would contact the police immediately if they were offered for sale. No, they'll be going to a private buyer, a very rich individual who will ask no questions about their provenance, who might even have commissioned the burglary in the first place."

"You think they've gone for good?" Pettersen asked.

"I fear they have."

He sighed. "Let's hope you're wrong. Ole Bull is a huge historical figure here in Norway. Losing his violins is a catastrophe, a national embarrassment. There's an alert out at all airports, seaports and border crossings. Every policeman in the country is on the lookout for them."

"If they didn't leave the country the night they were stolen," I said.

The inspector's mouth twisted into a grimace. "That, I'm afraid, is all too likely. But what about you? How was your trip to Aurlandsfjord?" He seemed relieved to be changing the subject.

"You tell him, Gianni," Antonio said in Italian. "All this English is wearing me out."

"There's not much to tell," I said to Pettersen, then described our encounters with Helga Valstad and Arne Falk.

"You know who made the fiddle now, at least," Pettersen said.

"But nothing more. We're still no nearer finding out who killed Rikard Olsen."

I was troubled. Pettersen seemed to have good grounds for suspecting that Michael Berg had been involved in the theft of the violins, but it still didn't make sense to me. Whatever the evidence, I just couldn't see him as capable of organising, and executing, a crime like this. It was no trivial burglary, after all. It had taken professional skill and netted two instruments that between them would be worth several million euros.

Back in our room at the hotel, I put my reservations to Margherita and Antonio.

"We all met him," I said. "Does any of this seem credible?"

"It does appear very unlikely," Margherita agreed. "He was a bit of a bore and he talked a lot, but a criminal mastermind? I can't see it."

"What about the evidence?" Antonio said. "We none of us knew Berg, and if I've learnt anything after twenty-five years in the police, it's that appearances can be deceptive, but facts speak for themselves."

"But do the facts have anything truthful to say?" I countered. "Fingerprints on the glass cabinets? That means nothing."

"What about the credit card receipt?"

"That's harder to explain away, I admit."

"And why did he stay on the island? Why didn't he leave on the boat like everyone else?"

"I don't know."

"The motive seems thin to me," Margherita said.

"Compensation for Oleana? All that happened two centuries ago. Why would Berg care much about what his ancestors had to go through? That all felt like harmless talk. And why would he go on about it at the café if he was planning to steal the violins that night?"

"That's a good point," Guastafeste conceded. "I'm not convinced about the Oleana connection, either."

"So if Berg wasn't involved, what do you think happened?" Margherita asked me.

I had no convincing answer to that. All I could do was speculate.

"Maybe his death was just an accident. He slipped on rocks and fell into the sea. That's why he missed the boat back."

"And the credit card receipt?" Antonio reminded me again.

"That's the bit I can't figure out. Unless he didn't go to the cove, but turned round and went back to the house instead. You know, to take another look at it."

Guastafeste shook his head. "Aina and I were on the cafe terrace all the time. We'd have seen him if he'd come back."

Margherita gave him an amused, slightly sceptical look. "Are you sure your attention wasn't focused on other things?"

Antonio flushed a little and smiled self-consciously. "Okay, maybe we wouldn't have noticed. But if he *did* come back, how did his body end up in the sea?"

I had no answer to that either.

"What we do know for certain," I said, "is that the violins have gone."

"A slick, professional job," Guastafeste said. "The thieves come in at night on a boat. They land on the far side of the island, where no one can see them, and break into the villa when everyone has gone home. I'd bet they were working to order. Like you said earlier, Gianni, someone commissioned them to go in and steal the violins. But who? Gianni?"

I was staring at the wall across the room. I'd just remembered.

"Gianni?" Antonio repeated.

"Pardon?"

"Are you all right?"

"The boat," I said. "I saw a boat."

"When? What are you talking about?"

"Do you remember?" I said to Margherita. "When we climbed the tower on the hill in the middle of Lysøen. There was a boat offshore to the west. A red and yellow boat."

"Was there?" she replied.

"I thought nothing of it at the time, but now, maybe it has more significance."

"You saw a boat?" Antonio said. "You think it was the thieves?"

"Red and yellow," I said. "Aksel Sørensen's boats are painted red and yellow."

Guastafeste gazed at me intently, already seeing where I was headed.

"It was a Sørensen boat?"

"I can't be sure. It was too far away for me to see if it had his company name on the side."

"There are probably lots of boats painted red and yellow," Margherita said.

"Probably," I agreed. "But how many of them belong to rich men with a passion for violins?"

"Are you saying what I think you're saying?" Antonio said.

249

"Do you think it's possible?" I looked at him. "When we went to his house, he said he'd tried violins by all the great makers – with one exception: Guarneri del Gesù."

Guastafeste finished the thought for me. "And one of Ole Bull's violins was a Guarneri del Gesù."

We were all silent for a time. Then Antonio said, "I think we should give Dag Pettersen a call."

He rang the inspector on his mobile and put it on speaker.

"That's a coincidence," Pettersen said. "I was just about to call you."

Antonio gave a start of surprise. "You were? Why?"

"We've been checking Ingvar Aandahl's office computer. There's an email in his inbox from Aksel Sørensen. Let me read it to you, translated into English, obviously. 'Ingvar. I'm really keen to get hold of Olsen's Hardanger fiddle. I'm tired of his stalling. Offer whatever it takes, but just get it done. Aksel.'"

Antonio was too stunned to speak for a moment. Then he found his voice.

"Sørensen told us he had no interest in Hardanger fiddles."

"I'll come and pick you up," Pettersen said. "We'll go and see Sørensen together. Now, why were you ringing me?"

"You wait here in the car until I call you in. Is that understood?" Pettersen said.

Antonio nodded. "Yes, we understand."

We watched the inspector and his team of officers go into Aksel Sørensen's house. The weather hadn't improved since our last visit. The rain was lashing down, hammering on the roof of the police car and running down the windows, making them virtually opaque. The wind was blowing a gale. It howled across the headland, flattening the grass and pounding the lone trees dotted across the landscape until they were almost bent double. Just another balmy summer's day on the Norwegian coast.

"I hope we're right about this," Guastafeste said.

"So do I."

I could feel the tension in my stomach, feel my heart-beat, though we were doing nothing more energetic than sitting in a car. It had taken a few hours to get to this stage and it was now mid-afternoon. Pettersen and his superiors had pondered long and hard before coming to the decision to search Sørensen's homes. The businessman was an influential person, wealthy and well-connected – exactly the kind of citizen the police, whatever their nationality, are always loath to upset.

What had swung it, I believe, although we hadn't been party to the discussions, was Pettersen's own doubts about exactly what had happened on Lysøen and the police chief's desire – desperation, perhaps – to do something that might give them a breakthrough in the case. The break-in at Ole Bull's villa was more than a simple theft to the Norwegians; it was a violation of a sacred monument and an insult to their pride. Add in the fact that Michael Berg, a US citizen, had died in suspicious circumstances and it was easy to see why the police felt it was worth taking a risk to find the missing violins.

Guastafeste and I weren't involved in the search, of course – that was solely a matter for the local police. I knew that was immensely frustrating for Antonio. He was itching to go in and help, but there were other reasons why we were there: Antonio to talk to Sørensen about Rikard Olsen's Hardanger fiddle and I because of my job. I'd spent fifty years making, and authenticating, string instruments. To the police, one violin was going to look pretty much like any other violin. Identifying a Guarneri del Gesù or a Vuillaume – particularly the two that had belonged to Bull – was a task that would be way outside their competence. But it wasn't hard for me. I'd inspected the violins only a few days ago. I'd know them immediately if I saw them again.

I looked at my watch.

"How long does it take to search a house?" I asked Antonio.

He shrugged. "Depends how thorough they are. It's a big house. Certainly a few hours."

I steeled myself for a long wait. Like Antonio, I'd rather have been inside the house than outside in a police car, but I could appreciate why Pettersen had kept us out of the action. We'd only have got in the way of his officers. I wondered whether Sørensen was at home. I guessed not. It was a working day and he'd more likely be at his office, or out on an oil rig.

Forty minutes later, my guess proved correct when a helicopter scudded in from the direction of Bergen and landed around the back of the house. I couldn't see who disembarked from it, but it could only be Sørensen, no doubt alerted to the police presence by one of his household staff. A further hour elapsed before a uniformed officer came out to say that we could go in.

Pettersen was in the music room. So was Aksel Sørensen. He was sitting on the sofa next to the grand piano and didn't look happy.

"You?" he said in English when he saw us. "You are part of this?"

"The violins are over here," Pettersen said. "We found five."

The instruments were still in their cases, the lids open. I did a perfunctory inspection, just glancing briefly at each of them, and my heart sank. I could see at once that none of these violins were the ones we were looking for.

Sørensen came over from the sofa and lingered in intimidating fashion by my shoulder as I made a closer appraisal – more for form's sake than because I needed to.

"So you know your violins, do you?" he sneered. "You see a Guarneri del Gesù there, or a Vuillaume? No? Oh, that's a surprise. You think I'm a thief, eh? You think that I steal violins? And not just any old violins, but Ole Bull's violins. You think I need to do that? You think I can't afford to buy them?"

He was understandably angry. It was uncomfortable being the target of his displeasure, more so because I knew I was partly responsible for this intrusion into his home.

"Is that a del Gesù?" he said as I leant over one of the cases. "Oh, no, it's a Gasparo da Salò. By coincidence, exactly the same Gasparo da Salò you saw the last time you were here. And what about that one? It looks remarkably like a Jean-Baptiste Vuillaume, doesn't it? Oh, no, wrong again, it's a Giovanni Gagliano. This is ridiculous. You come here, you search my house, imply that I'm a thief. How dare you! I have a reputation to think of, a good name that you're dirtying with these outrageous allegations."

He kept going as I went through the motions of checking all the violins, giving me the same savaging that I knew he would already have lavished on Pettersen, the "do you know who I am?", "heads will roll for this" harangue that is the common refrain of the affronted rich. I couldn't blame him. He was right. This *was* ridiculous. But, in my defence, it hadn't seemed so ludicrous a few hours earlier. A long shot, possibly, but nothing like the debacle that was now taking place in front of my eyes.

"Well?" Pettersen said as I finished my inspection. I could see hope in his eyes, a hope that I had no choice but to dash.

I shook my head. "They're not here."

He looked at the violin cases, searching for a straw to clutch at.

"You're absolutely sure?"

"Yes, I'm sure."

The inspector's face fell. He took out his phone and walked away across the room. He made a couple of calls, speaking very softly, then hung up and beckoned Antonio and me over.

"Nothing from the other two search teams, either," he said. "At Sørensen's apartments in Bergen and Stavanger."

He glanced apprehensively at the businessman and Sørensen, no doubt well practised in sensing weakness in an opponent, moved on to the attack.

"Are you satisfied?" he barked at the three of us, then he turned on Pettersen and laid into him furiously in Norwegian, a tirade that I was glad I couldn't understand.

Pettersen, to his credit, didn't flinch. He let Sørensen

burn off his anger, then took out a sheet of paper and said in English, "Perhaps you could explain this, Herr Sørensen?"

"What is it now?" Sørensen snapped, snatching the paper from the inspector's fingers. He read the text of the email and stiffened. Then he looked up defiantly.

"What of it?" he demanded.

"You admit you sent that email to Ingvar Aandahl?"

"Yes. So?"

"And you know that Rikard Olsen was murdered in Cremona and a Hardanger fiddle he had with him disappeared?"

"Yes, I know that. What makes you think that was the fiddle I was interested in?"

Pettersen hadn't expected that. "What?"

"You think Olsen only had one Hardanger fiddle?"

"You're asking me to believe that you were interested in a different instrument?"

"Can you prove that I wasn't?"

Pettersen didn't reply. He looked at Guastafeste, who joined in the exchange.

"When we were here before," he said to Sørensen. "You said you have no interest in Hardanger fiddles."

"Did I? I don't remember that."

"Yes, you say it. Gianni hear you, too. Don't you?"

I nodded. "Yes."

"So how do you explain your email to Ingvar Aandahl?" Antonio continued.

"I don't have to explain anything," Sørensen snarled. "Least of all to you, an Italian with no jurisdiction in this country." He tossed the sheet of paper back to Pettersen. "I think we're finished here. Get out of my house. You haven't heard the last of this."

He was an intimidating man, but Pettersen stood his ground.

"Where were you three days ago, between half past five and half past six in the evening?"

Sørensen gave a contemptuous laugh. "Now you're being silly. You think I had anything to do with Ingvar's death? You're even stupider than you look."

"Answer the question, please."

"I was in Stavanger. At a board meeting of my company. Fifteen people – fifteen very influential people – can vouch for me."

Pettersen hesitated. "I'll have to check that."

"Check all you like."

"In the meantime, I'd like you to come into the station to answer a few more questions."

"You're arresting me?"

"If I have to, yes. But I'd prefer you to come voluntarily at this stage. I'm sure you would, too."

I expected another explosion, but Sørensen was too astute, too controlled, to let his temper get the better of him.

"I'll call my lawyer," he said. "You can talk to both of us."

FIFTEEN

Guastafeste and I didn't sit in on the interview. That was just Pettersen, Sørensen and Sørensen's lawyer, a smooth, well-fed man in a dark suit, who was waiting for us when we arrived at Allehelgens gate. But we did stay on at the station, drinking coffee in a corner of the squadroom while the officers around us got on with their work.

I was acutely aware that the searches of Sørensen's homes had been a disaster, and that I was mainly responsible for it. I felt embarrassed and ashamed. I'd come up with a wild, wafer-thin theory and persuaded the police that it had enough substance to justify the raids, a reckless – and fruitless – act of folly that had probably damaged Pettersen's career and done absolutely nothing to further the search for the missing violins.

Only one thing kept me from curling up into a ball and wishing I could disappear: the need to make amends. I'd got it wrong, seriously wrong. If possible, I had to find a way of putting things right. But how?

I thought back to our visit to Lysøen, about our tour of the house, trying to remember everything that had happened: where we'd gone, what we'd seen, who else had been on the tour with us apart from Michael Berg. Then I moved on to the time afterwards, to our lunch on the cafe terrace, to our conversation with Berg and then our walk into the interior of the island and that moment we'd parted company with the American. What had happened after that? That was the key to the entire mystery.

I recalled our meeting with Pettersen in his office, his theory that Berg had somehow been involved in the theft of the violins. One fact had bothered me then, and it was still niggling away inside my head now.

"Are you all right, Gianni?" Antonio asked.

"Pardon?"

"You seem distracted."

"I'm just sorry about all this. The abortive search."

"It's not your fault."

"Of course it is. It was my idea."

"And it seemed like a good idea."

"Not in hindsight. Now it just looks stupid."

"Pettersen agreed with you. So did I. It might have been right."

"But it wasn't. That's all that counts. It was wrong."

"Don't blame yourself. Sørensen didn't have Ole Bull's violins, but he's hiding something. We know he's lying about Rikard's Hardanger fiddle. Let's see what Pettersen gets out of him."

We didn't have long to wait. The inspector was out after only twenty minutes. He came into the squadroom, looking pale and a little shaken.

"I need a cigarette," he said.

We followed him down the stairs and out into a yard at the rear of the police station. Pettersen lit up and took a long drag on his cigarette. I felt I had to apologise to him.

"I'm sorry about this. I hope it doesn't harm your career."

He gave a wry grin. "I've always wanted to direct traffic in Tromsø."

"How did it go? With Sørensen."

His mouth tightened, his upper lip receding into his moustache.

"Not well. He was, indeed, in a board meeting in Stavanger when Ingvar Aandahl was murdered. And he was on an oil rig in the North Sea when Rikard Olsen was in Cremona. Whoever killed them, it wasn't Sørensen."

"And the Hardanger fiddle?"

"He's sticking to his story that he was interested in another fiddle, not the one Olsen took to Italy. I don't believe him, but I can't prove it – and he knows it. So does his lawyer. I had to let him go."

"You have other leads in the Aandahl case?" Antonio asked.

Pettersen sucked on his cigarette, then shook his head.

"We've finished interviewing his friends and his neighbours, the businesses and homes near his office, but no one saw or heard anything. And we have no forensic evidence from the scene that might help us."

"We both know Sørensen is lying about the Hardanger fiddle. Why? What does he know that he's not saying?"

The inspector shrugged. "I put that question to him,

but he declined to answer."

We stepped aside to let a police car enter the yard. Two officers got out and went into the building. Pettersen took another drag on his cigarette, then coughed violently, turning away and covering his mouth.

I gave him a moment to recover before I said, "And Ole Bull's violins?"

Pettersen looked back at me, breathing hoarsely. "That's a separate matter."

I hesitated. I didn't want to be wrong a second time, but I had, at least, to put my theory to the inspector.

"I have another idea about them."

Pettersen regarded me dryly. "I hope it's better than your last one."

It was a valid point, but I couldn't allow it to stop me.

"Let's assume that Michael Berg didn't break into the villa that night."

"I deal in facts, not assumptions," Pettersen said.

"But facts are what you don't have. You don't know what happened. If he didn't break in, how did his credit card receipt end up on the floor under the glass cabinet? And why?"

"You're going to tell me. Is that what this is about?"

I didn't answer directly. "You said after our visit to the morgue that there was another witness who heard Berg saying that Bull owed his family compensation, but you didn't give a name."

"What of it?"

"If I tell you who that witness was, will you give me your attention?"

Pettersen blew smoke away across the yard.

"Go on," he said.

He had courage, I'll give him that. And a forgiving nature. Most people in his position would have declined to give me the time of day, but Pettersen indulged me. He heard what I had to say, questioned the reasoning behind it, then lapsed into a quiet reverie in which he thought long and hard about my proposition.

Then he looked at Guastafeste, wanting a second opinion from another professional.

"What do you think?"

Antonio didn't hesitate. "I think it's worth a try."

Pettersen fell silent again. I knew little about him, about what kind of man he was. A smoker, a sailor, a family man with two sons and a seasick wife. He seemed solid and reliable, the epitome of the honest copper, but there was obviously a streak of the gambler in him for he gave a brief nod and said, "Okay. What do we have to lose?"

That was the crux of the matter, of course. He knew that he was in trouble. Aksel Sørensen was no doubt, at this very minute, on the phone to the chief of police, or the minister of justice, or whoever ran the law enforcement system in Norway, shouting and screaming about his treatment. Pettersen had to do something drastic, and do it quickly, to salvage a few soggy bits of flotsam from the wreck of his career. And at the moment, I was the only person offering him a shred of hope. Sheep and lambs. If he was going to swing, he might as well do it in style.

"Let me make a few calls," he said. "I'll pick you up from your hotel in an hour."

*

Margherita was in our room, reading a book in the armchair. I felt bad about the amount of time she'd been left on her own. This holiday we'd planned had already been encroached on too much by Antonio's investigation. Now I was adding a different police inquiry to the mix that was going to take me away from her once more.

"It's not a problem," she said gently, and I could've given her a hug for her tolerance and understanding. "You don't need to feel guilty. Go and do what you need to do and stop worrying about me. I'm quite capable of spending an evening by myself."

"What will you do?"

"I don't know. I'll probably have something light here to eat in the hotel. I don't feel like a big meal, anyway, especially at Norwegian prices. Then I'll find something to occupy me." Her eyes glinted mischievously. "Maybe I'll go out to a bar and find some gorgeous young blond to entertain me."

"Well, good luck with that," I said, and leaned down and kissed her.

The police team was still on Lysøen, the island still closed to visitors. We took a police launch out from Buena Kai and walked along the path to Ole Bull's villa. It was nearly eight o'clock, but at this time of year it wouldn't get dark for hours. The twilight had that strange, ethereal quality that you only get in northern latitudes in summer, a pale, translucent tint, as if the sun had been swathed in gauze.

Pettersen assembled his officers in the huge drawing room and briefed them on the task they were going to carry out. Antonio and I sat on chairs at the back of the room, letting the incomprehensible Norwegian wash over us. My eyes strayed up to the carved ceiling and I marvelled again at the work that had gone into it. How many craftsmen with chisels and gouges had it taken to sculpt all that pine? How many months had it taken them to do it? A modern, computer-controlled cutting machine could probably duplicate the whole thing in just a few days and I daresay most people wouldn't notice the difference, but it wouldn't be the same. You can't separate a work of art from its creators, for they have put something of themselves into it: the touch of their hands, the sweat of their brows, the breath from their lips. The gouge lines and tiny blemishes, that from down here on the floor were invisible, were the makers' marks, their signatures that no machine ever leaves behind.

They say that robots will soon be taking over most of our jobs. My children, steeped in the technological wonders of their generation, like to provoke me by claiming that before long all violins will be made by machines, but I don't believe them. Perhaps a robot could master all the skills that go into the construction of an instrument – though I have my doubts about that – but the finished product could never match a hand-made violin. It would have no heart, no soul and, most importantly, no voice, for whatever else robots can do, they cannot sing.

The officers were splitting up into groups now and heading off to their appointed locations, the first stage in the plan that Pettersen and Antonio, with some input from me, had drawn up on our drive south from Bergen. I don't want to claim any undue credit for the scheme, but sometimes it takes an outsider to give

263

fresh impetus to an investigation that has stalled. The forensic teams had been all over the crime scene and the bay on the west of the island where the thieves were believed to have landed, and then departed, by boat. The police across the country, and beyond, had been looking out for the missing violins, but they still hadn't been found.

I'm not a police officer, but I've known Guastafeste long enough to have learnt something about police work, to have absorbed a couple of simple maxims: first, if you're not finding something you're looking for, perhaps you're looking in the wrong place; second, if a clue is too obvious, maybe there's a reason for that.

It was time to drop all assumptions and start from the beginning again, to look at the evidence from a different angle and see if it produced a different picture. Pettersen, to his credit, had been willing to do that. I hoped, for all our sakes, that it was going to lead somewhere.

There were three sub-divisions in the police team, each consisting of several officers with a sergeant in charge. The largest unit stayed to search the villa, inch by inch, from the basement to the roof; a second was doing the same to the café and outbuildings and the third was despatched to Gamletunet, the small cluster of about half a dozen houses down by the harbour. It was the logical thing to do, but the police had not, so far, done it. They'd picked up a trail across the island and been so intent on following it that they'd neglected the source of the scent.

Once again, Guastafeste and I weren't involved in the searches; we just had to stand by and watch. It was a boring few hours. Violins are not tiny objects –

concealing them would be quite difficult – but it was a very big house, full of nooks and crannies that the police took their time examining. When the team reached the drawing room, Guastafeste and I got out of their way and went outside onto the gravel forecourt.

It was gone ten o'clock, but it didn't seem to have got much darker. The sun was hovering somewhere out of sight on the other side of the island so the forecourt was in shadow, but across the water, the buildings on the mainland were glowing in a dusky light. I saw a man on a ladder painting his house, another mowing his lawn. They reminded me of hibernating animals – the long, harsh winter was over and they had to make the most of the brief summer before the darkness returned.

"How do you think it's going?" I asked, betraying my inner anxiety.

Guastafeste's reply was non-committal. "Hard to tell."

"Nothing so far."

"No."

"That's not good."

"It's early days."

"It's been a couple of hours."

"That's not long."

"They're not going to find them, are they?"

"We don't know that, Gianni. Let's wait and see."

I was getting restless. The knot in my stomach was tightening.

"Let's go for a walk."

We went down the path to the harbour, taking our time. The sun hadn't gone down yet, but the temperature had dropped. It was cool, a sharp breeze gusting in from the sea. The water was choppy and opaque, tinged with grey and a hint of purple. Waves were lapping against the shore, making a soft slapping sound on the rocks.

There were three boats in the harbour: the police launch that had brought us here and two other, smaller, vessels with outboard motors that must have belonged to the residents of Gamletunet. There were no shops on the island. The few people who lived here would have to go to the mainland for all their provisions.

Two police officers came out of one of the small, one-storey cottages and headed for a tiny outbuilding. I watched them go inside, then, less than five minutes later, come back out.

"They're running out of places to search," I said.

"It's a big island," Antonio said, trying to reassure me.

"Mostly forest and rock."

"They could be buried."

"Not violins like those. The weight of the soil, the damp. You couldn't risk that kind of damage."

The police officers were moving on to another house. In the harbour, the boats were bobbing on the swell. It was so quiet I could hear the soft, strangled screech of the mooring ropes as they were stretched tight by the motion. A seagull swooped down from nowhere, like the flutter of a handkerchief, let out a cry that pierced the silence, then was gone over the pine trees.

"What if I'm wrong?" I said.

"It won't matter," Guastafeste replied.

"Won't it?"

"Police work isn't science. You can't predict results. Sometimes it's like beachcombing. You turn over rocks and see what crawls out."

"And if it's nothing?"

"No one will blame you. They should've done this earlier. Pettersen knows that."

As if on cue, the inspector suddenly appeared on top of the rock outcrop that separated the harbour from Gamletunet. He saw us and clambered down to join us.

I waited for him to speak. When he didn't, I knew he had nothing positive to report, but I had to ask him, anyway.

"Well?"

Pettersen gave a facial shrug, his mouth puckering, squashing his moustache between his lips and nose. He didn't say anything. I looked over at the houses beyond the rock outcrop.

"Which one..." I began.

Pettersen knew what I was asking and shook his head.

"Nothing?" I said. I needed to hear him confirm it.

"No," he replied. "Nothing in any of them."

"So that's it. What about the villa?"

"The same."

"And the café and outbuildings?"

He shook his head again and touched the radio receiver clipped to his jacket.

"I'd have heard if there was anything."

I nodded, feeling the clammy touch of disappointment creeping through my body. It had been a long shot, I knew that. But, nevertheless, I'd hoped for more.

"Is there anywhere else?" I asked.

Pettersen gestured with a hand. "There's a timber shed over that way that the foresters use when they're cutting trees. I've sent a couple of men to search it."

I glanced at Antonio. There was sympathy in his eyes, but no surprise. He'd expected this to happen.

The police team was coming out of the hamlet and assembling on the path beside the harbour. Pettersen walked over to them and had a brief discussion, then the officers began to make their way back up to the villa, the inspector leading the way. Antonio and I followed them. We didn't speak: there was nothing to say.

The other two teams were out on the forecourt by the villa. They had the tired look of men and women who can't wait to knock off and go home. Pettersen addressed them, obviously thanking them for their hard work, then the group broke apart and the officers headed down towards the harbour, and the launch that would take them back to their families.

Pettersen came across to us. I sensed he didn't really want to, but he had no choice. I couldn't blame him. Twice now I'd persuaded him to do something, and twice the outcome had been failure. He was going to have a long, sleepless night, wondering what his superiors would do in the morning.

"I'm sorry. This wasn't – " I started to say, but he cut me off with a curt shake of his head.

"You'd better go. You don't want to miss the boat."

I took a final look around – at the ornate villa with its Moorish carvings and Russian Orthodox dome, at the view across to the mainland, at the forest that closed in protectively on the hill behind the house. This was almost certainly the last time I would ever see this place. Despite the disappointment of the evening, I would always have happy memories of

Lysøen. I thought of that tranquil, magical moment by the lake, watching the reflections in the water with Margherita beside me, of the spectacular panorama from the tower in the middle of the island.

The tower.

"Gianni, we have to go," Guastafeste said. "Gianni?"

I turned to him. "What?"

"The boat will be waiting for us."

I looked at Pettersen. "There's one other place."

He shook his head dismissively. "We've looked everywhere."

"No, there *is*," I said urgently. "The tower up there on the hill. We haven't been there."

"Tower?"

"We have to check it."

"We've finished now. My officers are going home. We have to go, too."

He'd had enough of me and my suggestions, but I wasn't going to let him deter me.

"It's the one place we haven't searched."

"Look, Signor Castiglione," Pettersen said impatiently. "I'm not going to – "

I didn't let him finish the sentence. "It won't take long. I'll do it."

Before they could attempt to stop me, I hurried away around the side of the house and onto the path up the hill.

"Gianni? Gianni, what on earth are you doing?"

"Signor Castiglione, stop now! I order you to stop."

I heard their voices behind me, but ignored them. I was moving fast up the path. I may be sixty-five years old, but I've been a hiker all my life. The Alps, the Dolomites, the Apennines, I've walked in them all, and this hill behind the villa was a mere pimple in comparison. Antonio and Pettersen were following me – I could hear the scrunch of their feet on the path – but they wouldn't catch me, not if I kept going.

It was an easy track to negotiate, even in the fading light, and I'd been up it before. It was quite gentle to start with, then it got steeper. I slowed down a little, pacing myself. I didn't want to run out of steam and have to pause to recover.

The forest was relatively sparse on this part of the island, the rocky ground and thin soil made sure of that. There were trees around me, but spaced out so I could see where I was going. It had to be midnight, but the sky was still light, the waning sun now supplemented by a rising moon.

"Gianni?"

"Signor Castiglione!"

They were still there below me, but their voices weren't getting any closer. I could feel the strain in my legs, hear my breathing becoming more laboured, but I didn't ease off. There would be time for that when I reached the top.

But where was it? I looked up, squinting through the branches of the trees. It was hard to tell. The path twisted to the left, then to the right. I almost slipped on the thick carpet of pine needles, but regained my balance and kept climbing. Maybe this wasn't such a good idea. My heart was thumping in my chest, my lungs heaving. I glanced over my shoulder. Antonio and Pettersen were narrowing the gap between us. I made one last painful effort and suddenly I was emerging from the forest onto the bare summit of the hill. The stone tower was there in front of me, silhouetted against the sky. I stopped, gasping for air.

"Gianni, are you mad?" Guastafeste said breathlessly as he caught up with me.

Pettersen was right behind him. "This isn't helpful," he snapped, his panting taking some of the sting out of his anger. "The boat will have to come back for us now."

"I had to make sure," I said, trying to placate him. "I remembered something from when I was here before."

I went across to the tower. Set into the stonework at the bottom was a small wooden door, about fifty centimetres square. I tried the handle. The door was locked. I looked around for something to use as a tool.

"Here, let me do it," Antonio said.

He found a thin piece of rock and slipped it into the gap between the door and its frame. He gave the rock a sharp hammer with the base of his palm and the wood splintered away from the lock. The door swung open.

Antonio moved aside and I knelt down and peered into the cavity. It was too dark to see anything so I used my sense of touch instead. My hands found something soft and yielding, like cloth. I squeezed and felt a more solid object underneath. I lifted it out and placed it carefully on the ground. There was a second, very similar, object in the cavity. I pulled that out, too.

They were towels. Ordinary cotton bathroom towels. My heart was pounding again, but this time with excitement. Antonio and Pettersen crouched down beside me. Very gently, I pulled aside the folds of the towels to reveal what they were hiding: two violins. Two polished, very beautiful violins gleaming in the twilight.

271

SIXTEEN

Guastafeste and I were alone on the top of the hill, sitting in the shadows beneath a small stand of pine trees. We were hidden from sight, but had a clear view of the stone tower, only five metres away across an open stretch of rocky ground.

Pettersen had gone down to the harbour to let the residents of Gamletunet know that the police intended to return in the morning to carry out a thorough search of the whole island. He would then have taken the launch back across to the mainland – or, rather, pretended to, for the boat was going to circle round and drop him back unseen in the cove on the west side. If everything went to plan, we were pretty sure that whoever had concealed the violins would be back to retrieve them that night.

My pulse had returned to normal, but I couldn't entirely shake off my feeling of elation, the mixture of excitement and joy that had surged through me when we'd found the violins, when Pettersen had shone his torch over them and an inspection confirmed their identities – a Jean-Baptiste Vuillaume and a Guarneri del Gesù, neither of them any the worse for their brief sojourn in the base of the tower. The discovery by itself was enough to make me happy, but I had the additional personal pleasure of knowing that I'd redeemed myself. The first part of my theory had been proved correct. Now we had to wait and see if the second part would be, too.

We sat in silence, trying not to move, to make any noise that might give away our presence. We were sheltered in the trees, but I was starting to feel the cold, the damp seeping up through the earth. It was the middle of the night now, but the darkness felt somehow thin and insubstantial, the sky washed with a sheen of moonlight. A scent of pine and the sea wafted up the hillside.

It had been a long, eventful day. I was tired, but not sleepy. I was too much on edge to doze off. Antonio was the same. I could sense him alert beside me, listening intently for any sound that was out of place. We heard the rustle of leaves, the creak of branches and the occasional distant call of a bird, but nothing moved in our immediate vicinity. There were animals on the island – squirrels, probably rats and mice – but they'd pick up our scent and keep well away. Fortunately for us, the human sense of smell was much less sensitive.

Maybe an hour passed – it was too dark to see the face of my wristwatch – then I felt Antonio stir. I turned my head and I heard it too: the faint crunch of footsteps on rough ground, too heavy to be anything other than a person coming up the path. No, that was wrong. I listened harder. It was more than one person. Certainly two, maybe three, it was difficult to be certain.

I peered out and saw a figure come over the rise, the tall figure of a man. Behind him were two other men.

"Signor Castiglione, Signor Guastafeste?"

It was Pettersen. I got to my feet, my legs and back stiff from inactivity, and stepped out of the trees. Guastafeste came with me.

"Here."

Pettersen turned.

"I assume nothing's happened," he said.

"No."

"I've brought two of my men. Is this the only path to the summit?"

"Yes."

"I'll send one man a little way down to hide in the woods, to cut off any retreat. The other will stay with me." He surveyed the area. He had a torch, but he didn't turn it on. The light would be seen from a long way off. "We'll wait over there, in the undergrowth behind the tower."

"Okay."

"If anyone comes, you let us make the first move. They could be violent. I don't want you getting hurt. Is that understood?"

"Yes, we understand."

"No more impetuous acts, Signor Castiglione. This is police business."

Pettersen and his colleague walked to the tower, crouched down and crawled into a clump of bushes. Antonio and I retreated into the trees and settled down on the ground again. It felt colder and harder than before. I shivered, hoping that we weren't going to be there all night. I rested my back against a tree trunk and stared out towards the tower. It was just a black cut-out against the sky, a tapering cylinder with the slim dark line of the flagpole protruding from the top.

I felt more drowsy now. My eyes were heavy. I resisted the urge to close them in case I fell asleep. Talking was out of the question so I had to think of another way of keeping myself awake. It's not something I usually have to do. Getting to sleep can sometimes be a problem. Then, I find repetitive thoughts can help relax me, to lull my active brain into submission. I don't count sheep, I count vegetables. I picture my kitchen garden, the beds overflowing with produce, and I walk along the rows in my mind, counting onions and lettuces and courgettes. Maybe the same technique could work in reverse with my eyes open. Maybe the counting could stimulate my brain and keep me conscious.

It couldn't.

I came round with a jolt as Guastafeste shook my arm. How long had I been asleep?

"There's someone coming," he whispered in my ear.

I listened. Footsteps on the path. Only one person this time and clearly audible. They weren't trying to creep up on us unawares, which was reassuring. They obviously had no suspicions that anyone might be lying in wait for them.

A bulge appeared on the silhouette of the tower – the outline of a man. He crouched down by the wooden door. I heard the rattle of keys. He couldn't possibly miss the broken lock, but what would he do? Panic and make a run for it? Or stay to check his loot was still there?

The latter, it seemed. He was opening the door and reaching in. Was that a faint sigh I detected as his fingers grasped the violins – rewrapped and put back exactly where we'd found them?

We did as Pettersen had instructed and let him make the first move. He waited a few seconds, allowing the new arrival time to remove the instruments from the tower. Then he pounced. Burst out suddenly from the undergrowth, his torch clicking on. The beam illuminated a man kneeling down on the ground with a violin in each hand. His face was turned away from me so I couldn't identify who it was.

It was fortunate that the instruments were still partially swathed in the towels, for the man gave a start of surprise and dropped them. Then he scrambled to his feet and stumbled away down the path. Pettersen shouted something – a warning, a command, it was hard to know exactly what – and we heard sounds of a scuffle lower down the hill: feet scraping, men grunting, a cry of pain. Maybe a minute went by, then Pettersen's torch picked out the figures of two men coming back up to the summit. One was the officer who'd been posted by the path. The other was a shorter man with fair hair and rimless glasses. He had his wrists cuffed behind his back, the officer's hand gripping one of his arms.

Pettersen's torch beam hit the man in the face and we looked into the frightened eyes of Erik Rasmussen, the guide who'd shown us around Ole Bull's villa.

It wasn't until mid-afternoon the next day that we got a full picture of what had happened. After Rasmussen's arrest, we'd taken the launch to the mainland and then been driven back to Bergen, Rasmussen travelling separately in a police van. Guastafeste and I went with Pettersen, the Vuillaume and Guarneri del Gesù – undamaged and still wrapped protectively in their towels – on the back seat next to me. They wouldn't be returned to Lysøen until the security measures at the villa had been reviewed and improved.

We made formal statements at the central police station before being taken back to our hotel. By then it was almost four o'clock in the morning. Margherita stirred momentarily as I slipped into bed beside her, then, reassured that I was safe, lapsed back into sleep. I didn't need to count vegetables or anything else. I was out like a light and slept deeply until mid-day. We were having a late lunch in the hotel coffee shop when Pettersen phoned, summoning us back to Allehelgens gate.

He obviously hadn't been to bed in the interim. He was still wearing the same clothes, a little more crumpled than the night before, and was unshaven and red-eyed. There was a half-drunk mug of coffee on his desk, a faint aroma of cigarettes indicating that he'd recently come back in from a smoke. He leant back in his chair, put his hands behind his head and looked at us, his eyelids drooping with fatigue.

"Rasmussen's made a full confession," he said. His voice was matter-of-fact, without a hint of satisfaction. He might have been telling us the time.

"He has?" I said, to prompt him to go on.

"Took us a while to get it. He denied everything to start with, of course. Spun us some tale about how he was only trying to help the police investigation. How

278

he'd suddenly remembered the store cupboard in the tower and thought he'd search it to save us the trouble. But that didn't stand much scrutiny. He soon began to crack and admitted he'd been planning to steal the violins for months. He knew all about the alarm system, the cameras. It was easy for him to disable them. He had the keys to the villa, but he needed to make it look like an outside job. Hence the broken locks, the signs of a boat landing on the other side of the island."

"So there wasn't a boat?"

"No, you were right about that." His mouth curled sheepishly. "You were right about a lot of things, Signor Castiglione. He faked the landing, the footprints on the beach. He took the violins, then decided to lie low for a while, hide the instruments until the heat died down a bit and it was safe to take them off the island. We already thought they'd gone, on their way to some crooked dealer or a rich, unscrupulous buyer. Why would we even think of looking in the tower on the hill? He might have got away with it, too, if he hadn't got too clever for his own good."

"What do you mean?"

"If Michael Berg hadn't put a spanner in the works, shown up unexpectedly and spoilt all his well-laid plans."

Pettersen yawned and stretched his arms. There were patches of sweat on the armpits of his shirt. We waited for him to continue.

"Those are the things you can never anticipate. They catch a lot of criminals out, make them do stupid things. You already know that Berg went over to the west side of the island and that he missed the last boat back to Buena Kai. We still don't know why. We can only guess the reason. Did he just lose track of time? Did he lie down somewhere in the sun and fall asleep? All we know is that he came back to the villa some time around seven o'clock in the evening and caught Rasmussen in the process of stealing the violins."

"He caught him in the act?" I said.

Pettersen nodded.

"He came past the side entrance to the house and must have seen that the door had been broken open. He went inside and there was Rasmussen with a crowbar, forcing open the glass cabinets to remove the violins. Rasmussen was taken by surprise and – so he says – he reacted instinctively. He lashed out with the crowbar and hit Berg on the forehead, killing him instantly. Rasmussen is adamant he didn't intend to kill him. He went to the body and was stunned to find that Berg was dead."

"Do you believe him?"

"Yes, I think I do. I think it probably *was* an accident. Rasmussen doesn't strike me as a violent man. He broke down when we questioned him, wanted to make a clean breast of what he'd done. I think it was troubling him."

"And Berg's body?"

"Rasmussen panicked. He'd killed a man. Somehow he had to get rid of the body. He picked Berg up and half carried, half dragged him along the path to the cliffs just south of the villa. Then he threw him into the sea."

"That's not all he did, is it?" I said.

Pettersen half smiled at me. "Yes, that's another thing you were right about. He needed to know who he'd killed, so he went through Berg's pockets and found his passport and driving licence and also the credit card receipt for lunch in his wallet. He'd already recognised him as the American tourist he'd overheard talking about Oleana and Bull's violins on the café terrace."

"So he planted the receipt inside the villa."

"It seemed the perfect opportunity to muddy the waters, to deflect attention onto Berg who, of course, wasn't going to be around to defend himself."

"And then he told you about the conversation on the terrace."

"Yes. I have to thank you for your help. You were ahead of us all along."

"It makes up for my mistake with Sørensen. Are you in trouble over that?"

For a second, Pettersen's tired eyes came alive.

"Not now," he said dryly.

He stood up and yawned again.

"I won't keep you any longer. I need to go home, take a shower and get some sleep."

We shook hands and said goodbye. Antonio was very quiet on the walk back to the hotel. I could sense the tension in him, could feel how frustrated he must be, but I didn't press him to talk. He'd open up when he was ready.

We were on the landing outside his room before he gave voice to what was on his mind.

"We've failed, Gianni," he said bluntly. "No, I'm sorry. I didn't mean that. This is nothing to do with you. I've failed."

"Now, don't be – " I began, but he didn't want to hear my feeble reassurances.

"I *have*," he interrupted. "I've come all this way, run up a huge bill and got precisely nowhere. Made absolutely no progress in finding out who killed Rikard Olsen."

I couldn't deny that was true, but I couldn't stand by and let him blame himself for it.

"It's not your fault, Antonio."

"That's how the chief will see it, how my colleagues will see it. I've had a fun trip to Norway, spent half the department's annual budget on expenses and come back empty handed. That's not going to look good."

"You can't find something that's not here," I said.

"But that's the point," Guastafeste fired back. "It *is* here, I'm sure of it. The answer is here in Norway, but I haven't been able to find it."

He unlocked the door to his room and paused, giving me a look that was part apology, party dismay.

"I'm sorry for dragging you into this, for wasting your time." He held up a hand to stall my protests. "No, don't say anything. It's over, Gianni. My time has run out. I have to go back to Italy."

SEVENTEEN

Margherita and I could have stayed on without him, maybe had a proper holiday in Norway, but neither of us felt like it. Disappointment is contagious and some of Antonio's troubled emotions had inevitably spread to us. We didn't feel much like prolonging our stay. We'd seen some of the country, had one or two glorious moments, and that was enough for the time being. Besides, the rain was beginning to depress us. We needed to get back to some warmth and sunshine.

Aina drove us to the airport. Antonio had spent his last night and last breakfast with her and was in a pensive, sombre mood. There were undoubtedly regrets about leaving without any breakthrough in his investigation, but maybe also regrets about leaving Aina. He didn't confide in me, but I could see that he was upset, that Aina clearly felt the same.

Margherita and I tactfully gave them some private time together in the terminal, then looked away while they had a final kiss and a hug before we went through security. We headed for the barrier and had almost passed the point of no return when Antonio suddenly seemed to have a change of heart and turned back. I thought he was going to give Aina another parting embrace, but instead he pulled out his phone and showed her a photograph.

"I took this at Budal," he said. "What does it mean?"

I looked at the picture, too. It showed the grave of Laila Halvorsen. Aina studied the words on the footstone.

"Og jeg skal nok vente for det lovte jeg sidst."

She gave a start, then her eyes found Antonio's and I saw a question in them.

"It's a quote from Solveig's Song, in *Peer Gynt*. It means, 'And I shall surely wait, for I promised that last'."

Antonio reacted with the same surprise as Aina. He glanced at her, his eyes suddenly soft and tender, and I realised that this gravestone engraving had a meaning that was personal to them as well as to whoever had commissioned the inscription all those years ago.

"From *Peer Gynt*?" he said.

Aina nodded. "It's Solveig singing of her love for Peer, how she'll always wait for him, and if he dies before they meet again, then they'll be reunited in heaven."

"Thank you."

Antonio put away his phone and his fingers touched Aina's one last time. They smiled at each other, then Antonio turned and walked quickly away through the barrier.

I bought three ugly, ludicrously over-priced stuffed toy trolls for my grandchildren in the duty free shop and half an hour later we were in the air, the plane climbing out over the sea through thick cloud, then turning south towards Italy.

Antonio waited until we'd reached cruising height and the cabin attendants were wheeling out the drinks' trolley before he took out his phone again and looked at the photograph.

"The question is," he said reflectively, "who was Laila Halvorsen waiting for?"

I suspect he was pondering that, and other questions, for most of the flight, for he barely spoke a word, other than to buy a coffee and some biscuits from one of the attendants. I could understand his silence. He must have had a lot on his mind. He was right about his boss and colleagues. They wouldn't be impressed by him returning with so little to show for his time in Norway. That would be eating away inside him. He was a conscientious police officer with a reputation for hard work and a track record of success. Going back to the *questura* with nothing was going to be a humiliation for him.

"Aandahl," he said suddenly.

I looked at him. "Pardon?"

"Why was he killed?" It wasn't really a question, but more a statement. And it wasn't addressed to me. It was Antonio thinking out loud.

"I don't know," he went on. "Pettersen doesn't know. The whole thing is a mystery."

We'd been over this before, but Antonio wanted to go through it all again. The circumstances of the murder, the method, the weapon used, the aftermath, the lack of progress in the police investigation. He reiterated every detail, as if the act of repetition might reveal something he'd missed. But it didn't. By the end, he was no nearer figuring out who'd killed the dealer, and why.

"What's the link?" he said, the question that had preoccupied him immediately after Aandahl's death and was still at the forefront of his mind. How did it connect to the murder of Rikard Olsen? "There has to be a link."

I didn't interrupt his train of thought. I couldn't help him. If the Bergen police, with all their resources, hadn't been able to solve the case, what chance did I stand?

Guastafeste looked out of the window. We'd crossed over the Alps and were beginning our long descent into Malpensa. Maybe he was thinking about that, for he turned to me and said abruptly, "The violin case Aandahl had with him when he left Italy. Could he have had two instruments inside it?"

"Two?" I replied.

"The Gasparo da Salò, and also the Hardanger fiddle."

"It depends on the case. You *can* get cases that hold two violins, or sometimes a violin and a viola, but they're generally rectangular. Didn't the VIP lounge supervisor say the case was shaped like a violin? That doesn't sound like a double case."

"But it's not impossible?"

"No, not at all. It could've been double thickness. I've seen cases like that. One violin in the base, one in the lid. You still think Aandahl had the Hardanger fiddle with him?"

"I don't know what to think. But I want to talk to the supervisor again."

I could feel his impatience during those last minutes of the flight. He was tense and fidgety, anxious to get off the plane as quickly as possible. The long wait to reclaim our baggage did nothing to calm him. He fretted and twitched beside the carousel and when our suitcases finally appeared, he was off like a hare, almost running out into the arrivals hall. Poor Margherita drew the short straw again and was left minding the luggage while Antonio and I went over to the VIP lounge. I wasn't strictly needed, but I'd been such an integral part of this whole affair that it seemed only natural for me to be there.

Signora Vasari was busy flattering and facilitating her pampered charges, but she managed to escape for a few minutes and took us into her office. Guastafeste explained what he wanted and the supervisor gave him a perplexed look.

"I really don't remember much about it," she said. "Except it looked like a violin case."

"Was it a big case?"

Signora Vasari shrugged. "It was the size of a violin, I suppose."

"How thick?" Antonio held up his hands, giving her different dimensions to consider.

"I'm afraid I didn't notice, I'm sorry."

"What about other bags? Did Signor Aandahl have any hold luggage?"

"Let me check."

She logged onto her computer and typed in Aandahl's name. "First name, Ingvar, that's right, isn't it?"

"Yes."

"Flew out June the eighth, Malpensa to Zürich. Yes, he had one other item of luggage. I don't know what it was or how big. There are no standard baggage allowances on private flights."

"What did you say?" Antonio asked with a frown.

"There are no – "

"No, before that. Did you say Malpensa to Zürich?"

"Yes, that's correct."

"Not Bergen?"

"No."

"You're sure about that?"

"Of course. We have a record of the flight plan the pilot filed."

"Do you know why it went to Zürich?"

"That's not information I have here."

"Was it refuelling?"

"I wouldn't have thought so. It was a Gulfstream G280. They have a range of several thousand miles."

"Or when it left Zürich to go on to Bergen?"

"You'd have to ask the Swiss authorities that question."

"Thank you, signora."

We'd come to the airport in Antonio's car, but he made me drive the return leg so he could use his phone to make a call to his colleagues at the *questura*. We were dropping Margherita off outside her apartment in Milan when he got a call back from Cremona. He listened for a while, then hung up.

"The plane landed at Zürich at eleven hundred hours, then left for Bergen ninety minutes later. There were two passengers on board – Ingvar Aandahl, and Agnetha Sørensen."

"Sørensen's ex-wife?" I said.

"Curious, eh?"

"She probably uses his jet all the time."

Antonio didn't seem convinced.

"Maybe. But I'd still be interested to know what

she was doing on that plane."

Coming back from holiday – if our trip to Norway could strictly be called that – is always a bit of a shock to the system. I like being home, with all its familiar comforts, but the downsides are the rather less appealing familiar chores. No food in the house so shopping to be done, a mountain of dirty washing from my suitcase and a garden out of control.

The temptation to do nothing is almost irresistible. To sit down in an armchair with a glass of wine and just ignore the things that need to be done. But I know from experience that that is the worst course of action. Chores do not go away. Food does not miraculously appear out of thin air, dirty clothes do not wash themselves, the weeds in the vegetable patch don't suddenly wither and die and eject themselves from the soil.

Life isn't that easy, I'm afraid. That glass of wine might be very pleasant, but once it's downed, nothing has changed. The guilt is still there, nagging away at the corner of your mind, the fridge and cupboards are still bare, but the alcohol has gone to your head and made you even less inclined, and less fit, to tackle the problem.

The solution is to knuckle down and do it all immediately, to get on with it before that lazy, whining little devil in your brain can deter you with his "put your feet up for a couple of minutes," "have a nap," "leave it until tomorrow, it's not important."

So that's what I did. Unpacked my case, put my clothes in the washing machine, made a list of provisions to buy, then went out into the garden to see what vegetables I didn't need to get from the shops. My mange-tout peas had gone mad in my absence, grown so big and fat that they could be shelled, my French climbing bean plants – the purple variety that turn green when you cook them – were laden with long, tender pods and my courgettes had mutated into huge marrows that I knew would be difficult to do much with. One alone is enough to last me a week and finding appetising things to do with them isn't easy. I once made stuffed marrow for my grandchildren when they came to stay, filled one with mince and onion and chopped tomatoes and basil, but it didn't go down well. "We really like the filling, Grandpa," they told me, "but please don't bother with that horrible bit on the outside again."

I picked as much produce as I could handle, then drove to the shops to stock up on other things. Returning home, I made a simple pasta dish of rigatoni with peas and courgettes, then treated myself to the glass of red wine I'd been longing for all afternoon – and it tasted all the better for having been delayed.

I was sitting on the terrace, letting the warm evening sun soak into my bones, evaporate all that Norwegian rain that still lingered inside me, when Guastafeste rang and asked if he could come out to the house. He hadn't been home since I'd last seen him; he'd gone straight to the *questura* and continued working.

"Have you eaten?" I asked him when he arrived, knowing what the answer would be.

"Well, no, but – "

"Wait there."

"Gianni, you don't have to – "

"I won't be long."

I poured him a glass of wine and left him on the terrace while I went into the kitchen to rustle up a meal for him. He doesn't like me to fuss, but it was no trouble. I'd made enough rigatoni to have some left over to eat cold in a salad so I gave him that with some porcini mushrooms, a few tomatoes, some of my garden peas, which are always tastier raw than cooked, a dressing of oil and balsamic vinegar and a dusting of Parmesan cheese.

"Thank you, Gianni."

"Don't mention it."

He picked up one of the gigantic courgettes I'd harvested earlier and weighed it in his hand.

"Is this really a courgette?"

"Take a couple," I said. "If you don't eat them, you can always use them to strengthen your biceps."

I sat down at the table and drank my wine while he ate. The sun was dipping lower, glancing through the branches of my fruit trees. I had a good crop of plums this year. That was another task I'd have to get down to sooner rather than later – picking the fruit before the birds and the wasps had the lot.

"I've been on the phone to Zürich," Antonio said, sitting back in his chair and rubbing his stomach with the palm of his hand. "You know what I like about the Swiss police? They're such good linguists. There's always someone who speaks Italian. And they don't hang around. You ask them something and they get back to you in a couple of hours."

He paused to drink some wine. "Agnetha Sørensen flew into Zürich in her ex-husband's Gulfstream jet on June the seventh and hired a car from Avis at the airport, a top-of-the-range Mercedes Benz S-Klasse saloon, with air con and GPS. She had it for twenty-four hours and returned it the next day, just before she joined Ingvar Aandahl on the plane to fly back to Bergen. Avis, of course, keep a record of the mileage on all their cars. Agnetha drove seven hundred and seventy-four kilometres in the time she had the Mercedes, quite a lot for a country as small as Switzerland. Now, interestingly, the distance from Zürich to Cremona, by the most direct route, is about three hundred and eighty kilometres, so a return trip would be seven hundred and sixty or thereabouts, almost exactly the mileage she did."

I stared at him. "You think she drove to Cremona?"

"It's possible. It would only take about five hours each way. She could easily do it in twenty-four hours. Switzerland and Italy, as you know, are both Schengen countries. There are no checks at the border, no records of who comes and goes. And, curiously, she didn't switch on the GPS system in the car so that can't tell us where she went."

This was such a startling turn of events that I was struggling to take it in.

"Are you saying you suspect her of killing Rikard Olsen?"

"Well, she's his former partner, someone he left for another woman."

"But that was years ago. Why on earth would she kill him now?"

"For the Hardanger fiddle."

"Agnetha Sørensen? Why would she want the fiddle?"

"There's another interesting thing about her. Her maiden name was Falk. She's Arne Falk's daughter."

"The strange old man up in the mountains?"

Antonio nodded. "A violin maker with links to Håkon Halvorsen, the man who made the fiddle. And Agnetha was also a close friend of Ingvar Aandahl."

I was momentarily speechless. I felt as if the air had been punched out of me.

"I've been in touch with Dag Pettersen," Antonio went on. "I'm flying back to Bergen tomorrow. Why don't you come with me?"

EIGHTEEN

Dag Pettersen was waiting for us at Flesland Airport. We got into an unmarked car with him, but we didn't drive far – just around the terminal building to a heliport where a police helicopter was parked on the apron. Inevitably, it was raining again, the sky almost black with clouds, the ground glistening with water.

"We've spoken to Agnetha Sørensen's office," the inspector said. "They said she's away for a couple of days."

"Oh." Guastafeste was disappointed. "Do you know where?"

Pettersen nodded. "According to her sons, she's gone to see her father at Budal."

"That's quite a long way," I said, remembering our visit to the village.

Pettersen inclined his head towards the helicopter. "Depends how you travel."

He'd made all the arrangements. Helicopter to Aurland, where we landed on a patch of flat ground beside the fjord, then a police car up the mountain to

Budal. After that, we were on our own. There was no way up the rough track except on foot. There were four of us. Pettersen had brought along a female officer named Lund, a young, fit-looking uniformed constable who could probably have sprinted up the track without breaking sweat, but had to tag along patiently, pausing every hundred metres or so for us out-of-condition males to draw breath. The rain had stopped just inland from Bergen and it was now a cool, but bright, day.

The scent of woodsmoke again told us we were nearing Arne Falk's house, then we rounded the rock buttress and saw the ramshackle wooden cabin and outbuildings in front of us. Agnetha Sørensen came out of the cabin as we approached. Gone were the high heels and clinging dresses of the city. Out here, she was wearing trainers, loose trousers and a thick woollen pullover. Her blonde hair was tied back at the nape of the neck, a couple of gold studs gleaming in her ears.

She stared at us, her expression passing from surprise to anxiety and then to a frown of puzzlement. She said something to Pettersen in Norwegian, which had to be something along the lines of, "What on earth are you doing here?" and he replied in English.

"If you don't mind, Fru Sørensen, can we speak in English? Detective Guastafeste would like to ask you a few questions."

"Questions?" Her eyes flicked from Pettersen to Antonio and I saw another fleeting look of anxiety in them. "Questions about what?"

"Perhaps we could go inside the house."

A wood fire was burning in the hearth, a few

charred pine logs glowing red, giving off tendrils of smoke that drifted away up the chimney. There was a bucket and mop on the floor by the sink, a pair of blue rubber gloves on the table which I guessed Agnetha had removed when she'd come out to meet us.

"I'm afraid my father doesn't keep the place very clean," she said by way of explanation. "He doesn't notice the dirt."

She picked up the rubber gloves and tossed them into the sink. Mingling with the acrid smell of smoke was a more chemical odour, some kind of cleaning fluid Agnetha had been using on the wooden floor. She seemed a different woman today, no longer the glamorous former fashion model turned businesswoman but a practical, down-to-earth countrywoman who could turn her hand to any tasks that needed doing: scrubbing floors, lighting fires. I could see her milking a goat, handling a hunting rifle, even skinning an elk and butchering the carcass like her father. Perhaps all Norwegian are like that, still essentially frontiers people beneath the veneer of modern living.

"Where *is* your father?" I asked.

She hesitated for only a fraction of a second.

"He's gone for a walk."

"By himself? Is he all right? A vulnerable, elderly man like him."

"He does it all the time." She paused, gazing at me quizzically. "What makes you say he's vulnerable?"

"Well, he seemed it last time we were here."

Her eyes opened wide. "You've been here *before*?"

"Last week. We came to ask him about the Hardanger fiddle that Håkon Halvorsen made."

"Is that why you're here now? To question him again?"

It was Guastafeste who answered. "No, it is you we want to speak to. About your trip to Zürich a couple of weeks ago."

She stiffened. "My trip to Zürich?"

"Why did you go there?"

"Please, sit down."

Agnetha pulled out some chairs and then took one herself. I had a feeling she was giving herself time to think. Pettersen, Guastafeste and I sat down. The female constable, Lund, remained standing near the door.

"I went on business," Agnetha said, her tone casual, perhaps slightly perplexed, as if she couldn't see any reason why anyone might be interested in something so mundane.

"That's your clothing design business?"

"Yes. I go to Switzerland quite often. My clothes are expensive, high-end fashion. I only sell through certain, select outlets and there are more of those in Switzerland than most countries."

"You were visiting clients?"

"Yes."

"Just in Zürich?"

"Yes."

"How many clients?"

Her friendly, obliging manner slipped a little. Her brow furrowed.

"Look, what's this about? Why are you interested in my business trips?"

Pettersen interjected to answer that question.

"This is an official Italian police investigation, Fru Sørensen. It has the full support of the Norwegian police. We'd appreciate it if you answered these questions as fully as you can."

Agnetha's cool blue eyes bored into the inspector. "Am I under suspicion for something?"

"We're just trying to clear up a few things," Pettersen replied evasively, glancing at Antonio to go on.

"Where did you stay in Zürich?" he asked. "A hotel?"

Agnetha hesitated. I got the feeling she was weighing up whether to cooperate or shut down this interview immediately, calculating which might be more advantageous to her.

"I stayed in a friend's apartment," she said finally.

"You were there on the night of June the seventh?"

"Yes, just that one night."

"And your friend can confirm that?"

Her lips twitched apologetically. "I'm afraid not. She was out of town for a few days. She left me a set of keys."

"Did you go anywhere other than Zürich?"

"I went for a drive into the mountains. Switzerland's a beautiful country."

"A long drive?"

"I forget."

"The mileage on your hire car was seven hundred and seventy-four kilometres."

"Was it? I must have gone further than I thought."

"Did you cross over the border into Italy?"

"No. Why would I have done that?"

"You did not go to Cremona?"

She gave him an incredulous look. "To *Cremona*? No, of course not."

"Did you kill Rikard Olsen?"

It was blunt, but effective. Agnetha recoiled, as if he'd slapped her.

"That's ridiculous. Why would I kill Rikard?"

"For the Hardanger fiddle."

She laughed. A cold, humourless laugh that sounded forced. "Are you serious? For a *violin*?"

"A violin with Laila Halvorsen's face on it," Antonio said.

"I don't know who Laila Halvorsen is."

"But your father does, doesn't he?"

She looked at him, but didn't reply.

"Are you sure you didn't go to Cremona?" Pettersen asked.

"I've already answered that question. Do you have any evidence that I went there? No, I didn't think you did. Now, please, stop making these ludicrous accusations."

"What about Ingvar Aandahl?" Pettersen said.

"I told you everything I knew when you interviewed me in Bergen. I have nothing to add now."

"He was a friend of yours. You saw him a lot. You had access to his office. Did you kill him?"

"That's enough." Agnetha pushed back her chair and stood up. "If there's anything else you want to ask me, you'd better do it in the presence of my lawyer."

She walked across to the door and held it open for us. Antonio and I exchanged looks with Pettersen and he shrugged. There was nothing more we could do.

We went out of the cabin. I gazed up at the mountain behind us, wondering where Arne had gone for his walk. We'd come all this way. It was bitterly disappointing to be leaving with nothing to show for it. My eyes came to rest on the outbuildings. The smaller of the two, I already knew, was a smokehouse. The larger, I'd assumed on our previous visit, was Arne's workshop, but was it? I had a sudden urge to see inside.

Antonio, Pettersen and Lund were walking away. They were police officers. Their actions were strictly controlled by rules and legal procedures. I, however, was a civilian. I was subject to no such regulation.

Agnetha was watching us carefully from the doorway, but she was a few metres away. I didn't think she could move fast enough to stop me. Heading off as if to follow the other three, I made a sudden deviation to the left and dashed across to the outbuilding. I heard Agnetha's sharp cry of protest, but by then I was pushing open the door and stepping inside.

I stopped dead just beyond the threshold. Some time in the past it must have been a workshop, for there were workbenches around the walls and tools and violin moulds hanging from racks. But it wasn't a workshop now: it was a shrine. A shrine to Laila Halvorsen.

Her image was everywhere. Photographs of her covered almost every inch of the walls, many of them duplicated, some blown up into life-size prints. Her smiling face filled the room with her warmth and beauty. Laila by a fjord, Laila on a boat, Laila on a beach, Laila in a restaurant with a group of friends, Laila cross-country skiing in the mountains, Laila warming herself by a blazing log fire – a poignant record of her young, all too short, life.

Another face stood out in this gallery of pictures: a stocky young man who was posing next to Laila in most of the photographs. He was shorter than her by a few centimetres, dark haired and handsome. From their expressions, the intimacy of their poses – holding hands, arms around each other – it was obvious that

301

they were more than just friends. He'd changed a lot in the intervening fifty or so years, but I knew at once who the young man was: Arne Falk.

My gaze strayed around the room. There were other photos that, on first sight, didn't appear to be about Laila. One section, near the window, was devoted to pictures of a violin, taken at various stages of its construction. But given that the violin was the Hardanger fiddle that Rikard Olsen had brought to Cremona, that, too, was really a memory of Laila. Some of the photos showed the carving of the front and back plates, the insertion of the mother-of-pearl purfling and the complex marquetry on the fingerboard, but most of them concentrated on the scroll, on the gradual process of sculpting Laila's head from the block of maple. A rough cut first, then the more detailed work: her eyes, nose, lips, hair, the perfect likeness emerging from the wood.

I could feel the deep love that had gone into that creation, even from these photographs that were beginning to fade and curl with age, but as I turned to inspect the display on the other side of the window, I sensed a different emotion in the images: not love, but grief. While most of the room was a celebration of Laila Halvorsen's life, this particular area was a record of her death.

There were cuttings from different newspapers that had been glued to pieces of card. The headlines and text were in Norwegian, but I could see from the dates – June, 1962 – and the photographs of a wrecked car beside a road that they referred to Laila's tragic end. Other photos showed her funeral, the mourners outside the church at Budal and then by Laila's grave in the churchyard. One was a close-up of the headstone, another – much newer photo – of the footstone and its inscription. *Og jeg skal nok vente for det lovte jeg sidst.* I gazed at the words, understanding now whom Laila was waiting for.

"Get out!"

Agnetha was in the doorway, her face tight with fury.

"Get out!" she yelled at me. "This is private. You have no right to be in here."

She snatched a rusty old chisel from one of the tool racks and took a pace towards me. I saw an anger and aggression in her face that was frightening in its intensity.

"Get out!"

She raised the chisel like a dagger and took another step. Then hands locked onto her from both sides, Pettersen and Guastafeste taking an arm each, immobilising her. Antonio reached out and prized the chisel from her fingers. Agnetha fought back, screaming at them in Norwegian and struggling to escape, but they were too strong for her. Lund came in and, in one swift, practised movement, cuffed Agnetha's wrists behind her back. Agnetha's anger seemed to ebb away in an instant. Her shoulders and head dropped and she allowed herself to be led outside.

"Where's your father?" Pettersen demanded.

Agnetha didn't reply.

"Where *is* he? Where did he go for a walk?"

Agnetha spat out something in Norwegian and turned to me. There was ice in her eyes.

"You shouldn't have done that," she snarled. "That's personal to my father. It's none of your business."

"Listen," Guastafeste said.

"What?"

"Listen." He had his head turned to one side, his ear cocked.

Then I heard it, too: the faint, distant sound of a violin carrying to us on the wind.

"Where's it coming from?"

"Up there."

"Leave him alone," Agnetha yelled. "He's a sick man. Leave him alone."

Pettersen glanced at Lund. "Keep an eye on her."

We hurried round the side of the cabin and headed up the hill, the path steep and rough under foot, the surface pitted by frost and heavy rain. Arne Falk was just a few minutes away, a small, hunched figure sitting on a boulder outside the mouth of a cave that seemed to penetrate deep into the mountain. Next to him was a waterfall that cascaded down a sheer rock face into a small pool, and then over another cliff into a yawning chasm. The spray from the waterfall was drifting across and landing on Arne, silvering his hair with tiny droplets, but he didn't appear to notice. He didn't notice anything, even our arrival, he was too absorbed in his playing.

The Hardanger fiddle was under his chin, his bushy beard and long hair enveloping the lower bouts of the instrument so that it seemed to be growing out of his body. The music he was playing was like nothing I'd ever heard before. It was eerie and ethereal, full of an immense sadness, the sound amplified and distorted by the cave behind him. This wasn't the merry dance music for which the Hardanger fiddle is renowned: it was something darker and more profound.

The violin is a magical instrument. It can produce the most wonderful sounds, but the magic can be both good and bad. To my ears, what Arne was playing sounded like a man's soul calling out in agony. It was a painful cry into the void, the musical equivalent of the Munch *Scream*.

We approached him tentatively, sensing that he was lost to the world, in a trance that had to be broken gently or the reaction might be unpredictable. I was remembering, and I'm sure Antonio was too, our previous encounter with him. A Hardanger fiddle wasn't a hunting rifle, but who knew what he would do if we upset him.

A few metres away from the boulder, we stopped. Arne still hadn't registered our presence. He was staring in our direction, but whatever he was seeing, it wasn't us. I couldn't help wondering how the young, attractive Arne in the photographs had turned into this gnarled, disturbed old man. Then Pettersen spoke.

"Herr Falk?"

Arne didn't appear to hear him. The bow was still gliding over the fiddle strings, the drone strings vibrating too, more softly so the sound seemed to come from the cave, from some strange, diabolical creature lurking deep in the bowels of the mountain.

"Herr Falk?"

Arne stopped playing. He lowered the fiddle. Around his neck, he was wearing the silver locket containing Laila Halvorsen's hair. He gazed at each of us in turn, his expression puzzled. If he recognised us, he didn't show any signs of it.

Pettersen said something else in Norwegian. It seemed to confuse Arne. He stared at us, his eyes sinking deeper into his face, darting from side to side as if he scented danger. He stood up and backed away, the fiddle clutched tight to his chest. Then he started shouting at us. Loud, angry yells, flecks of spittle showering out onto his beard. I stepped forward.

"Arne, it's me, Gianni. Don't you remember? We had a drink together. I make violins, too."

It was the English again, the change of language that seemed to trigger some mechanism in his brain, to shut down, or open up, some pathway that made him pause to think. He stopped shouting. His eyes were fixed on me.

"Drink?" he said.

"Yes, drink," I replied. "Would you like a drink, Arne? Shall we go and have a drink?"

He glanced nervously at Pettersen and Guastafeste.

"We're friends," I reassured him. "You remember Antonio? He was here before, with me."

"Give us the violin," Pettersen said, moving forward, his hand outstretched.

"Inspector, that's – " I began, but it was too late. It was the worst thing he could have done.

Arne gripped the fiddle even tighter and started screaming again. He backed away to the edge of the cliff above the lower waterfall, his feet only inches away from the drop.

"*Nei, pappa!*" a voice shouted behind us.

I turned. Agnetha was running up the path, her hands still cuffed. Lund was a few metres behind her, with blood on her face.

"*Pappa!*" Agnetha stopped and called out to her father, obviously pleading with him to come away from the edge.

"Agnetha?" Arne squinted at her.

"*Ja, pappa*. Agnetha."

"It's mine," he said in English, his brain still muddled. "Mine." He pressed the fiddle to his heart.

"Yes, it's yours," Agnetha replied, speaking English now. "Come away from the waterfall."

"You're not having it." Arne glared at Pettersen. "It's mine. It's my Laila."

"Yes, we know, *pappa*," Agnetha said. She came nearer, twisting round to show Pettersen the cuffs on her wrists. "Take these off me."

"I don't think − "

"Only I can deal with this. He's my father. Take them off."

Pettersen hesitated, then nodded at Lund. She produced a key and unlocked the handcuffs. Agnetha edged towards her father.

"Come to me, *pappa*." She was still speaking English, sensing that he was responding better to a foreign language. He had to think harder and that made him less likely to do something impetuous.

"It's time now," Arne said.

"Time for what, *pappa*?"

"To meet her. To meet Laila."

"Not yet, *pappa*."

"Yes, it's time. She's waiting for me."

Arne turned the violin so he could gaze at the scroll. "She's beautiful, isn't she?"

"Yes, she's beautiful."

"She died."

"I know."

Tears welled up in Arne's eyes and trickled down his cheeks into his beard.

307

"She died. I must go to her."

"Not now, *pappa*. I need you here. You have me."

Agnetha took a step nearer. Arne shuffled to the edge of the cliff. The ground was wet and slippery. One false move and he was gone. Agnetha paused. She held out her arm.

"Take my hand, *pappa*."

"I wasn't there," Arne sobbed. "I should've been there. I loved her."

"I love you, too, *pappa*. And you love me."

"She's waiting."

"So am I. Take my hand."

"No, I have to go to her."

Arne lifted the fiddle and kissed the face on the scroll. Tears rolled down onto the wood.

"Don't leave me, *pappa*."

"What?"

"You can't leave me."

"She's waiting."

"I'm waiting, too. Come to me."

"Come to you?"

"Yes. Come to me, not Laila. I'm here, *pappa*."

Arne turned and looked down over the precipice. The spray from the waterfall merged with his tears. He swayed on unsteady legs.

"It's time," he said. He folded his arms around the fiddle, Laila's face next to his.

"Leave Laila with me," Agnetha said.

"What?"

"Give me the violin. You don't want to hurt Laila, do you?"

Arne blinked at her uncomprehendingly. "Hurt her?"

"You'll hurt her, *pappa*. Give it to me."

"I love her."

"I know you do. Come here."

Agnetha reached out and gently pulled her father away from the edge. He was weeping uncontrollably, shaking with distress. I stepped forward and took his other arm. Together, we guided him back down the mountain.

NINETEEN

"Let's start at the beginning, shall we?" Pettersen said, taking charge of the interrogation while Antonio and I watched from the side of the room.

Agnetha didn't answer. She was looking anxiously at her father who was slumped in an armchair by the fire. The Hardanger fiddle was still cradled in his arms. He was rocking to and fro, murmuring to himself, as if he were lulling a baby to sleep. The tears had stopped, but there was a look of acute sorrow in his eyes, which were fixed on Laila's face on the scroll of the violin.

"Fru Sørensen, did you hear me?" Pettersen went on.

"Yes, I heard you," Agnetha replied, her voice laced with contempt. "I've already told you, I have nothing to say until I see my lawyer."

"As you wish." Pettersen turned to Lund, who was watching over Arne. "Take the violin away from him and handcuff him."

"Yes, sir."

"No!"

Agnetha was on her feet, starting towards the hearth. Pettersen grabbed her arm and pushed her back down onto the chair.

"Sit down!" he barked.

"Leave my father alone. He has nothing to do with this."

"He has everything to do with it. He has the Hardanger fiddle that was stolen from Rikard Olsen after he was murdered. If you won't help us, we'll have to arrest your father."

He nodded at Lund. She took the handcuffs from the leather pouch on her belt and stepped nearer Arne. Reaching down, she tried to remove the fiddle from his grasp. He let out a howl, like a wounded animal, and clutched the instrument tighter to his chest.

"Use force, if necessary," Pettersen ordered.

Agnetha erupted from her chair again, but the inspector blocked her path. Agnetha yelled something furious in Norwegian. Pettersen didn't yield an inch. He replied in English, calm and polite.

"Your father is in possession of stolen goods, which implicate him in the murder of Rikard Olsen. He will be arrested and taken back to Bergen for questioning."

"He's a very distressed old man," Agnetha snapped. "What kind of a police officer are you?"

"What kind of a daughter are you?" Pettersen retorted. He glanced at Lund. "Carry on."

Lund took hold of the neck of the violin and attempted to wrench it away from Arne, but he hung on to it grimly, shouting and screaming at the officer. Agnetha tried to get up again. Pettersen pushed her down. Lund put her knee on the arm of Arne's chair and leaned over, her left forearm ramming him back into the upholstery while her right hand tugged on the violin. Arne let out a cry, part pain, part anger, his anguish echoing around the room. I couldn't stand by and watch this happening.

"Inspector, is this really necessary?" I asked.

"Keep out of it, Signor Castiglione. This is a police matter."

"But you can hear how upset he is. Surely there's another way to do this."

"Oh, there is," Pettersen said. "Isn't there, Fru Sørensen? It's in your hands."

Lund was still fighting with Arne. His anger gave him a strength that belied his age and frailty, but he was still no match for the young police officer. She forced open his fingers and whipped the fiddle away from him. Arne screamed, as if he'd been stabbed, and struggled to get up from the armchair, his arms lashing out wildly at Lund. I stepped in quickly, taking the violin away from her while Guastafeste restrained Arne. He was sobbing again now, tears flooding down his face and into his beard.

"Cuff him!" Pettersen said curtly.

"No! Don't touch him," Agnetha cried. "I'll tell you what you want to know." Her eyes were moist. She was staring in agony at her father. "Don't hurt him. Please, don't hurt him."

Lund moved away. Guastafeste let go of Arne's shoulders.

"Give him back the violin," Agnetha said. "He's waited so long for it. Don't take it away from him now."

I held out the fiddle. Arne snatched it from my hands and wrapped his arms around it, his cheek pressed to the scroll.

"Laila," he whimpered. "My Laila."

Pettersen pulled out a chair and sat down. He looked at Agnetha.

"Well?"

She kept her eyes on her father for a moment, reassuring herself that he was all right before she turned to the inspector.

"Promise me you'll leave him out of this. He had no part in it."

"If he had no part in it, then, yes, I can promise that," Pettersen replied. "But I want to hear what you have to say first."

"He loved her, Laila Halvorsen," Agnetha said. "Never stopped loving her. He met her in Oslo when he was a young man. Laila was a student at the university, my father was a violin maker – like Laila's father. He'd just finished his apprenticeship and was thinking about setting up in business for himself. They fell in love. They were inseparable, did everything together. You can see that from the photos in the workshop. You can see the love in their faces."

She paused, glancing at her father again to see if he was listening, but Arne was in a world of his own, murmuring incoherently to the violin in his arms.

"This was the early nineteen sixties," Agnetha went on. "Before Norway discovered oil and became rich. It was a drab, depressing place to live. My father wanted to get away, to see more of the world, so he went off travelling for a few months – to southern Europe and North Africa. Laila couldn't go with him because of her studies. It was while he was away that she was killed in a car crash. He didn't know anything about it.

314

No one knew where he was, or how to get in touch with him. By the time he found out and came straight home, Laila was buried – down the hill in the churchyard at Budal. He was devastated. The love of his life was gone and he hadn't been there for her. He'd been roaming around Spain and Morocco, enjoying himself. He blamed himself for her death. If he'd stayed in Norway, he would have protected her, looked after her. She'd never have got into that car with the drunk driver.

"I don't think he ever got over it. He settled down for a while, making violins. He met my mother a few years later and I was born, but they split up very soon afterwards. The torch he carried for Laila was crippling. He could never love another woman the way he'd loved her. It hollowed him out, made him incapable of forming a lasting relationship with anyone else. It affected his mind, too. The obsession, the infatuation, the guilt all started to unhinge him, to turn him a little mad, I suppose. Look at him."

She turned her head. Arne was stroking the scroll of the Hardanger fiddle, caressing the carved wooden hair as if it were real. There was a look of pure happiness on his face.

"He's got her back now," Agnetha said. "He's finally got his Laila back after all these years."

"It's a beautiful piece of work," I said. "Håkon Halvorsen was a fine craftsman."

Agnetha rounded on me instantly. "Halvorsen didn't make it, my father did. It's *his* violin. He's got back what belongs to him. He made it in the sixties, not long after Laila died. Carved the scroll from a photograph of her and made a special compartment

315

for the silver locket she'd given him before he went off travelling. He hung it on the wall of his workshop. I lived with my mother after they separated, but I visited *pappa* regularly. I was fascinated by the fiddle, by the beautiful face on the scroll. Even then, I could see how much it meant to my father."

"This was where? In Oslo?" Pettersen said.

"Yes. But he took it with him when he bought Halvorsen's house and workshop after his death. It was on the wall there, too. Well, until it was stolen. I think that was when my father started to go downhill mentally. The loss of the fiddle was too much for him. It was like losing Laila all over again. I still don't know what happened."

"A man named Knut Karlsen took it," Guastafeste said. "Another man who'd loved Laila in his youth."

"Knut Karlsen? I've never heard of him."

"He grew up in Budal, then moved to Bergen. It was when he died that Rikard Olsen acquired the fiddle."

"I didn't know about Karlsen."

"But you knew Rikard had the fiddle, didn't you?"

Agnetha nodded. "I saw his appeal on the internet."

"And you decided to kill him for it."

"No!" Agnetha's eyes flashed with anger. "That's not what happened. I tried to buy it from him. I offered him a good price, but he was stubborn. Rikard was always stubborn, always difficult. I begged him to sell it to me, told him how much it would mean to my father, but he wouldn't budge. I kept trying to persuade him to sell. That's why I went to Cremona, to ask him again. But he still refused. I lost my temper. I was furious with him. I hit him and he fell into the canal. I

316

panicked. I didn't know what to do. I just ran away. It was an accident, something that happened in the heat of the moment. I didn't mean to kill him."

"Are you sure that's what happened?" Guastafeste said.

"Of course. Don't you believe me?" Agnetha replied.

"Gianni and I met Rikard in Cremona. He showed us the fiddle. He knew very little about it. He didn't know who'd made it, didn't know who the woman on the scroll was. That doesn't fit with what you just said. If you were telling the truth, Rikard would have known about your father and Laila Halvorsen."

"I *did* tell him," Agnetha insisted.

"Then your version of what happened in Cremona does not ring true, either," Guastafeste went on. "You did not go there openly. You went to Zürich and hired a car, then crossed the border. You knew there would be no record of your entering Italy, no record of your staying in a hotel. The whole thing was planned. It was not an accident. You went there with the intention of killing Rikard."

"For a *violin*?" Agnetha sneered.

"You wanted the violin," Guastafeste said. "I believe that part. But there was another reason, too, wasn't there? Revenge."

"Revenge for what?"

"For your son."

Agnetha stared at him. The colour had drained from her face.

"My *son*? What are you talking about?"

"For Rasmus. You forget, we've met him. We've met both your sons. The younger one, Johan, looks just like his father, Aksel Sørensen. But Rasmus looks like Rikard.

317

He's not Sørensen's son, is he? He's Rikard Olsen's."

"Is this true?" Pettersen interjected.

"A DNA test would soon prove it," Antonio replied. "Rikard was a..." He gave me the word in Italian and I translated it.

"Womaniser."

"Yes, a womaniser. Let me guess what happened. You were together, you became pregnant and then he abandoned you. Am I right?"

Agnetha took a long time to reply. I thought she was going to stonewall, to deny everything, but she'd obviously decided to make a clean breast of it.

"Rikard was a shit," she said, and I was surprised by the venom in her voice. "I was three months pregnant when he walked out on me. Left me for that bitch Kamilla Nygaard. He knew it, but he didn't care. He didn't care about me, or about our unborn child. All that mattered to him was himself, what he wanted. That's Rikard right through, a selfish, uncaring bastard."

"So you hatched a plan to kill him, "Pettersen said. "That's right, isn't it?"

Agnetha said nothing.

"You waited a long time," Pettersen went on. "How old is your son now? How many years did you nurture that violent hatred for Rikard Olsen?"

"This isn't about Rikard," Agnetha snapped. "It's about my father. It's all about my father."

Her gaze went back to Arne, who was still totally absorbed with the fiddle in his arms. Agnetha's expression softened. There was tenderness in her eyes.

"I couldn't bear to watch him deteriorate," she said. "You've seen what he did to Halvorsen's workshop. He stopped working, stopped making violins. All he

318

could think about was Laila. He spent hours in there, just looking at her face on the wall. He wasn't interested in anything else. I'd visit and he'd barely speak to me. He'd simply shut himself away in the workshop and be alone with his memories of Laila. I thought that getting the fiddle back might bring him back to me, that somehow he'd recover his senses and be the father I remembered, be the father I loved. That's what I hoped, anyway."

Her eyes were glistening. I could see how emotionally agitated she was, how close to breaking down. Guastafeste must have been aware of it, too, but he was a police officer. He could remain more detached from it than I could. Whatever her feelings, whatever her motives, there was no getting away from the fact that she'd killed Rikard Olsen.

"You worked it all out, didn't you?" Antonio said. "You could have killed him here in Norway, but that was too close to home. You preferred to do it in Italy, where there'd be no trail leading back to you."

Agnetha didn't respond.

"And Ingvar Aandahl?" Pettersen said. "Why did you kill him? What wrong had he done you?"

The softness fell away from her face, a hard defiance taking its place.

"Ingvar was a fool," she said forcefully. "I flew back from Zürich with him, the fiddle hidden in my suitcase. But he guessed what I'd really been up to and tried to blackmail me. Tried to extort money in return for silence. Well, he's silent now."

"He was trying to buy the Hardanger fiddle, acting for your ex-husband, we believe."

"Yes, Aksel told me just a couple of days ago. He

319

wanted to do it for me. He knew the story, of course. He knew about Laila and my father, but he didn't want to approach Rikard directly. He used Ingvar as an intermediary."

She looked at her father again.

"He's happy now. That's all I wanted. Have you finished? Have you asked all your questions?"

She stood up. She seemed tired. The fight had drained out of her.

"Let's get this over with."

TWENTY

It was late by the time we got back to Bergen, even later when we'd finished making our statements at the police station. We went to our hotel and had a beer in the bar. Antonio was subdued. He'd just seen his murder investigation brought to a successful conclusion, but he gave no sign of satisfaction.

"Are you all right?" I asked.

"Yes, I'm fine," he replied wearily.

"You can close your case now."

"I know."

"Isn't that cause for celebration?"

"Do you feel like celebrating?"

"No."

"Me, neither."

He glanced away pensively across the room. There weren't many other people there – a middle-aged couple nursing small glasses of red wine, a lone man with a laptop and a rowdy group of six or seven men in suits and open-necked shirts who looked like salesmen unwinding after a day of meetings. Their table was littered with glasses and empty beer bottles.

"I never do, really," Antonio said. "Back home, after a case like this, we always go out for a drink. The whole team. We laugh and we slap each other on the back and the boss congratulates us on a job well done. But what are we celebrating?"

"The end," I said. "Isn't it good to bring things to a conclusion, to find the answers you've been looking for?"

"Maybe. But it doesn't change the basic facts. Rikard Olsen is still dead. So is Ingvar Aandahl."

"And Agnetha Sørensen has confessed to their killings. Isn't that justice of a sort?"

"I suppose so. I know I ought to feel happy – and perhaps I will later – but right now I just feel tired and depressed. Okay, we've got our solution. We've tied everything up neatly, so why does it still feel like a big mess?"

"That's life," I said. "Whatever we do, it's always a mess."

I thought about Agnetha, pale and quiet in the helicopter as we flew back to Bergen, and I thought about her father, that sad, lonely, disturbed old man hugging a fiddle and talking to a face carved out of wood. Love, hate, greed, fear, I recalled Antonio listing the reasons why people killed, the primal emotions that drive our actions. Agnetha had been frightened of Ingvar Aandahl, but what had been her motive for killing Rikard Olsen? Hatred? Perhaps. Or was it mostly love? Love for her father, a love that wanted to bring back his sanity and make him happy again. An unrealistic, selfish desire, undoubtedly, but that didn't make it any less heartfelt.

Were there ever good and bad reasons for murder, or was it always an absolute crime? All that counted was the act itself, the motive was irrelevant. I'm sure moral philosophers would have opinions on the matter, probably many contradictory opinions, but I'm not a philosopher. I'm a violin maker. I could make no sense of any of it.

"What happens now?" I asked.

"It's out of my hands, thank God," Antonio replied. "There'll be a lot of arguing about jurisdictions, about extradition and trials, but that's up to the lawyers. It's not my worry." He drained his glass of beer. "You want another?"

"At these prices?"

"The Cremona Police Department is paying. Come on, Gianni, I think we've earned it."

We flew back to Italy next morning and I saw nothing of Guastafeste for a fortnight. Then he came out to my house for dinner one evening and announced that he was returning to Norway.

"For the case?" I said.

"To see Aina," he replied.

"You're still... together?"

He nodded. "She's learning Italian and I've been learning Norwegian. *Snakker du italiensk?* Do you speak Italian? *Hvor mye er hvalbiffen?* How much is the whale steak? That should do for starters."

Margherita and I drove him to the airport. At the departure barrier, we gave him a present – a sturdy black umbrella.

"You're going to need it," I said.

We watched him disappear into the snaking line through security and Margherita said, "Do you think it will last?"

"I hope so," I replied. "He's a good man. He needs a good woman." I looked at her. "We all do."

We went back to my house and I made us lunch, then afterwards we went into the music room to play duets. I took out my selection of Ole Bull compositions and chose *Saeterjentens Søndag*, The Herd Girl's Sunday. I looked over at Margherita as we played. What did Solveig say to Peer Gynt about the reality of his existence? In my faith, in my hope, in my love. That was how I felt about Margherita.

The lyrical melody of Ole Bull's music filled the room. Margherita caught my eye and smiled. I knew that, like me, she was thinking of that warm afternoon on Lysøen, of sitting in the forest, the scent of pine in the air and the sunlight dancing on the surface of the lake.

AUTHOR'S NOTE

Ole Bull, the Norwegian Paganini, was one of the most celebrated violinists of the nineteenth century - and probably of all time.

For information about his life, and his ill-fated colony in the United States, I am indebted to the following books: *The Life of Ole Bull*, by Mortimer Smith (Princeton University Press); *Ole Bull: A Memoir*, by Sara Chapman Thorp Bull (Houghton Mifflin and Company) and *Oleana The Ole Bull Colony*, by Paul W. Heimel (Knox Books).

ENJOYED THIS BOOK?

Why not try another of Paul Adam's enthralling
Cremona Mysteries?

Paganini's Ghost

'Superb...captivating but never transparent...enriched by
meticulously detailed historical intrigues'
Publishers Weekly

A dazzling young Russian virtuoso performs a sell-out
recital on Paganini's violin in the cathedral in Cremona.
Then one of the audience, a shady Parisian art dealer, is
found dead in his hotel room, a fragment of sheet music
belonging to the virtuoso hidden in his wallet. But how did
the dead man get hold of it? And why?

Violin maker Gianni Castiglione is drawn into the murder
investigation by his friend, detective Antonio Guastafeste,
and the two men find themselves at the centre of a
tantalising story of love, deception and greed. Following a
trail that leads back to Paganini, his lover Elisa Bonaparte
(Napoleon's sister), Catherine the Great of Russia and a
long-lost priceless treasure, Gianni and Antonio must
unravel another mystery that has gone unanswered for over
a century, one that may hold the answer to the modern-day
murder.

Filled with remarkable history and musical lore, *Paganini's
Ghost* plays at a breathtaking tempo that will keep you
reading until the very last page.

ISBN 978-0-9557277-2-6
Available from all good bookshops or online

Another great title by Paul Adam
KNIFE EDGE

'Paul Adam writes fiercely topical thrillers
which deliver anxiety along with the excitement'
Literary Review

Knife Edge is a timely, chillingly plausible thriller that lifts
the lid on the secretive links between people smuggling,
illegal agricultural labour and Britain's supermarkets.

Crime reporter Joe Verdi investigates the murder of a
Kurdish immigrant by Turkish people-traffickers in London.
The dead man's wife Irena, the key witness to the killing,
flees to East Anglia where she disappears into the murky
underworld of gangmasters and exploited foreign workers.

The police are unable to trace Irena so Joe goes undercover
as a migrant labourer to try to find her. But he's not the only
one looking for her – the Turks are also on her trail.

Meanwhile, Joe's colleague Ellie Mason is following up an
outbreak of typhoid. The only link between the victims seems
to be the supermarket chain where they bought their food.

As the two reporters' investigations come together in a
heart-stopping climax, the shocking truth about our
industrialised system of food production is uncovered.
There is a price to pay for cheap food – and sometimes that
price is people's lives.

ISBN 978-0-9557277-1-9
Available from all good book shops or online.